FINE BOYS

MODERN African Writing

from Ohio University Press
Laura T. Murphy and Ainehi Edoro, Series Editors

This series brings the best African writing to an international audience. These groundbreaking novels, memoirs, and other literary works showcase the most talented writers of the African continent. The series also features works of significant historical and literary value translated into English for the first time. Moderately priced, the books chosen for the series are well crafted, original, and ideally suited for African studies classes, world literature classes, or any reader looking for compelling voices of diverse African perspectives.

FINE BOYS

A NOVEL

Eghosa Imasuen

OHIO UNIVERSITY PRESS • ATHENS

Ohio University Press, Athens, Ohio 45701

ohioswallow.com

Printed in the United States of America
Ohio University Press books are printed on acid-free paper ⊗ ™

31 30 29 28 27 26 25 24 23 22 21 5 4 3 2 1

Library of Congress Cataloging-in-Publication Data
Names: Imasuen, Eghosa, 1976– author.
Title: Fine boys : a novel / Eghosa Imasuen.
Other titles: Modern African writing.
Description: Athens : Ohio University Press, 2021. | Series: Modern African writing
Identifiers: LCCN 2021003007 (print) | LCCN 2021003008 (ebook) | ISBN 9780821424575 (paperback) | ISBN 9780821447437 (pdf)
Subjects: LCSH: College students—Nigeria—Fiction. | Secret societies—Fiction. | Nigeria—Social conditions—1960—Fiction. | Nigeria—Politics and government—1960—Fiction.
Classification: LCC PR9387.9.I47 F56 2021 (print) | LCC PR9387.9.I47 (ebook) | DDC 823/.92—dc23
LC record available at https://lccn.loc.gov/2021003007
LC ebook record available at https://lccn.loc.gov/2021003008

For Arorivho "Riscoe" Onyoh, friend and brother

There is fiction in the space between
the lines on your page of memories.
. . .
Sometimes a lie is the best thing.

—Tracy Chapman
"Telling Stories," from the album *Telling Stories*

YEAR ONE

January 1993–March 1994

1

I REMEMBER something my father told me after I went with him on a visit to one oyibo oil executive. I was thirteen, in class three; I wore my Federal Government College Warri white-and-white and had been impressed by the white man's office. He was Canadian, I think, and he had a potbelly that jiggled every time he laughed. The office had that smell of air-conditioned Big Men, like chocolate and tobacco, like cheap cigars—not cigarettes—big cheap cigars that go out on their own if you do not puff on them. When we had left, I told my father that the oyibo man's office smelled of money. Daddy had already put the 505 in reverse. He stopped the car, shifted to neutral, and looked at me.

"Ewaen, money doesn't smell like that. Money fucking smells like smelly fucking armpits, balls, and shit. You understand? Armpits, balls, and shit. The rest is all fucking show."

My father said "fuck" a lot. He could use the f-word five times in a fifteen-word sentence—the twins and I had counted.

"You have to understand, Ewaen. You do not make money by standing around in clean suits making yanga. You must get dirty and smelly. And on Friday, when your fucking payslip is ready, you can fucking have a bath, splash on some Old Spice, and then smell good. But be under no illusions, sonny. Money doesn't smell good when it's being made, when it's really being made."

3

He had a point. I had smelled crude oil, and it smelled like shit—like armpits, balls, and shit. I do not know why I remember this, here at the start of this story of youth and lost innocence. What did I learn that day? That beneath facades was always the smell of dirt? That real life was not clean, not antiseptic? My father always had funny things to say—funny, rude things.

Daddy had made his bones as an engineer with Scallop Oil in the early seventies. He was a Scallop scholar, among the first in a set of exceptional chaps the oil company thought were brilliant enough to be trained as the earliest indigenous engineers for its Niger Delta operations. Daddy had told my brother and me about his training in England. The group had been taught ballroom dancing, etiquette, and other oyibo mannerisms. The company wanted to mold these chaps into highfliers—brilliant and well-behaved young men who would come back home to take control of their country's destiny and protect the industry. Those were the actual words Daddy said the oyibo director used when he spoke to them after they graduated in '69. And it seemed the oyibos believed them too. That is, until Daddy, at the staff camp for the gas terminal in Forcados, broke a snooker stick on an oyibo man's head for saying "Black men lack the intellectual capacity to understand a gentleman's game like billiards."

I once asked Daddy if he did. That is, if he understood billiards. He did not. But that was not the point, he said. He told us in those days the only foreign engineers who agreed to work in the mosquito-infested swamps were ex-mercenaries and such. The goat who had made the comment was a semiliterate expatriate technician—the typical specimen: balding, not properly bathed, with dirt-encrusted fingernails that always scratched at an itchy crotch. Daddy, a London-trained engineer, was not going to take that nonsense from anyone. My father had gone to university in the UK in the swinging sixties—the Summer of Love, he called it, as though the three years he spent in England had been one big sunny holiday. He was there when, in 1968, the children of Europe erupted in demonstrations and rioting against their parents, who had survived two world wars. My father was "too angry," "too educated," did not know when to shut *the fuck* up and bear it. By 1978 he had left Scallop, "resigned," he said. I think he was fired.

By the early nineties, Daddy was tired of sweat and shit. He wanted to clean up his money. The process had started in '88, when he invested in a bureau de change. After handling dollars for four years, the next step was easy: set up a bank. Daddy drew up the papers and applied for a license to start a building society. Maybe the money the mortgage bank made would smell better than armpits and balls and shit.

IN MID-1992, CNN reported that sixteen-year-old Amy Fisher had just shot Mary Jo Buttafuoco. The report said something about Amy wanting the older woman dead so Joey—the bloody cradle snatcher—Buttafuoco could be free. I remember Amy was my age. Germany was unified, and British MPs had just elected a woman as speaker of the House of Commons. The Soviet Union had been over for less than a year, and the Russian-speaking part of Ukraine was threatening secession. The police officers who kicked Rodney King's head in were getting acquitted for the first time. Grunge rockers were breaking their necks to that song "Smells Like Teen Spirit"—inspired by the smell of latrines, I think—and African reggae singers were in a panic, rewriting songs, rearranging LPs, and pushing back release dates now that Mandela was *really* free. Fuel prices here increased for the first time past the one-naira mark. We had civilian governors and a military president. I was awaiting my matriculation exam results, hoping to make it into the University of Benin to study medicine. I was learning how to drive on the busy Warri streets. I was being a good son.

By October of the same year, five months after my matriculation exams, I was seething, this feeling of being on the edge of the boil, about to explode, bored but not idle, working but not busy, feeling like a kettle with a hiccupy whistle. It was supposed to be a period to put on weight, to do nothing, to forget everything I had learned in the previous six years of secondary school. I had my university admission and was supposed to have started in early September, but universities were on strike. I was stuck working at my father's bank. I was the purchasing clerk. Daddy was training me to handle money.

MY JOB involved liaising with the on-site manager, supervising the building of the edifice that was to be our head office, and then, armed with a list of requirements, scouring the spare-parts markets and building-materials depots in my beat-up Peugeot 505. This was not as easy as it seemed. Warri's go-slows were notorious. It could take up to two hours to make a run for extra nails and hammers, in part due to the long time it took to haggle.

I was also in charge of the school run, which meant I had to be the one to wake up the twins, prep them for school, put them in my 505, and travel around Warri to both sides of town. Eniye was in SS2 in the Federal Government College (FGC) at Ogunu; Osaze was in the steel company's staff school near Aladja.

One afternoon, I was driving back from FGC Warri with Eniye in the front seat. Eniye was the dark twin; her complexion was like coffee before you poured the milk in. The girl who looked like our father. She still grew her hair long then and in a weave, her cornrows matted close to the scalp in simple designs quite unlike the very complicated head they adorned.

There were small fires on either side of the road. A smoky haze glossed over the dirt and grime of the expressway, making everything seem like a faded watercolor done to the sound of cackling dust devils. Harmattan was about to begin, and soon dust clouds would join the brush fires. The painting would fade even more. My sister had started another argument.

"Ewaen, I don't know what you're saying o. I'm telling you, the juniors nowadays are so rude. You can't even punish them again."

"Of course you can," I replied. "The main thing is the degree of punishment. It has to be just right."

"But we should be able to punish. I was punished. Why can't I deal—"

"Eniye, you can't kill someone's child because you think she was rude to you."

An insect slammed into the windshield. I turned on the wiper and watched the spray of soapy water fog up the expressway for a millisecond before the wiper blades kicked in. I downshifted, accelerating past a lorry.

"See, it's not like when you were in FGC. Times have changed."

This was typical Eniye. To her, I had left FGC Warri ages ago when, in fact, it had been only two years since I was moved by my mom to Osaze's school after a bullying incident had left my back scarred with the horizontal slash marks of a senior student's belt. There was no winning an argument with my younger sister. She was like our father. She always got her way, always got her point through. I ignored her last sentence, not needing to wonder what she would do to any junior who tried her. I was tired, and we still had the long drive to her twin brother's school.

Osaze and Eniye were a paradox—both intense rivals and soulmates. It was as though they had been fighting from inside

7

Mommy's womb. Their arguments were like two elephants fighting in the rain forest; it was the grass that suffered. If anyone was foolish enough to intervene or take sides, the twins ignored their own disagreement and ganged up on the unfortunate fool. I had many times been a victim of my own good intentions.

We reached Osaze's school. It was nestled in the third housing estate of the decrepit steel company built by the military in the late seventies and run aground by the short-lived civilian regime that followed. On the other side of the estate was the DSC Primary School III, where Osaze, Eniye, and I were legends. We had topped the common entrance exams in our different years, Eniye finishing second only to Osaze. Both schools were built by an Israeli construction company and were intended to serve the children of the nonexistent staff of the steel company. The school buildings themselves looked like something out of a kibbutz—red with faux-brick walls that were solid concrete cast from prefabricated molds, all arranged in a square with the back windows of the classes facing outwards in a defense configuration. It had made dodging class very difficult. The secondary school had evolved into a private enterprise with a reputation for strict discipline reinforced by a principal of the "old school." Mr. Sambawa did not subscribe to the opinion that caning was bad. He felt that corporal punishment was the best way to keep naughty children in line—liberal doses of it. I remember the shock I felt when I left the FGC, where the law banning caning in federal schools was circumvented by delegating the work to senior students, to come to a small disciplinarian college where the teachers flogged with glee. It seemed to work. There were no reports of the kind of bullying that happened in FGC Warri here.

I parked the 505 and was about to get out when one of my brother's classmates, a girl playing ten-ten on the lawn with several other pinafored, plaited-haired girls, shouted to me that Osaze had already left. I knew where he would be. I kicked the car into reverse and drove to Wilhelm's house.

WILHELM, ONE-HALF of my crew of best friends, lived on the steel company's estate. His father was an engineer who had made the mistake a decade and a half earlier of leaving a well-paid job in Germany. Although Wilhelm always said his father complained that the Germans were all closet racists—too ashamed almost half a century after the end of the Second World War to show their real selves, which I thought was odd since he married one of them—Papa Wilhelm must have rued his decision to return in the late seventies. Wilhelm said he came back because he wanted to contribute his quota to the building of his fatherland; he wanted to bring his oyibo-trained expertise back home where it was needed. My father said the Udoji salary award of the mid-seventies that tripled the salaries of federal civil servants lured people like Wilhelm's father back. According to Daddy, this increase was made because the Gowon military regime wanted to extend its tenure and needed to bribe its civil servants and appear magnanimous at the same time. What happened was that food prices tripled in tandem. The regime was promptly overthrown in the dry season of '75, although that was scant consolation for people like Wilhelm's father. He had become a poor man with only the slightest of pretensions to Nigeria's long-vanished middle class. Wilhelm believed that their return to Nigeria was also the reason his parents always argued. His mother missed the shopping, hated the sun, and, above all, hated the Niger Wives club for foreign wives of Nigerian men.

Good old Willy; he spent most of the time at home, so if I did not come to pick up Osaze from school early, my brother would go hang out with him. Wilhelm, like me, was "awaiting admission." He and I would start medicine in Uniben as soon as the lecturers' strike was called off.

I drove into Wilhelm's mother's garden to find the pair having a kickaround. My brother stood backing the car, a football at his feet. The tall ebelebo tree in the backyard cast shifting shadows on the playing field of loamy, kicked-up earth. Two upturned paint cans marked a four-foot-wide goal on the far side. The 505 was too noisy for him to pretend he had not heard me drive in. From the hunch of my brother's shoulders, the way he pushed the ball from right foot to left and back, I knew he was about to score a goal, poke the ball through my friend's legs, or bend his waist in a cruel pantomime of show-me-your-number. Wilhelm, facing us, looked up.

"Your brother don come o," Wilhelm said, the look of almost-fear clearing from his face. Despite being mixed-race, Wilhelm's Pidgin English was very good. I think it made up for the fact that he could not speak a word of Ishan, his father's language.

Osaze turned, waved at me, and ran to the base of a Queen of the Philippines to pick up his bag. Wilhelm, already at my side of the car, leaned in, said hi to Eniye, and turned to me.

"Ewaen, how far na?"

I caught my reflection in his thick glasses. "I dey o, Willy," I replied. "We get gist."

"Hmm. About wetin?"

About nothing. I just wanted to whet his appetite for Saturday, for our weekly know-your-mate video game tournament. "No worry, shebi you go come Kpobo house next tomorrow?"

"Of course. I've been practicing my Chun-Li. Get ready to be thoroughly thrashed."

"You wish. No worry, I go gist you then," I said.

"Okay."

There was a quizzical look on Wilhelm's face, as though he wanted to ask what gist I had that I couldn't tell him right there. Instead, he turned, shouted Osaze's name, and told him to hurry. Osaze came to the car, started an argument with Eniye about who would sit in front, lost, and got into the back seat.

"YOU ARE a scatterbrain! A useless boy!" It was Saturday, and I was receiving a routine scolding from my father. My mind was on the tournament that Wilhelm and Kpobo would already have started. We lived on the outskirts of town in a two-and-a-half-story brown building behind the Effurun Police Barracks. The "half" was the bedroom wing, which wasn't actually on either story. It stuck out, not quite upstairs and definitely not downstairs, riding on the building like a child carried on its mother's back.

Daddy continued, "I should never have taught you to drive. You go around town fucking around instead of getting your fucking job done."

Fucking around. The words were a family synonym for wasting company time. Daddy's face belied his bad mouth, his quick wit, his swinging moods. He was very handsome—dark, not fair like me—with dark eyes, the eyebrows always close together as if in a thoughtful frown. The sides of his head were beginning to show their first peppering of white-gray hair, the same color as his mustache, a sparse brush that stopped just before either side of his thin, always-pressed-too-close-together lips. Looking at him, you'd expect a brooding personality, few words, small laughter, mild temper, and no rage. I remember when I was shorter, younger, and too young for expletives to be thrown at me. I remember raw backsides.

My parents did not punish their children by making them assume contorted, almost-impossible positions, nor did they send us on impractical errands whose only conceivable motivation could be to register their discontent with any crimes eight-year-olds could have committed. We never knelt with our arms raised and kept apart, never touching; we never "picked pins," right index finger touching the ground, left leg in the air, all the weight on a shaky right foot; we were never made to do the "angle ninety" with our backs against a stuccoed wall, knees flexed with bums perched on an imaginary stool. We were never sent to "fill the bottles," to stand in front of the filter, watching the water trickle into old Treetop Juice glass bottles, swatting away mosquitoes as they feasted on our exposed legs. No. Daddy and Mommy had strict limitations on what they thought constituted cruel and unusual punishment. Instead, they either sent you to a dark room—a veritable dunce's corner—or they beat you. They beat the shit out of you with slaps, spanks on the bottom, and knocks on the head but never with a closed fist, never with a cane. A cane, to them, was cruel and unusual.

"Imuetiyan, leave the boy alone." Mommy sometimes let her voice rise above its habitual whisper. It didn't now. She came into the upstairs sitting room. My mother only called Daddy by his full name when she thought he was being unreasonable. She rested her hands on her kitchen apron, the dishrag slung over her shoulder. Mommy shouted something back at the help, something about watching the soup to make sure it didn't burn or she'd send her back to the village. Now here was the person I resembled. Fair with a wide, square face, she always had the embarrassment of having to prove she was Itsekiri and not Igbo. This was made more difficult because she spoke Igbo beautifully; she grew up in Aba; her father had been a port official working in nearby Port Harcourt. She always told us that the "curse of languages" was something we had picked up from her side of the family. We only had to look at her and her sisters because not one of them spoke their mother tongue.

She took me by the shoulder and led me out of the sitting room, leaving my father fuming. She had a paunch, a small bulge that she hid well with her wrappers and an exceptionally sturdy girdle. She blamed the twins for the paunch. I always noted a tone of nostalgia whenever she made this accusation.

Out of earshot of Daddy, she said, "Don't mind him, you hear. He's in a bad mood because one of the new managers at the bank crashed the station wagon."

"I heard," I replied. "The manager forced the driver to let him drive."

"Your father sha, he no dey hear word. I queried him on the wisdom of hiring a fifty-year-old who couldn't drive. I said, 'Tiyan, where has this man been all his life when his mates were learning how to drive?' I mean, what kind of manager can he be?"

"So where are you going to?" She asked the question with her back to me while untying the apron.

"Kpobo's house."

"The commissioner's son?"

"The former commissioner's son," I replied.

"Will you be driving?" She continued, "When you leave your friend's place, try and check me at the shop. Maybe we'll drive back together. Phone first o." She paused, "In short, don't bother. The phones probably won't be working. I'll be there till seven. Just come; don't ride okada back home. Those motorcyclists are lunatics." Singing the words as she turned to face me, she threw the apron over her right shoulder, her paunch bouncing in rhythm to what she said.

She smiled and left me at the half-turn staircase. She was going to her bedroom to get ready for work. She owned and ran a supermarket, although she was a biochemist, a profession she had never practiced because Warri had no universities, no labs where she could have worked. I was born the day before her final exams. She said this was the reason I was brainy; my father said it was the reason I had a big head.

2

CHUN-LI WINS!

"Kpobo, hold me o. I go kill am o!" Wilhelm screamed.

He had just walloped my Guile with an upside-down helicopter kick from his Chun-Li.

Kpobo said, "Wetin dey do you, Ewaen? Where is your mind? You're not concentrating." He came round to my right and took the control pad from my hands. As he sat he continued, "How you go let this mumu win you? Just chill make I finish am for you."

I watched as he and Wilhelm started a best-of-three between Ken and Chun-Li. We were in the children's parlor in Kpobo's home at Marine Quarters. Kpobo's father had built his mansion just behind the hustle and bustle of Enerhen Junction. What marked out their compound as special was the change in tempo as you crossed from the mud-splattered and very noisy "Center of Warri" into the quiet and tree-shaded Marine Quarters. Their house was just beside the epicenter of all of Warri's go-slows. But I had never, throughout the time we were in Technical High School, heard Kpobo complain of being late because of a traffic jam. All he had to do was walk across the gridlock to where the traffic flowed better, hop into a taxi, and voilà, he was in school minutes later. He enjoyed all of this while we, his friends, had to run the gauntlet of traffic jams and assault-rifle-armed policemen and their checkpoints. He was lucky.

"I've had sex," I said.

Wilhelm noticed first, his attention not completely in the game since he was getting thoroughly thwacked by Kpobo. As the echo of Chun-Li's death cry rang out, he turned from the TV screen.

"Wetin you talk?" Wilhelm asked. He took off his glasses and wiped them on his shirt.

Ken wins!

"Wetin he talk?" Kpobo asked as I dragged the pad from Wilhelm's hands and sat on the stool directly facing the TV.

"Hey, no spoil the controller," Wilhelm said. He continued, this time speaking to Kpobo, "I think he said he don sex. Talk true, Ewaen. You don nack? You don pop the cherry?"

Wilhelm knew all the terms. I selected a character, Balrog this time, and motioned for Kpobo to do the same.

He ignored me and asked instead, "Is it true? Have you done it?"

"It's nothing," I said.

It was fun to see their faces: Wilhelm wide-eyed, his glasses misting up from anticipation, his hair a shade lighter than the wispy beard he had just started growing; Kpobo, darker, pretending not to care if I gave an answer or not. He still had not picked a character. He turned from me, faced the TV, and moved his cursor around the character-choice menu. Kpobo was the shortest of the three of us; he was the hairiest, though, having his first facial hair when we were in class four. He now had a fowl-scratch beard, full sideburns, and no mustache. We always teased him about the no-mustache thing; he said it was genetic, and that it was the reason his father and older brothers were always clean-shaven. Wilhelm's new beard, which he attributed to generous and regular applications of methylated spirit to his chin, meant that I was the only naked-faced one left.

But I was the first to have had sex. Although, strictly, Kpobo could not be considered a virgin. He had *lost* his at the hands—and I use "hands" decidedly here—of a nanny at the tender age of twelve. Wilhelm and I always insisted that this did not count.

I continued, "Abeg, choose character. Make I beat you."

He ignored me and threw his pad on the floor. "Talk now. Talk or we won't play anymore."

So I told them about Tessa, a girl I had just met, and about the ride to her place in the afternoon two days ago, not sparing any detail. Midway through my narrative, Kpobo and I commenced our bout. The climax of my story coincided with my knocking his avatar out.

The quiet only lasted a few seconds before Kpobo spoke. "Ewaen, you sleep with ashewo."

"Shut up, Kpobo. She wasn't a prostitute," I said.

"Yes, she was. You just told us she has an expatriate boyfriend whose *Playboy* and *Penthouse* magazines she then used to hook you."

"So? She got tired of her oyibo man and wanted me."

"On the day you guys met?" Willy asked.

He gave up any pretense of wanting a reply when I shot him a hard look. He made a show of inspecting his control pad and sniffled, a curious tic he used in readjusting his glasses when they slipped down the bridge of his nose. I was not about to let my friends ruin this for me.

"Wilhelm, na you remain o." Kpobo only called our friend Wilhelm whenever he wanted to annoy him.

"Shut up. This is the only part that you enjoy, Kpobo. Isn't it?" Wilhelm only spoke good English when he was irritated or wanted to make a serious point.

"What are you getting upset about? Sex?" I asked, still aglow at being first in this gaggle of geeks.

"I don't blame you," Kpobo said. He changed the subject and asked, "So how far with una preparations for school?"

Beneath the abrupt change of subject, I felt it: Kpobo was still uncomfortable talking about university. It was in his eyes—the way they stuck to the screensaver of the video game, the way they stopped moving around the room. He was not entering university this year. This was no fault of his. The center where he had written the national University Matriculation Exams had started an hour and a half late because the question papers were stuck in traffic. The chap who had the highest scores in the certificate exams in our second secondary school was made to write a three-hour exam in just one hour. He did not pass. So while his best friends, Wilhelm and me, would enter the University of Benin to study medicine as soon as the strike was called off, Kpobo would be at home for an entire year. But maybe he was luckier. He had told us that his father was going to send him to England to resume, with the February admissions, a course with combined honors in computer engineering and telecommunications.

"Oboy, we are waiting for the university to open," I said.

"I hear the head of state has threatened to sack any lecturer who doesn't resume by the end of November," Wilhelm added.

"My father says he's a joker. With the presidential elections slated for June next year, he can't be seen to be just another heavy-handed military dictator. He predicts that before the start of December, the federal government would have capitulated, and then you guys can resume," Kpobo said.

BAD BOYS, friends, cultists, fine boys, and jokers. Life in the University of Benin, and in every university in the country, needed its students to straddle lines that were blurred by new definitions of badness, of love, of friendship, and of loyalty. What was the difference between survival and actual living?

How much do children need to know on their first visit to adulthood?

One evening, four months later, Wilhelm and I sat in the University of Benin's hostel car park, resting after the day's lectures. We really were sitting *in* the car park, in the gutters that ran along the entire length of its western wall. Behind us the coed hostel, Hall Two, loomed in the darkness. Shadows like blocks of Lego from a juju-man's nightmare seemed to lean over, threatening to fall on our heads. Small flickering snatches of light from candles and from smoky kerosene lamps appeared in windows, going off, coming on, moving around the facades of each of the blocks like a slow-motion version of the same juju-man's idea of Tetris. Wilhelm and I waited for the rest of our new friends. Two of them were walking back from Six Candles.

Six Candles—that was what we called the small market that woke up in front of Hall Two every evening. Not really lit by candles but by very smoky kerosene lanterns converted from old spray cans, the small illegal stalls were owned and run by nonacademic staff of Uniben and their families. They sold drinks, cigarettes, and snacks like the moin-burger, a contraption made from a bun—really a small, highly compressible, bromate-saturated loaf—and moin-moin. It was just as well that they had something to do to make ends meet. They were not receiving their salaries as their breadwinners were on strike and the authorities were enforcing the government's "no work, no pay" policy.

As soon as the academic staff union, ASUU, had called off its strike and we, the new students, had finished registration and clearance, the Non-academic Staff Union, NASU, went on strike, claiming it deserved a slice of the pie, too. It was a small pie: the government had to redefine the salary structure of the university lecturers—a salary structure that was stuck in the eighties when the naira was worth twenty times what it was now. The rolling strikes had begun in the mid-eighties and still continued, shifting from sector to sector. As soon as rail workers were taken care of, hospitals went on strike. Once doctors and nurses were taken care of, coal miners and oil workers went on strike. It was part of the reason we sat out in the dark, lit only by cars that came to pick up girls from the female hostel, Hall One. The generators were not working and the National Electric Power Authority, NEPA, had "taken the light." Before the generator operators downed tools, they took away the keys to the generator houses serving the hostels, the labs, the school health center, and the teaching hospital. But we were in university. We learned to manage; we learned to bear.

Five of our friends were out with us this evening: Ejiro Ogbodo, a nineteen-year-old engineering student from Warri; Tuoyo Ogbe, twenty-three, general all-around laze-about, also from Warri, who had finally decided to seek a degree in engineering; Omogui Idogun, the only Bini boy here apart from me, was twenty and studying history. He was not very bright, though. Coming back from the stands of Six Candles were the last two, the only others who smoked cigarettes apart from Tuoyo: Kayode (Kayoh or Knockout) Erhahon, eighteen but with the body of a forty-year-old, his Lagos-fed tummy already capitulating in its battle with gravity; and Clement (Oliver Tambo) Unegbu, who was in agric econs though he hated the course and had never been on a farm in his eighteen years of life. Sitting, legs dangling into the dark emptiness of the gutter, were Wilhelm and me, the youngest in the group.

We spent these evenings yabbing each other, throwing careless and sometimes very painful insults at ourselves.

Kayoh reached where we sat and said, "Wilhelm, wetin you dey do here? Isn't the prof supposed to be tucking you into bed now?" He jumped into the gutter beside Wilhelm, hugged him, and blew a cloud of Benson and Hedges in his face.

Wilhelm lived in the staff quarters with an uncle, a professor of accounting. Kayoh thought he had been first to tell me that the professor wasn't really Wilhelm's uncle. I knew this already; the professor's wife was a member of Niger Wives, a Ukrainian doctor whom Wilhelm's mother had contacted when he got his admission into Uniben. Wilhelm hated the arrangement but could hardly defy his *momsie;* she did not want her son developing any rash on his blemish-free skin in some hostel. Wilhelm took any opportunity he had to stay out late. He had told the professor that he had a zoology seminar with some friends and would not be returning that night. How could he prefer sharing my iron-spring bed in my mosquito-infested room to what he had in the prof's house?

"Yeah," shouted Omogui, "leave here for the men."

Wilhelm ignored Omogui and pulled himself away from Kayoh's embrace. Everybody braced for it: Wilhelm's tongue was barbed. Barbed and poisonous.

"See this jambite o," he said. "See this mumu who took bike from pharmacy to main café. You're talking. You no dey fear?"

Everyone burst into laughter except Tambo. He had not heard the story.

"Wetin happen?" he asked.

I told him, "No mind the big fool o. He was standing in front of the pharmacy department. That was about two weeks after we started school. Instead of looking at signboards, the idiot asked a group of staylites where he could take a bike to the main café. Almost out of control with laughter, I think, they told him to walk about two hundred meters to the library and take a bike to the main café."

Tambo was already laughing, but I could not resist delivering the coup dc grâce.

"You can imagine Kayoh's face after the bike man brought him back to the pharmacy and pointed across the street to the largest building in Uniben, saying that was the main café."

"I no blame you," Kayoh said. "Na because I tell una, shebi?"

Everyone had such stories to tell. We had all been fazed at one time or the other by the staylites, quite rabid and extremely mischievous sophomores who lived for the next opportunity to humiliate a freshman, a jambite. Even old men like Tuoyo had been fazed. It was normal. It was expected. The staylites told us, just like the traditional October rush for girls that seemed to be permanently postponed to February because of the scattered school calendar, we would faze others in our second year too.

Kayoh was not finished, "Because I told you, eh? You, Ewaen. You who, just a few weeks ago, begged mommy to fill his clearance and registration forms." He stopped talking, put his left thumb in his mouth and pretended to suck.

The conference exploded in laughter as they always did each time the story was repeated. My mother, sha. She had really embarrassed me during the two days she spent with me while I settled in. It started during the drive down from Warri. While Michael—the driver—drove, my mom proceeded to give me what she felt was much-needed motherly advice. As I cringed ever further into the car seat's upholstery, Mom touched on cleanliness, tidiness, reading, girls, sex, condoms, and AIDS. The day did not get better.

But I had developed a hide of steel. It came from having been teased all my life. I could take anything this crowd could throw at me. Wilhelm, my classmate in FGC Warri and friend and classmate now, said that if he was told half of the things I heard to his face, he would be in a fight every evening. Did having a thick skin make me the butt of jokes? I do not think so. I think it was because of an intense shyness I had never gotten over. The only time I spoke up was when it was time to yab the nicer chaps like Kayoh. Kayoh—now there was a guy. He was the most jovial, most nutty bobo there ever was. After that first day in the queue at the clearance center when he had teased me, a stranger, about my mother filling my forms, we had remained fast friends. Of course, Kayoh, as was typical, had ingratiated himself to Wilhelm because he knew his guardian was a professor of accounting. It was an investment. Who knew the rewards that could be reaped from being close friends with the charge of one of your professors?

The laughter had not yet died down when Tambo whispered, "See them Yibril and him crew."

We watched one of the bad boys in school cross the car park from Hall One towards where we sat. He was at the head of a line of about five others, all dressed in black. They were members of the Black Axe, or as Wilhelm told us Yibril insisted, the Neo-black Movement. It was one of the banned university confraternities; and it was the most popular, most uncouth, most overpopulated confra in any of the universities in Nigeria. Yibril was Willy's cousin, a poor relation from Uromi, a second cousin once removed.

As they approached, he nodded at us, at Willy. He was a short guy with a wide toothy maw that always seemed to smile. He stopped, waved his gang away and came over to us. Shifting, our other friends cleared a space for Yibril as he hopped into the gutter beside Tuoyo. They were neighbors from Obahor, a suburb in Warri's old town.

"Bros! We no dey see you o!" he said. "If I didn't know better, I go say you were dodging me."

Tuoyo, who was age-mates with Yibril and not at all afraid of him, said, "See this small rat o. Abeg comot your hand from my shoulder. You no dey fear? I go knock your head o!"

"Knock which head? My own?"

"Because you dey Black Axe? Oya call all those your boys come make I beat all of una."

A shadow passed over Yibril's face. For a millisecond only, a wrinkle formed over the middle of his brow. Yibril laughed.

"No play go there o. Those bastards are not very nice dudes. If they reach here them go naked you o."

It was all good-natured fun. After he and Tuoyo had gone through their fake wrestling match, he turned to Willy. "Cousin, how now?"

"Fine o."

Yibril smiled and climbed out of the gutter, jogging the short distance to where his troop was waiting. They vanished into the bushes surrounding Dreams, the drinking joint that was beside Hall One.

Tuoyo was the first to speak. "Careful, Willy. You know say Yibril wan' blend you enter confra?"

"No, no, na my cousin. My mama go beat am die," Willy said.

"I am afraid of that guy," I said.

"Who? Yibril?"

"Who? Shorty?"

Tuoyo and Willy spoke at the same time. Tuoyo continued.

"No mind Yibril, Ewaen. Na just big fool. Very fake guy those days for Dom Domigos; he enter university two years ago come dey blow hard guy."

"Yes, but na fine boy now," I said.

"Fine wetin?"

"Fine what?"

They had chorused again, one in pidgin, the other, Wilhelm, in English. Tuoyo continued speaking, "Ewaen, this place, this school, the whole environment dey change people. But some people will always be the same. Yibril can never fine."

"I just feel Willy should be careful around him, cousin or not."

But I knew my concern for Willy might be misplaced. I noticed that Yibril always took special care to ignore him, to keep him separate. Only Willy's very close friends knew about their relationship. Looking around our small gathering, I knew that some of my friends had already blended confra. The night, two weeks ago, when Tambo came back black and blue and all muddied, he had given the excuse that he fell off a motorcycle taxi. We all knew he had just come from an initiation cere-mony in the bush. Slowly, our new fellowship was breaking up. Inexorably, the new friendships forged several months before were ending. The possibility that they would turn into impla-cable enmity would shock those who sat in that gutter that night. Our definitions of badness, of love, of friendship, and of loyalty would change.

ON THE way to Hall One, I asked Wilhelm, "We dey go see Brenda?"

"Yep," he replied.

Cool. I had not seen Brenda in a whole week. She would say that her "boy-bestfriend" had abandoned her. She would laugh and jump all over me, hugging and blowing kisses.

"How you see this confra thing?" Wilhelm asked.

We were jumping the gutters closest to Hall One. Weaving in and around parked cars that had come to pick up girls for a lovely night away from the darkness of the NASU strike and NEPA, we walked into the porter's lodge serving the girls' hostel.

"I no know, man. I no know," I murmured.

"Hasn't anyone been to see you? Has no one asked you to blend?" he asked, staring straight ahead.

I put a hand on his shoulder to stop him. What was he talking about? Anyone who the confra boys thought possessed fineness had been hassled out of his wits with requests and, sometimes, quite fearful pressure to join up, to blend one of the university gangs. This was not a new topic of discussion. Why was Wilhelm bringing it up again? We had talked about it the last week before leaving Warri and the week after completing registration. We were special targets though: we were Warri boys, fine boys from the rugged city; we were from the town that produced the quintessential confra boy; we were supposed to possess innate *ruggedity*. But looking at him now in the dark, his face lit up now and then by the passing lights of cars and okadas, and catching my own reflection in his glasses, I laughed at the confraternities and their spokesmen and recruiters. Us, hard men? What a joke. We were just a couple of precocious sixteen-year-olds—going on seventeen—out to have a good time. And if in the process we caught an education, the better for us.

"Has anyone been on your case in particular?" I asked him.

"Na one guy from science department o. He's been on my neck since January. I threatened to report him to the prof the day before yesterday, and he told me I would see. Can you imagine that idiot with body odor telling me that I will *see*?" Wilhelm's complexion turned a bright red, and I knew he was serious because he was speaking good English again.

"But confra, sha," I said, trying to make light of it. "They stupid o—the guys they actually send to recruit us. I don't know if they think that anyone who actually considers himself a fine boy will actually *blend*." Wilhelm was already smiling, so I continued. "Imagine the guy who accosted me with a proposal that I, *a fine boy* according to him, should join the Buccaneers a week ago. Smelly, with a dirty yellow T-shirt underneath a black one and the dirtiest and most caked jeans I'd ever set my eyes on. You wan' know wetin I tell am?"

"What did you tell him?"

"I said if being a fine boy meant looking like him, I'd rather be ugly."

"You didn't."

"I did. It worked. He left scratching his head. Probably trying to figure out which confra I belonged to. Anything that would explain my liver."

We were now on the corridors of Hall One. As we made our way up the stairs of the three-story building, Wilhelm said, "You know both of you are in love, right?"

"Guy, that na nonsense talk. We are just friends. Just close friends. Wetin dey do you and your rotten mind? Everything between a guy and a girl must include sex to you?"

"No vex o. No vex. Just making small talk," Wilhelm laughed.

3

"EWAEN-BOOBOO! Ewaen darling!" Only Brenda could make that screech sound like a welcome. From her corner of the room, she hailed me and Wilhelm, almost knocking her cornermate's simmering pot of soup off its perch on the electric cooker beside her. The darkness in the room was barely lit by here-and-there candles.

"Oh, Fidelia. Come and carry this your soup before it injures somebody," Brenda said to an irritated Fidelia, who was napping in someone else's corner. Fidelia scratched herself, shifted her position, and ignored Brenda.

"Ha, Wilhelm, welcome o. I'm special, girls! See, two hunks came to find me."

"Yeah, you are, Brenda," the roomies chorused.

"Yeah, I am," said Brenda. "Oya, make way for my visitors. Come in. Come in." She still stood at her corner.

Barely seen above the lockers that were only four and a half feet tall, she beckoned to us like a Maggie Thatcher. Brenda Adolor was the daughter of one of my father's competitors. We had become friends when we escorted our fathers to the Warri Chamber of Commerce meetings that each hosted. This was while I was still in FGC, two years before I transferred to her school, THS. Brenda was feisty. She was beautiful. She was short. She was so alive that at times I wanted to search her back for the battery pack—definitely not Tiger batteries but

Duracell premium. She was, as she said, my "girl-bestfriend." Was I in love with her or she with me? No. But we were close. I was the shoulder to cry on whenever she was brokenhearted by the newest unfulfilled crush, which, with Brenda, was quite often. Her own part of the bargain—self-appointed—was to try and hook me up with any attractive and available friend she thought I might like. She was now studying law, which meant, unlike the old days when we were seatmates in the same class in secondary school, we only saw each other in the evenings when I took time out to visit her. *Visit her* because my room, filled to the brim with twelve-plus boys, was not a nice place to entertain girls, girl-bestfriend or not.

Wilhem and I maneuvered ourselves through a sea of pots and pans, lockers and minifridges, and grumbling girls to my girl-bestfriend's corner. On the bottom bunk of her bed sat Harry Igbudu. I had introduced them only last week at Brenda's insistence. He was studying engineering and, as all science students are in year one, we were in the same class—a massive lecture theater called 500 LT—but it should have been called 1,000 or 2,000 LT.

"Harry, how far now?" I asked as we shook hands and snapped fingers. He shifted to allow space for us to sit down while Brenda remained standing.

"I dey o," he replied belatedly. "Wilhelm, how far?"

Wilhelm, who was always uncomfortable around girls, replied in the Queen's English, "I'm fine and you?"

Brenda caught on fast. "See oyibo o. 'I'm fine and you?'" she mimicked. We laughed, including Wilhelm.

"You no go change," he said, finally relapsing into the medium of language he was more comfortable with.

We gisted plenty that night. The topics ranged from lectures and school to girls, toasting, and boys. The unrelenting assault by Fidelia's soup on our nostrils made us move to the

balcony when Brenda, after chastising the owner of the offending pot, suggested that we get some fresh air.

"The most annoying thing is the attention you get from
confra boys. They feel that just because they've blended, they
can get any girl they want." Brenda had been on about this
particular issue all night. "Harry, I hope you haven't joined
confra," she intoned.

"Of course not." I knew Harry had not blended. His brother,
who had been a don during his time at the state university in
Ekpoma, had asked a year-three student in one of the confraternities to look after Harry and make sure he was not harassed
into joining anything. Even if Harry wanted to blend, it would
be impossible with his caliber of guardian angel. This was one
of my reasons for suspecting that the whole confra thing was
rubbish.

"Ewaen. Willy. Make una no join confra o," Brenda said.

I leaned on the balcony's iron guards, gazing out into the
clear night sky. With the power out again, it was easier to see
the stars out. Far in the distance, I could barely make out the
silhouette of the medical complex where, if we passed the on-
slaught of year-one exams, the first set of which were coming
up in a month's time, Wilhelm and I would be receiving lectures next year. That was if they could complete the building in
time. I had heard that the foundation stone was laid by Gowon
twenty years ago. But work had now resumed at the site.

"Ewaen, won't you answer? Make una no join confra o."

"I hear, Brenda," I said.

About an hour after we got to Brenda's, we knew it was
time to leave. The closing of curtains and the gratuitously loud
yawns by her roommates made it clear. NEPA had "brought
light," the electric stove with Fidelia's pot of soup was back on,
and the fumes from the pot had snuck up on us outside and had
started assaulting us again. Brenda said her goodnights, holding

back Harry for just a little longer than I thought necessary. We then made our way back to our respective rooms in the guys' dorms. Harry left us at the gate to Hall Two, and Wilhelm and I continued through the dimly lit shortcut to Hall Three.

THE ELECTRICITY made the room too alive for 11 p.m. All my roommates were awake. After first scolding no one in particular about my kerosene lantern they had left burning, I paused at the spot where we hung it from the ceiling to blow it out. Ejiro was in his corner as usual. Deceptively quiet, he would erupt into an argument within minutes. His specialty was to quietly watch any developing disagreement and take the least-populated position. He lived for those moments when—after shouting everyone down with an aggressively driven-home point—he could smile and say, yes, he had won another argument. Ejiro shared the double bunk in his corner of the room with Tambo, who was not actually supposed to be there. He had followed Omogui back from a drinking session three weeks after we started school and had slowly, but inexorably, grafted himself into the room. Tambo was cool, though. Apart from disappearing for days at a time. He was always the first to wake up and the first to place our buckets at the tap shared by three blocks.

Omogui slept in the bunk beside mine. I was not surprised that he was not in his corner. He was in mine twiddling with my radio. The unmistakable California siren of Dr. Dre and Snoop whined, and I knew that only he would be presumptuous enough to hop in my private space and turn on my stereo.

After driving him away, I cleared the bed to make space for Wilhelm and me, dropped my clothes in the closet, and settled down to partake in the argument—about which video game console, Sega's or Nintendo's, was superior—that I was fortunate to meet. Ejiro, as usual, was taking the road less traveled, arguing that all video games were bad and the devil's work. We slept around three in the morning.

A109 WAS our room number. A room of twelve boys—legal occupants and squatters. The daily routine involved getting up in the morning, fetching water, bathing, and then looking for breakfast. Maybe lectures featured in this schedule. They were not priorities—not without the public address systems, which had been locked up by the striking university junior workers. The struggle to get food precluded all other concerns. The school did not feed students anymore. We had heard that the first students' riot in the university had been about food. It happened in the late seventies when the price for a meal ticket rose from fifty kobo to eighty kobo. The university eventually gave up trying and converted the main cafeteria into a lecture hall complex for arts and social science students. Small blocks of bukaterias were built just beside the hostels. This was where we ate. They served watered-down stew and rice, extremely soft eba, and some more water with egusi sprinkled in it. Very nasty stuff, but we managed. We learned to bear.

The main problem with food was not its availability or lack. We had no money. Every one of my friends had parents who still thought Nigeria was in the eighties. My father felt that the ₦750 he gave me monthly was too much. He felt he was spoiling me. All our parents felt they were spoiling us. Yet, my ₦750 barely lasted two weeks. By the fifteenth of each month, I was invariably broke. We were all broke. Kayoh, whose father was a director in an oil company, received five hundred naira a month. Five hundred! A meal was seven naira. That meant feeding in a day took twenty-one naira. A month took . . . do the arithmetic. This budget did not include money for beer and cigarettes or for toasting girls. But somehow, we managed.

After eating and maybe going for lectures or, more likely, lazing in our rooms all day like lions in the savannah, evening came, and we went to the car park and Six Candles. Those who drank and smoked scrounged around for beer, Chelsea gin, rum, and cigarettes, while Wilhelm and I, the teetotalers, sat in the gutter, waiting for our customary conference to start. So each evening, instead of looking for a class in which to read and dissect the day's barely audible lectures with my classmates, I spent it with my new friends, discussing girls and insulting ourselves. These meetings ended for me when I took leave to go and "mark attendance" in Brenda's room. The rewards for visiting Brenda could include a meal. After this, I went back to my room with or without Wilhelm, and the day began again. Routine. Boring. Until one night in February of '93.

THE CAR park in front of Hall One was almost empty when I left Brenda's room that night. It was six days to Valentine's Day. A girl in a miniskirt leaned against the door of a Range Rover. The driver glanced at me, winked, and continued talking to his babe. He didn't see me wink back. I walked across the car park. It had rained earlier that evening, and the air still smelled of freshly cut grass. The tarmac gleamed like the floor of a new Teflon frying pan. I entered Hall Three the long way around, through its porter's lodge. I stopped at the notice board to peruse a two-month-old mimeograph. It listed five students rusticated and three others expelled for cultism, for belonging to the banned confraternities.

On getting to my room, the first thing I noticed was my lantern on the ground just inside the door. This was odd. The room itself was in darkness as NEPA had not yet brought light, and the nonacademic staff were still on strike. My roommates stood around the door with some students from the neighboring rooms.

"Who threw my lantern outside?" I asked. Everyone was quiet. I repeated my question.

Ejiro was the closest to me and he said, "Ewaen, cool down. We were robbed."

It was then I noticed that everyone had gathered around Omogui. He had a small bruise to the side of his head and a fourth-year medical student who lived in the room next door was administering first aid. He looked shaken, but he smiled at me.

"What happened?" I asked.

Ejiro told me. When I left them at the car park, he, Tambo, Omogui, and Kayoh strolled back to the room. Kayoh and Tambo had left for Dreams to try and con someone into buying them drinks. Ejiro, Omogui, and some of the guys in the room had settled down to a small card game of WHOT when they heard a voice from the door saying, "Last card, check up!" Thinking it was one of the jokers from next door, they had been shocked when the chap came into the dim light of the lantern, wearing an adire-cloth mask that covered his nose and mouth and flashing a gun. As Ejiro described it, "It looked like a piece of cast-iron plumbing."

"Who were those in the room?" I asked.

There were the six of them: Ejiro, Omogui, and four others. No, like he said, Tambo and Kayoh had left to go and find who would buy them beer.

"Thank God for them," I said.

Ejiro continued. Two other similarly clad goons followed the first one into the room. Over the next ten or so minutes, they were told to empty their pockets, their bags, and their closets. Stupid Omogui had his head broken after he struggled with one of the robbers over a small parcel found in his bag. When the polythene-wrapped parcel tore in their hands, everyone was shocked to see that it contained cash.

"Imagine," Ejiro said. "And I was begging him just this evening for money to eat." I think Ejiro was more upset with Omogui for having money in the first place and for having the audacity to hide it. Also, Ejiro apologized that my entire *Playboy* collection had been stolen. One of the roommates had taken them from under my mattress and was completely engrossed when the crooks broke in. That one pained me.

While we were still gathered outside, the electricity came back, and we moved in to arrange our stuff. The roommate who was the cause of my magazines being stolen said, "Ha! We should leave everything, you know? Evidence, in case security decides to investigate after we make the report."

"Guy, shut up," Ejiro said. "Which report you wan' report? Who's going to follow you to come and check the hostel? Have you forgotten the hostel wardens and porters are on strike?"

Omogui, still groggy from the attack, said to Ejiro, "Leave him. Let's arrange this room."

We did that by putting stuff in the closets and scraping the shards of the broken lantern's globe off the floor. It was about this time that Tambo came back alone. We told Tambo what happened, and he joined in cleaning up. My radio, my iron, Tambo's cassette tape collection, our shoes, and mugs—everything of value was either with the thieves or lay in pieces on the floor. Later that night, as we were settling down to sleep, Tambo signaled for me and Ejiro to meet him outside. Moving quietly out of the room in our boxers and pajamas, we followed him down the passageway. He told us he wanted to discuss something. We settled for the corridors and sat along the edges of one. We waited for him to start.

He lit a cigarette—a St. Moritz—blew out the silver-and-blue-colored smoke, and spoke, "This thing that happened tonight pained me o. It really pained me."

Ejiro always rubbed his eyes in this odd way; he used his knuckles like a toddler and said, "Tambo, the thing pains all of us. Wetin you wan' tell us?"

I was getting impatient too. There were mosquitoes outside and they were buzzing worryingly close. I did not want to spend the rest of the night scratching. Tambo took his time. He dragged another hit of his cigarette, the glow lighting up lines of aggravation on his pimpled face. I knew he was upset about the whole robbery thing, but he was taking it badly.

"We can't even report the matter to anyone. The bloody idiots keep us in hostels when all the junior workers are on strike. It's not normal, I'm telling you. It's not normal." He took another drag and said, "I know one guy from Ekosodin who fit help us get our things back."

Ejiro was the first to pick up on what Tambo was really saying.

"Clement," he said, calling Tambo by his given name, "You dey crase? You want us to mix up with confra boys because our things were stolen?"

"That's like jumping from the frying pan into the fire," I said.

We paused as one guy passed, escorting a girl back to Hall One.

When they were out of earshot, Tambo said, "You guys, cool it. Listen to what I'm saying. This is someone I have heard of—someone who people say is very nice. It's not like I am that close to him. He's in my department."

"How can he help us?" I asked.

"Most of the student robbers live in Ekosodin."

"How do we know they were students?" I asked again.

"Ewaen, they were students. Who else get the liver to rob in the hostels?" Ejiro said. I saw the look. He wanted me to shut up so Tambo could continue. Tambo did.

"Students or no, at least they operate from Ekosodin. This guy lives there. He and his friends go fit help us. Look at them as a kind of civil defense outfit. They know people. They go fit catch these guys. They go fit punish them. They go fit let us re-cover our stuff. We get to try this chance. I mean, I don't know about you, but I can't let them get away with this."

"Wetin be your guy name?" Ejiro asked.

"TJ. And he no be my guy like that. As I have been saying, na just someone I hear say like to help people."

4

SIX OF us strolled down Green House Road in Ekosodin. Jumping puddles of water from burst water mains, Ejiro and I struggled to keep up. We flanked Tambo and TJ. TJ was about six foot five with a small head and a permanent smile on his face. A smile which, if not for his reputation, would have been seen as very annoying. He was the head—the *Capo di tutti Capi*—of La Cosa Nostra, Oliver Tambo had explained just before we went to sleep the night before. TJ was dressed in a white sleeveless vest and deep-blue jeans, which seemed out of place because faded jeans were in fashion. He was in his final year in the Agricultural Science department, Tambo's department.

I glanced behind us at the two chaps escorting TJ. They were his bodyguards, Lorenchi and Tommy. Lorenchi was nice; I liked him. He had smiled and shaken our hands so boisterously when we were introduced just thirty minutes before that it felt as if we had known each other for years. Tommy was another matter altogether. As Ejiro said when we first got off the bikes we took from the hostel, Tommy looked like a bad person. He wore a scowl that made him look perpetually constipated. They both wore nice pastel button-down shirts— Tommy's green, Lorenchi's gray—tucked into faded gray jeans.

SO, THIS was Ekosodin. I had never been to any of the university's suburbs. The school had placed a moratorium on building hostels after the confraternity crises of the mid to late eighties. They felt that the hostels, four as they were then, only served as breeding grounds for the gangs terrorizing the university. Professor Williams, the iron lady and then vice-chancellor, stopped building them. And since matter always moves to a place of least resistance, the excess students moved out to the surrounding communities of Ekosodin, BDPA—we pronounced this Bee-Dee-Pah—and Osasogie. A building boom followed in these places with villagers putting up fire-traps to serve as hostels for the desperate students. The confras duly followed.

The first student to die in gang warfare was killed in Osasogie, off campus, in '89, the year before the VC forced the students out. Ekosodin, itself, was at the back end of the school compound. It was accessed via a gate, nestled in the staff quarters, directly opposite the faculty of social sciences, which was manned by a spare detail of security men armed with batons. The off-campus residences were villages, small hamlets. The roads were unmotorable—steep lanes, the gradients of which would draw a gasp from a fit Ethiopian runner, with abrupt cut-offs caused by gully erosion, "cut-offs" being a euphemism for craters and vast chasms; and shrubs, elephant grass, and small forests sprouted in the middle of the streets here and there. Rats were the fauna and feral cats the predators.

We had left for Ekosodin at about nine that morning. Taking bikes from the hostel gates, after a bath and a brief "Good luck" from Omogui, the only other roommate who knew of our mission, we rode through the straight avenue that separated the library from the hostels to the Ekosodin gate. Then the stroll began. Jumping and dodging gutters, stopping a while to allow the occasional cat to jump out of a bush and chase after a rat, we walked for close to ten minutes before we got to Green House, where Tambo said TJ stayed. TJ was very nice.

He had taken us for a walk and asked us to gist him about what happened.

"That's very sad," TJ said. "And you, Ewaen. What did you lose?" We had reached a small beer parlor and he motioned us inside.

"My stereo—"

"Wetin you call am?" It was Lorenchi, the joker. "TJ, these boys be real aje-butter o! You're calling a deck 'stereo'? Tommy, when last did you hear it called a stereo?" He was laughing his head off as we took our seats around a squat square table.

Tommy gave a thin smile and replied, "It's been a while, dude." Lorenchi kept on laughing until a look from TJ shut him up.

We sat silent for a few minutes. Tommy grunted uncomfortably. Then Tambo leaned over to Ejiro and me and whispered. We were supposed to offer them drinks before any meaningful discussions could start. I mentally slapped my forehead. Tambo had told us to bring some cash for shacks and cigarettes. "You get to flow beer o. Beer is a good lubricant for gist," he had said. I signaled for the beer parlor attendant, a boy clad in shorts and a singlet, and told him to take their orders.

"A Gulder for me, two stouts for Lorenchi and Tommy and—"

"A bottle of Harp lager?" the boy asked.

Tambo nodded.

TJ looked at Ejiro and me. "What will you guys have?"

I knew before I answered that Lorenchi would burst into another fit of laughter.

"Two Fantas," I said. Lorenchi did not disappoint me. But something else bugged me. I could not put my finger on it, but I knew it was important.

"So, you were saying?" TJ wiped the head of lager that overflowed from the rim of his tumbler. Waiting for an answer, he flicked the foam on his fingertips away and stared at me.

I listed the items taken from me, omitting my magazines. No need for them to know about that. No need to give Lorenchi's mirth more ammunition. It was sunny outside, and the chilled-to-the-bone beer that I paid for loosened up their tongues, and TJ and his boys let loose an endless flow of gist on us. What was particularly interesting was the history of Uniben according to TJ. His perspective on events of his five sessions here was fascinating. He told us about the "engineering massacre" of 1989. According to him, this was caused by a quarrel—over a girl, a slap, who slapped her, and why—between members of the Maphite and Black Axe confraternities. This small misunderstanding had snowballed over many months, culminating in the first Uniben student confraternity killing of an FGC Warri alumnus who bled to death at the junction of Oba Ewaure and First. Two days later, the fatal stabbing led to the greatest clash of arms that any university in the country had yet seen. About forty boys from the rival gangs had fought for about twenty minutes in the faculty of engineering. The blood. The gore. It was a wonder no one died.

Professor Williams's response was characteristic. She expelled the Maphite confra into nonexistence. Somehow, the university authorities got hold of photos taken at a Maphite postinitiation party. When the senate disciplinary hearings were held, numerous denials were met with the inevitable photographs of the suspect holding a glass of beer and dancing with what seemed like reckless abandon while holding on to a girl's waist. The Black Axe was similarly decimated, although less so as no photos of them were found. TJ made no bones about his disappointment that members of the Black Axe had survived Professor Williams's purge. They, after all, owned the turf he lived on. The Cosa Nostra boys that lived here kept a low profile. As we found out over time, rearing your head up too high meant you risked getting it chopped off.

"You see, these guys are so crass. So rude. The boys who took your stuff are most likely Ah-kay boys," TJ said, using the term that everyone called the Black Axe members. Ah-kay. "Don't worry, sha. We will get it all back for you."

He then told us what it would take. He had his strong suspicions about who took our belongings. As we knew, Ekosodin was Black Axe territory. Thus, he, as a fine boy, could not make trouble where he was not strong. We would have to buy our stuff back.

Buy our stuff back? For what?

They were on their third bottles, so I thought he was not being serious. He was. There was nothing to worry about. We would have to give them a thousand naira, much less than our stuff was worth, and then Lorenchi and Tommy would leave for the suspects' "base of operations" and "negotiate" for our stuff. Within an hour or two, if we were lucky and these were indeed the thieves, we would be leaving Ekosodin with our things.

I glanced at Ejiro and Tambo and noticed how differently they were taking it. Tambo was silently encouraging me with his eyes, barely able to keep his mouth closed, buoyed as he was with two bottles of sweaty lager. Ejiro, on the other hand, was uncomfortable and leaned in to whisper in my ear, "Guy, I no trust these guys. What if they take our money run?"

"No worry. Nothing dey happen," I whispered back.

Why were Tambo and Ejiro leaving me to make the decision? They were both older. I decided it was a risk worth taking. True, true, wetin for fit happen? Nothing. Tambo would not knowingly take us to a place where we would be in danger, would he? I made up my mind.

"TJ, okay. But we only have seven hundred naira. Hope that will do?"

TJ rubbed his goatee, considered our offer, and said, "Sure. Why not? Bring the dough."

I counted thirty of the twenty-naira notes I had in my pocket and collected five more from Ejiro. We gave these to TJ, who, without counting, handed them over to Lorenchi and Tommy. He spoke to them—an odd language, it seemed a pastiche of words from mafia films and pidgin—and they left, hopefully to get back our stuff, or "loot," the word I heard repeated during the cryptic exchange.

Tambo stubbed out his cigarette and left with Lorenchi and Tommy. I bought TJ another stout and we continued gisting. He asked us where home was, and we told him.

"Ah! Warri boys. You guys are supposed to be hard guys now. Why you let this thing happen to una?" he asked.

Ejiro laughed and said, "What could we have done?"

These were my thoughts exactly. What did this guy expect us to have done? We had not even taken our matriculation oaths; the ceremony was coming up in three weeks' time. Our legs, as the sophomores reminded us on our hostel block, were one foot in, one foot out of the university. But somehow, I knew before TJ said anything more where the conversation was headed.

"You guys are fine boys now," he said. "You are supposed to be moving with fine boys too. If you were with me, under my protection, this could never happen."

He turned from his beer to look at the two of us. What a sight we must have seemed to him. Ejiro, my immediate senior in THS, fancied himself a bodybuilder. Very handsome with an aquiline nose I had seen replicated in all his siblings, he was finally losing his teenage baby fat and already had the wisp of a mustache shading his upper lip. I was a slight contrast to my friend. I was fair, shorter, and had an intense stare that girls in secondary school told me was unnerving—"bedroom eyes," they called them. We would make good additions to the Cosa Nostra confra.

Neither of us replied. We pretended not to know what he was talking about, so he continued. "Since you resumed, have any guys spoken to you about blending?"

Of course, yes. We told him so.

"Has anyone from the Cosa Nostra blocked you guys?"

"No," we chorused.

"That's because we don't just go around begging any Tom, Dick, and Harry. Ours is an elite club. The real fine boys, that's who we are. I mean, look una two. A fine pair. Well brought up and articulate. What the Cosa Nostra needs are boys like una two. What would you think about joining?"

Ejiro launched into his standard rebuttal to any request he received to blend. "You see, TJ, my father is a pastor. So is my mother. Forget say we be Warri boys. We didn't grow up in those parts of town. The last thing I was told before leaving for school was not to join any cult. They say you guys swear blood oaths. Ah, if I join una, my papa go kill me."

These should have been enough reasons for him not to dream of ever joining confra, right? The real reason why boys like Ejiro, Wilhelm, and I never thought of blending was an intense and very-difficult-to-hide sense of superiority. It was not morals. It was not fear. I just felt I was better than the lot. And from conversations with Wilhelm and Ejiro, I knew they felt the same. But TJ was another thing altogether. He was from our side of the tracks: upper middle class, articulate, an I-don't-care aura. Very enthralling. I did not feel superior to him. I admired the respect with which people treated him on Green House Road as they greeted him when we walked down to the beer parlor. His responses seemed sincere: a nod here, a firm, two-handed shake there.

He laughed when he finally digested what Ejiro had said. "Blood oaths! Where did you get that? Do you guys like mafia films?"

We both nodded.

"Haven't you noticed the way the dons carry themselves? With honor. Even among bad guys there must be honor. What the Cosa Nostra stands for is the protection of honor and dignity. No one should step on your toes, and if you're with us, God punishes the one who tries. Is that what your father told you not to join? Something that protects honor?

"Look at what is happening today. You guys came to me to get what was stolen from you. Not your stuff. No, not that. You came for your stolen pride, your lost dignity. Your honor. That is what was snatched away yesterday."

His beer was getting hot. He had not touched it for about four minutes. He was so intent on us, on convincing us with his logic. He would have pressed further but for the beer attendant who broke his train of thought by asking if there was anything else we needed. Then I saw it: the look in his eyes when he glared at the poor boy. It instantly vanished though, replaced again by the grin, the smile with which I suspected he camouflaged his ruthlessness.

I changed the subject. "Where for Lagos you dey stay?"

Glancing apprehensively at me, Ejiro shooed the beer parlor attendant away.

"Ikeja," TJ said. "Off Allen Avenue."

What I have since noticed is how common the deus ex machina is in real life. If I were telling a story and wrote what happened next, it would have been taboo. In fiction. But not here. No, not here. I pressed further. I don't know why I did. It was just to change the subject and to find out more about him, where he lived, what he did before he came to university, and who he was.

"Which side?" I asked. "I mean, I spend holidays with my aunt who lives on Oluwaleyimu. Do you stay anywhere around there?"

TJ's eyes lit up. "It's a lie. Where on Oluwaleyimu?"

"Opposite the snooker joint. Just after Washerman Dry-cleaners," I said, wondering what the look on his face meant.

"Are you serious?" He roared with laughter. "I live on Olu-waleyimu. Who is your aunty?"

"Alero," I replied. "Alero Tsewo. Do you know her?"

He was quiet for a moment. He reached for his glass of amber lager and drained it. Then he spoke, "The barrister! This world is a small place o. You are Justin's brother?"

"His cousin," I replied. Justin Tsewo was my big cousin. He lived with our aunt, a single mom, in her three-bedroom apartment in Lagos. He was finishing up a first degree in computer science at the University of Lagos. So TJ knew him. This was getting interesting.

"Me and Justin are like this," TJ said. He held up his left hand with the fore and middle fingers crossed. "Small world. He told me his smallie was entering Uniben this year. I am supposed to look after you. I'm supposed to protect—" He paused and looked away. "Small world," he repeated.

I was supposed to be on the lookout for this guy. My cousin had told me he had some friends in Uniben. I was to try and contact them if things became too hot with the confra issue. He did not want me to blend. He said his guys were connected and that they would protect me from "anyhow" confra boys. The irony. But the name he gave me was not TJ; it was Toju. No excuse. I should have made the connection. So the guy who was supposed to protect me from confra was the one toasting me to join up. TJ's face was back in his glass, which was empty now.

I said, hinting at our special relationship, "Na you be Toju? I'm supposed to block you if I have any problems."

TJ turned a dark purple and sighed. Ejiro had a confused smile on his face, signaling that he was glad with the direction the gist was taking even though he had lost track of it.

TAMBO CAME back with Lorenchi and Tommy. They were hauling a large brown traveling bag. My heart leapt. I recognized it as Ejiro's. Happy that we had our stuff back, he was smiling beside me. When we asked how things went, they only smiled and said that we should not worry.

TJ called me aside, and we spoke for a minute or two before I finally left with my guys. He told me not to tell Justin about what had happened. He would square things with me later on and since I now knew his place, if I had any problems all I had to do was holla at him.

"OMO-BOYS, you guys have heart o."

Kayoh had been talking for over ten minutes. We were in our room, gathered around the half-empty bag from which my roommates were each collecting their stuff—lost and found. No one felt the pull of the car park tonight. I had replaced the glass bulb of my lantern and the dull, still light of the yellow kerosene flame accentuated the lines on Kayoh's face as he showered praises on me, Ejiro, and Tambo.

"So Oliver, wetin happen?" I asked Tambo. He had been strangely evasive about the walk he had taken with TJ's goons, insisting that he would gist us when the car park committee members were all present.

"Yeah, Tambo, what happened?" Harry repeated my question.

Tambo smiled cryptically at all of us and insisted that we finish distributing the stolen items. Not everyone recovered what he had lost. I, for one, could not find my laundry iron. At least my radio was back. We finished up and followed Tambo outside to the raised walkways between the hostel blocks. Sitting, legs dangling over the edge, we waited for him to tell us how his walk had gone.

"After I had left with Lorenchi and Tommy, we went to one guy's room at the other end of Ekosodin. One of Yibril's friends, una no go know am. Bad Axeman, men! Anyway, I waited outside while the other guys entered and started the negotiations. Oboy, they quarreled o. The guy was denying everything. This was what I heard from the other side of the door until they offered him money to help them recover the stuff. Then the tone of the gist changed. He said that they should have said so at the beginning, and the next thing they came out with Ejiro's traveling bag, and the rest you know."

He stopped speaking, took a St. Moritz from his pocket, and lit it, caressing the blue-gray smoke with his lips before blowing it out into the dark, starlit night.

There were six of us out that night: Kayoh, me, Wilhelm, Ejiro, Harry, and Tambo. I think the presence of these friends prevented the fight from happening. Something had been bothering me since we sat in the beer parlor. It had just clicked.

I asked, "Where you talk say you know TJ from?"

I remembered the answer Tambo had given to the question that Ejiro had asked last night. He had said he did not know them personally; that they were just guys he knew by reputation. That was the reason he gave when he went in first to speak with them the moment we entered Green House in Ekosodin; that since they were not that well-known to him, it would be rude for the three of us to just barge into Green House.

"What did I tell you?" Tambo looked at me, suddenly suspicious, his stubby fingertips going to his mouth.

Kayoh, who couldn't abide his nail biting, pulled Tambo's hand from his mouth. I watched a thin strand of saliva stretch between Tambo's right hand and mouth. I watched it break when Tambo pulled away from Kayoh's grasp.

"I can't remember. Tell us again," I said.

He fidgeted with his cigarette uncomfortably and murmured something about my provoking him.

Wilhelm, confused by my tone, cut in, "Ewaen, what's wrong with you? Tambo na 'im organize the return of una things. Your radio, Ejiro's bag. If you have anything to say, say it and stop confusing us."

I did. "Tambo. You said you did not know these guys. How come TJ knew the exact brand of beer you drank?"

"Not TJ," Ejiro said. "It was the barboy. The barboy knew what he drank."

Tambo looked at me. They all looked at me. The only person with a measure of understanding was Ejiro since he was there. No one spoke. Ejiro kept on looking at me. He got it. But I would not be the one to explain this. No, not me. I felt it, I knew it, but I couldn't, wouldn't, say it. Tambo's posturing, his murmuring that I was looking for trouble, had worked. His eyes said it all; he knew people. He was now a confra boy.

Ejiro spoke, this time turning from his seat on the ledge to face the group. "Do you guys know that Tambo, our friend, left us with these guys make them toast us to join confra? To blend. And he said he didn't know them. He knows them. If he could lie about that, how do we know that these guys didn't organize this whole theft? First, to obtain our dough and second, to get some more boys for their confra. How do we know tha—"

"Shut up!" Tambo screamed and lunged at Ejiro. A flurry of sparks flew from his cigarette butt as it tumbled through the air and bounced off the concrete of the walkway onto the ground. "Idiot! Your father! You dey accuse me? I don't blame you. Devil solder your yansh!"

Ejiro, bodybuilding enthusiast that he was, shot his right hand up and in front of him. The rest of us struggled to our feet. Ejiro had Tambo by the throat; his right arm, a solid iron bar, seemed like a slave trader's shackle connecting both their heads. Ejiro had one single bone, no joints, in that arm.

I stood at Ejiro's side and whispered in his ear, "Guy, cool down. Cool down."

"Imagine the fool?" Ejiro said. "Because person quiet? Because person quiet he feel say we be fools. Na by force to join confra?" Ejiro's eyes had narrowed to thin slits.

I stared at Tambo. Both of his hands tried to pry open Ejiro's fingers. He was being helped by Wilhelm and Kayoh. Harry remained sitting, laughing his arse off, tears collecting at the corners of his eyes, and holding onto his sides. A very far-off squeak-squeak sound seemed to come from Tambo.

Kayoh shouted, "Ejiro, you wan' kill am? Stop. Stop!"

Ejiro finally let go. Tambo didn't drop to the ground like I thought he would, like we all thought he would. He took a step back, rubbed at his neck, and continued shouting.

"Na you too know me, Ejiro? Na you too know me? Ha! You don see me finish! This is pure see-finish!"

"I go beat you o," Ejiro said. He spoke quieter now. There was a hint of a smile at the corner of his lips. His eyes did not smile though.

Kayoh quieted Tambo down and asked him if he had anything to do with the theft. He denied involvement and told us this story: Tommy, TJ's dark bodyguard, approached Tambo after Kayoh left him the night of the theft. It was just on the side path into Hall Three. Tambo could still see Kayoh walking on towards his room in Hall Four when Tommy told him that his roommates had just been robbed and that if they wanted their things back, he should bring them to see TJ. That was all he knew. And yes, he knew them personally. We did not press on the point, content as we were with this strong confirmation that Tambo had blended Cosa Nostra.

"Ewaen, Ejiro, there is no need to be angry. The reason why I shouted just now was because it just dawned on me that I was being played. My mind was not there at all—all I wanted was to get our things back. Una know how much I owe you guys. You accommodated me when I no get anywhere stay, and una feel say I go betray una? I could never. I could never."

Tambo continued rubbing at his neck; I could see that a welt had developed just above his collarbone.

Kayoh was standing between Tambo and Ejiro. "Why didn't you call me back?" he asked Tambo. "I was right there, Oliver Tambo. You could have called me back."

Students passed us without looking up, suspicious that those bad A109 boys were at it again.

Tambo did not say anything.

We still had doubts: Did he really not know about the theft? Did the Cosa Nostra steal our things? Oliver Tambo said no, it was really Black Axe boys who robbed us. It seemed it was a scam they played. Take the things, put the word out that you had them, and then wait for any protectors the victims had to intervene and buy them back. The Cosa Nostra did not rob us. They just knew who did.

It seemed as though he was speaking the truth. I believed him.

5

THE NON-ACADEMIC Staff Union, NASU, called off their strike a week after Saint Valentine's Day. A month after full activities returned to the university, the academic staff union resumed their strike, protesting the salary increases NASU managed to get from the government. If NASU received a so-and-so percentage increase in salaries, it followed that the lecturers' union, ASUU, deserved their percentage too. So we were back home after three months in school.

The car park committee dispersed after a last plenary session in which we exchanged phone numbers and promised to keep in touch. Kayoh went back to Lagos to work in his father's petrol station; Ejiro would be in Warri at Enerhen Junction, opposite the old Kingsway Stores, working in his father's business center and barbing salon; and Wilhelm and I left school in one of Daddy's company cars. I would resume my vacation job as a purchasing clerk, while Wilhelm was to go back to his job as a general, all-around annoyance. Tuoyo had been in a car accident and broke his hand before the strike shut down the school; he was still busy with his physiotherapy sessions and called me—during one of the very small gaps in which the telephones worked—thanking God that ASUU was on strike because he had not yet learned to write with his left hand. Different strokes, I guess, although I should have been thankful too. I would have failed the end-of-semester exams booked for the end of April, but as things stood, I had a chance to catch up on my schoolwork.

Back home, I got the surprise I had been expecting. It was a year late, but it was coming. I knew this, but I was still disappointed. Mom was not at home. The first sign that something was wrong was the unusual quietness of Michael, our driver, during the ride from Benin. Any questions about Mom, my siblings, and the house were deftly deflected; Wilhelm was in the car to distract me from properly noting how reticent the driver was being.

The real first sign that my parents had quarreled again should have been the fact that Mom had come to my matriculation ceremony alone. I had tried to call the house and Daddy's office beforehand, but the telephones were down again. What finally confirmed it was when, after dropping Wilhelm off at DSC, I got home and saw that Iye, my father's mother, was there. My grandmother's presence meant trouble—either she was its cause, or she appeared after the fact. The timing seemed a bit off; Daddy and Mommy had their major quarrels every two years. It was like clockwork. Every even year I could remember, '82, '84, '86, '88, and '90, all had a month or two when we packed up and left with Mom to our other granny's, Nene. Most times, this displacement was preceded by a night of terror from which Mom emerged with a black eye here or a bruise there. But she always went back.

Ete, our Efik gateman, opened the gate for me and Michael. Osaze ran alongside the car all the way to the garage, hailing and screaming his welcomes. Eniye was waiting there with Iye.

"Ko'o, my pikin," Iye said as I jumped down from the car.

I walked to where she stood. She wore a toothless smile. *Haba!* She had forgotten her dentures again. She had once been beautiful, strikingly so, according to Daddy, whose somewhat biased opinion was confirmed by several stunning black-and-white photographs he kept in his room. She was very light skinned and had the most hypnotic stare, and below this, a short stubby nose with wide nostrils that were more expressive than any mouth. They flared when she was angry, they narrowed when she was moody, and they seemed to come together when she smiled. My sister had the same nose.

Daddy always regaled us with tales of Iye's prowess in business. "Iye is a great trader," Daddy would say. "Don't let her small stature and kind demeanor fool you. You can't outsell that woman." Small stature, yes. But kind demeanor? Who was Daddy fooling?

"Koyo, Iye," I said, unsure if I had pronounced the Bini greeting well.

She laughed. "Ko'o, my pikin. Obokhian!" she said again and again, each greeting followed by my replies that everything was fine; that yes, I had eaten; that I was not fighting in school; that Michael did not overspeed. The typical Bini greeting lasts minutes. On the receiving end, it can seem to go on for hours, like now. Iye finally broke the marathon session off and walked away, still repeating, "Ko'o, Ko'o." The bemused smile on Osaze's face summed up our usual reaction to a welcome from Iye.

Osaze went to Michael and collected some of my luggage from him. I lugged my box after my brother, and we struggled up the stairwell, turning at the first bank. Eniye, behind and not saying anything, which was unusual, followed us through the children's parlor into the bedroom wing. Down the corridor, to the right, was our room—the boys' room. The air-conditioning had tripped off again, and Osaze left us to go to the switchbox to turn the circuit breaker back on.

As the two-horsepower machine droned, filling the room with a steady stream of cool air, Eniye said to me, "Daddy beat Mommy."

Nothing more.

I understood.

Osaze came back into the room, and the twins told me all that had happened. Two weeks before my matriculation ceremony, Aunty Alero had visited from Lagos. She was fronting for property developers who wanted to dispose of some buildings in Warri. Aunty felt that her brother-in-law would be interested; she had beat the prices down to the last that her clients were prepared to take. Daddy was interested. Everyone was smiling until the question of saying thank you to Aunty Alero came up. Daddy, shrewd businessman that he was, jumped on the rule that estate agents were not supposed to demand gifts from prospective buyers. Alero was not his agent, he said. He was right, of course, but that was not the point. Aunty left days later without the houses sold, and then the arguments began. Daddy was upset that Mommy had not taken his side. He even accused her of "sabotaging" (Eniye remembered the word being shouted) the "family." The row had escalated and ended as their arguments usually did—Mommy left for her mother's. Why had Mom not said anything during my matriculation ceremony?

I UNPACKED my bags. Despite everything, it was good to be home. I missed my room and my bed, even though I would have to share it with Osaze since Iye was visiting. I looked around. Eniye and Osaze were wrestling with my traveling bag on what was now Iye's temporary bed. Behind them, through the window, I could see the pigeonholes of the children's dining room. Our bedroom was big. The walls were covered with deep-brown plywood paneling about a quarter of an inch thick. The floor tiles were in terrazzo, a light blue, and the poor lighting occasioned by the smallness of our windows was relieved by bright fluorescent lights that were tucked behind the dark-brown curtain heads. We had been living here since I was ten, but I was still a stranger in my own house. I was the victim of what Wilhelm called the firstborn syndrome: at ten I was put in a boarding house. The first term holidays saw me return with only the clothes on my back; then it was decided that the twins would not go to hostel in their first year in secondary school. The experiment was continuing, I knew. If my experiences so far in a university hostel were anything to go by, Osaze and Eniye would be off-campus residents by the time they got to university. Being firstborn came with its luggage.

I DROVE to see my mother later that afternoon. She was in the kitchen with Nene preparing some starch and owho soup for Osaze and me. We had left Eniye at home so it would not seem empty if my father came back from work early. Osaze and I watched pirate satellite television in Nene's parlor.

"Food don done o! Osaze and Ewaen, come to the table and eat," Nene shouted from the door of the kitchen. She was holding a tray with steaming ceramic bowls. She stood by the dining table after dropping her load and called for Mom to bring the cold water from the fridge. She smiled at us, her reading glasses steamed by the wisps of water vapor from the soup and starch she had been carrying.

Looking back, I think it was years later before I realized it was not normal for Nigerian grannies to wear bifocals. My Nene was special; the YWCA had educated her in the thirties. She had gone to school in Ghana—where she obtained her City and Guilds—and had come back to marry my grandfather. But a sweet little Mama Goose she was not; if you were her grandchild and expected to spend holidays with her spoiled and pampered, you were in for a shock. She checked our homework and had a mean left hook with the watering can.

We sat at the table to eat. I had just mastered—okay, "mastered" is stretching it—the manual dexterity needed for cutting the lumps of jelly-like starch down to a size amenable to swallowing. I found Osaze hadn't yet. His right hand was high in the air, a globular mass of yellow jelly connecting it to the plate, dangling, I swear, two feet from the table.

The plate fell, landing on the table with a terrible clang and Nene's shout. "Aha! Osaze, you still can't cut starch? Come, let me help you." She unstuck his fingers from the still-dangling lump, which she placed back on the plate. I watched as she pressed against the sticky mass with the outside of her right forefinger and miraculously produced a lime-sized piece which she dipped in owho and then put in my fifteen-year-old brother's mouth. *Seeing* it was different from *doing* it. Waiting, I placed my plate directly beside Mom's. She would have to do the whole single-finger magic for me. She and Nene were experts at it.

While Mom cut my pieces, she spoke. "I am resuming my part-time law in September o."

"Oh, that's good," I said. She was going back to school. In '88 she had had the epiphany that she did not like science after all. She decided she wanted to study law and enrolled for the six-year part-time program at the University of Benin. She had deferred the place in '91, with just two years left, because of the vehement protests of my father, who had insisted that it was a waste of family time and a waste of company time—here he was trying to refocus the family financially and she was gallivanting in university. So now she was going back. Mom and I in the same school? Cool.

"Yes, good," she repeated. She was not looking at me; she was seemingly concentrating instead on the plate of starch in front of her. "But Daddy is still against it."

Nene kissed her teeth, "*Kpsscheeew*"—a squishing sound made by drawing air into the mouth through clenched teeth. She glanced at Mom and shook her head, "You're still his mumu, shebi? Omasan. Omasan."

"Yes, Ma."

"Omasan. How many times did I call you?"

"Three, Ma," Mom replied.

"You want this man to kill you, abi? You want this Bini man to kill my daughter?" Nene said so quietly I had to strain to catch the words.

"Nene, please. The children."

"Shut up." Nene spoke louder. "Which children? Doesn't he see the children when he's using you as a punching bag? I just can't understand him." Nene stopped talking. There was a look of discomfort on her face. She placed her right hand on her left shoulder, alternately caressing and squeezing the joint. She had not washed the hand, and when she removed it, there was a yellow soup stain on the white jacquard blouse.

My mother's eyes took on an expression of half-fear, half-exasperation. She pushed my plate of starch, the one she had been helping me cut, away. "Ah, Nene, are you taking your medicine? Don't get yourself upset. The doctor said you should take it easy o. Ewaen, go to Nene's room and bring the pink pillbox you see on the dressing table. She needs her glyceryl. Hurry."

As I stood up to go, Nene put her left hand, the clean one, on my shoulder. "Don't worry, my son. I'll be fine." She was taking slow, deep breaths and the look of agony that had crept onto her face seconds ago slowly cleared. She leaned back into the dining chair, bent her head backwards, and with her eyes closed said, "What kind of a man did you marry? I mean, your father, he was no saint. But he never raised a hand to me. God rest his soul, not even in anger." She smiled quietly, remembering. "What he did was a lot worse though. He would just stop talking to you."

Mom smiled too. "He did that to us. I wanted to die anytime Papa used the silent treatment."

Osaze and I watched this exchange between mother and daughter like good African children: seen, not heard. I took and started swallowing the lumps dipped in the soup. I was staring across the table at the two-foot mask balanced in a corner of the room. As far back as I could remember, Nene had had this carving. Mom had told me that it was a drum. It had Portuguese sailors' heads for its plaits, its cheeks stretched down to the floor in tribal-marked jowls, and on its crown was stretched a piece of cowhide. I remembered one of the pictures in an album at home. It was taken just after Osaze and I came back from our only trip abroad in '80. I was four and just inches taller than the mask beside me in that photo. My face was a lot smoother then, with none of the angles that developed from too much suffering in FGC Warri. Daydreaming about the British accent I had developed in a month and struggled for years afterwards to keep in Warri's brutal environment, I barely heard the continuing discussion between Nene and Mom.

"This time, my daughter, you are not going to go back just like that. If I had my way you would not go back at all. Nonsense! Have any of his relatives called yet?"

"His brother called. He was all apologies, explaining that it would all get better; that Imuetiyan was like that from childhood; that he really loves me but is very poor at handling stress."

"It is a weak man who uses anger and rage to show fear. You married a weak man, my daughter. Enough. Never mind them, my dear. Worry about your children. How are they taking it?"

"Nene, I'm blessed o. Look at these two—no problems. Throughout all the wahala of my marriage, Ewaen and Osaze have been fine despite my fears that they'd be like their father. They are going to be complete gentlemen, especially Ewaen with his head always in books—"

"Just like you when you were a child."

"It's Eniye I'm afraid for. She's too much like her father. Not just in appearance and complexion. In character too. Do you know that when he was chasing me around the swimming pool, Eniye was running after him, screaming for him to stop? She has his anger."

"My granddaughter. Not like her twin at all. Where was Osaze when all this was happening?"

Mom reached for Osaze with her left hand, the clean one, and scratched his head. "It only adds to my fear—"

"What fear?"

"That they will fight their father one day."

"Oh. But they will, Omasan. And it might not be because of you."

"Osaze just strolled up to Imuetiyan, as if he appeared from nowhere, and told him quietly to stop beating his mother. And then he walked to where I was lying in the grass, pulled a wrapper over me, and led me into the house. Eniye stood there glaring at her father. She fights her brothers. She cannot be talked down from any course she's chosen to take."

"Omasan, don't worry. She will mellow by the time she turns sixteen. She's always been a tomboy. These things change."

"I hope so. Ewaen, stop playing with your food. Oya, eat! Before it gets cold."

6

DADDY NORMALLY came home from work at around seven in the evening. That first night back from school he did not return until after nine. Osaze said it was because he had been working very hard. Eniye said that this was a lie and that Daddy had a girlfriend. I believed Osaze. Mommy had told me at my matriculation that Daddy had fired some of his new managers at our new bank. The first to go had been the accountant who could not drive, then the personnel manager, the treasury manager—sad, I liked him—and the banking hall manager. Daddy had next promoted their assistants to the newly vacant positions and was essentially running the bank himself. Of the original, most senior staff, only the general manager remained. My father, an engineer by training, was running a bank—albeit a small savings and loan—all by himself. Like he would always say, he was a good money manager and, thus, was suited to handle things at his new office, unlike those fucking bastards who wanted to rob him blind.

We did not talk much that first night. Daddy came home tired. It was a Wednesday. For some reason Wednesday was always a particularly difficult day at the office. Daddy saw me, said his welcome, and went into his room, requesting that his supper be brought there. He looked tired. My father had aged in the three months since I last saw him. The worry lines on his forehead were more deeply set, looking like they had been tattooed in. There seemed to be more gray in his hair.

Daddy called me into his room on Sunday morning. He asked about school. I told him about the confra boys, about smelly toilets filled to the brim, about the classes that we took in stadium-sized lecture halls without microphones, and about the cost of living, food, and handouts.

He laughed, "I know where you are going with this, son." His eyes glittered as though he had caught me in a lie.

"What?" I said. But I knew. Daddy was playing defense, preventing me from even beginning the necessary request for an increase in my pocket money. The mischievous and embarrassed smile on my face gave me away. We laughed together even as I said, "But, Daddy, the money is not enough. Seven hundred fifty naira can't last two weeks. I barely manage."

"But that's the point, sonny-boy. You're supposed to manage it. When I was in school, I don't think I ever sent home for extra money more than four times." He had started again with this old story.

"Daddy, that's because you had a full scholarship that paid for everything. You even told me that you used to forge lists to send to your brother so you would have extra cash."

"Children. Don't you forget anything? When they call off the strike, I'll see what I can do," he said.

Right, I thought, *you're planning to give an increase of a mighty fifty naira.* "Thanks, Dad," I said. Then I remembered something. "Dad, when I was in 500 LT, I noticed I couldn't see the blackboard from the back of the class—"

"What were you doing in the back of the class? If you went earlier, you would have been in front."

"Not that," I said, slightly irritated with the interruption of my flow. "I then tried on one of my friend's glasses, one Osayeni—"

"That's a Bini name."

"Yes, he is Bini. I put on his glasses and everything was clear. And my friend is short-sighted. I want to see an optometrist. I think I might need glasses."

"That's no surprise," he said.

Completing the sentence for him in my mind, I knew he meant to say, *Your mother is short-sighted. I was wondering which of you inherited that trait from her.* Instead he said, "Write up a list when it's time for school and we'll go through it together."

I turned to go, whispering a thank you, but he stopped me. He went to the small fridge in the kitchenette in the left-hand corner of the room. While I waited for the treat I knew he had just put in the microwave, I looked around. As usual, his wardrobe doors were open. Hanging from the brown mahogany doors were his trousers. Worn only once, all of them. The twins and I called them our bank; we would sneak into his room when he was not in—either taking a stroll around the garden or at work—and steal the loose change he had forgotten there. At times, our withdrawals reached three thousand naira, and I was asking for an increase from seven-fifty. But, like Daddy said, he was training us to handle money.

He came back into the room proper holding a tray of fried meat and a bottle of blackcurrant juice.

He asked me to get two glasses from the tray on top of the fridge. As I ambled to the fridge, I contemplated what we were going to talk about that warranted this luxury. I knew it would have something to do with Mommy. I was going to delay the gist. As I came back to the cream upholstered parlor chair, I said, "You didn't come for my matriculation."

"My son."

"You didn't come. Only Mommy came. It was the most important day of my life so far, and I was really expecting my whole family. But you guys didn't come. Why?"

"Ewaen, listen to me. The most important day of your life *until now*, yes. But I'm your father. My expectations for you . . . look, getting into the university is nothing. The day that will make me proud is when you graduate. My children are not for matriculation; they are for graduation! As you get older, you'll know that this day was nothing. Anybody can matriculate. The most important day will be your graduation, your convocation. You'll see." He was really trying to make me feel better. Was it working? I did not know. The logic was sound. What did I know about life?

I said, "You're wrong, Dad. The most important day I'm expecting next will be when I pass my Second MB exams."

He laughed. I joined in.

He turned serious and said, "Ewaen, you are getting older now. There are some things we need to talk about." Here it comes. Whenever this was the topic, he always said I was getting older and that there were things I needed to know. "Have you seen your mother since you came back?"

I wasn't getting drawn into this conversation. Not actively, if I could bear it. "Yes," I said reluctantly. I would keep quiet for the rest of it.

"It's her sisters."

I shifted uncomfortably, staring straight down at the patterned Persian rug at the foot of my father's bed.

Daddy continued, "You know everything was fine before Rosan came back from England and started filling your mother's head with nonsense about politics. See, a woman's place is by her husband, not gallivanting all over town. I warned your mother. She said I was clipping her wings. That I had been preventing her from progressing ever since we married. Imagine that. That was how they started the House of Reps thing. Okay, so Rosan gets elected. The next thing I hear is that my wife wants to move to Lagos to be with her sister as her personal assistant. Thank God for the coup. We would certainly have divorced. Your mom doesn't understand that she's the only one still married amongst her sisters. This is Nigeria. She doesn't understand . . . then that small one that I watched grow up . . ." He paused and cast his eyes down momentarily, as if apologizing for his temper. "That Alero comes prancing in here trying to cheat me . . ."

He continued talking. About the time he stopped Mom from pursuing her doctorate in biochemistry, insisting that she had children to raise. About the plans he had for setting up a pharmaceutical company for his wife to run. But her attitude . . . about the time he had to fire her because they were taking the quarrels from the house into the office and vice versa. I remembered that one. It was morning. I was six and had watched my mom being led back into the house with her nightgown torn, escorted by our secretary, Felicia, who provided the wrapper that covered my mother's nakedness. I did not say a word. But, oh, I wanted to ask him so many questions. How come I have never heard both of you say you love each other, Dad? How come you always get back together only to break each other all over again? Why have I never seen you two exchange a tender touch? Why did you get married? Why do you beat her, Daddy? Why?

We spent about an hour together. It was a marathon monologue. After he finished, I felt the way I always did when he offloaded on me: angry, broken, starting with a display of thunder and lightning and ending with the depressing rain that quenched fire but did nothing to disperse the ashes that remained of my soul. All he had to tell me always left me numb. I do not know why he did it. Mom never spoke about him in the same way. Never. Was he expecting me to hate my mother? I could not understand any of it. All I knew was that I could never hit a woman. I would never.

MOMMY AND Daddy settled their quarrel two months later. I had spent the day at Wilhelm's house with Kpobo and Brenda. We sat down to eat a German dish that Wilhelm's mom had made—something that tasted like meat but looked a lot like bread. Wilhelm was angry that I was skipping out on *Street Fighter 2* Saturdays. I left the three of them after thoroughly reminding them who was the "king" and drove home. When I drove back home by four that evening, I met Michael driving out of the gate with Iye in the back seat. Nobody had told me Iye was leaving. Dad was in his room, and since he was not seeing her off, I guessed that Iye had had enough of her stubborn son. Later that evening, a horn blared out from the gate. Mommy was back. No ceremony. She parked outside the garage, came down, gave us each a perfunctory hug, and walked straight to her room.

The rest of my "holiday" went by quickly. Mommy and Daddy slowly warmed up to each other. They sat together at night under the white streetlights that surrounded the pool and watched us swim. They both teased me about nonexistent girlfriends I was supposed to have in school. June and July passed quickly, routine months only lit up by the controversy over the June 12 election and its annulment. Daddy, who saw an undertone of conspiracy in everything, was convinced that the university lecturers' strike was allowed to last this long because the military government did not want the students in school during the elections. That concentration of educated and, in most cases, crazy young people would have been like a jerry can of nitroglycerine in the back seat of a 404 pickup van driving on an old potholed road.

The lecturers suspended the strike in August, a week after the Interim National Government was sworn in. The stuttering riots in Lagos protesting the annulment had been brutally put down. The junta said they were "stepping aside" to let peace reign. There was this Ikeja lawyer on the pages of newspapers who wrote screaming op-eds about not letting those who murdered a journalist in '86 go free. Noisy period, it was.

7

A LUTA Continua! Vitoria e certa! School was like an army camp. Everywhere you turned, there was a police van surrounded by gun-toting Mobile policemen. The government was taking no chances. The tension in the university was like a rubber band stretched too tight. Every evening, in front of Hall One, a de facto meeting hall was set up. Students like Thompson TT Talabi, Nna Ojukwu, and our Students' Union president, Mike Igini, climbed the soapbox and spoke truth to power. I remembered stopping once or twice to listen. They recalled the history of Nigeria from amalgamation onwards; they reminded us about the promises the junta had made—promises which they said had been broken at every turn; they spoke about "Maradona," our military president, in not-very-flattering terms; and they punctuated everything with the name of the great Mandela. *A Luta Continua! Vitoria e certa!*

I just wanted to get back to schoolwork. The newspapers had saturated me with enough about June 12. The television stations—not national, mostly CNN and the BBC—ran intermittent specials on the state of the giant of Africa. They gave a balanced view, allowing the inevitable government spokespeople, who invented an art form out of overturning logic, and the usually disheveled pro-democracy activists, who looked like they needed a haircut, like bohemians without the style, like beat poets without the talent, to present their perspectives. I had spent my strike holiday reading and catching up on the A-level schoolwork that Nigerian university students do in year one. I was in a rush to get back to class. But not everyone felt the same. The arguments we held in the car park often spilled over into the room and into sleeping time. Ejiro had an uncle in prison, accused as a civilian collaborator in the Orkar coup attempt of '90. Ejiro held an unshakable position on what the pro-democracy activists should have done to the head of the junta. Others, like Omogui, felt that the acclaimed winner of the June 12 elections, MKO Abiola, was not a saint.

"See, Kayoh, Ejiro. We don't know what might have informed their decision to annul the elections. MKO is the general's close friend. Maybe he knows that he's a bad guy," Omogui said.

It was 10 p.m. that night in A109. Kayoh was spending the night with us and lay beside me on my bed, facing the wall and backing Omogui in disgust. Ejiro paced around the center table, stopping now and again to kick it in anger.

Omogui continued, "I mean it was you, Ejiro, who said that MKO was involved in the '83 coup, that he bankrolled it. How can we allow a guy who did that become president?"

Ejiro replied, "That is not for IBB to decide."

"But no be only him decide, na. The Army Council voted unanimously to annul the election. Isn't that a kind of democracy?"

"Haba," Kayoh whispered beside me. I giggled and nudged his back. He said, "This Omogui na big fool o."

"Na 'im politics. Leave him with his views. Everybody is allowed one."

Ejiro said to Omogui, "Even if, as you say, it was a collective decision by the Armed Forces Ruling Council, it was not theirs to make. The Nigerian people decided. And don't give me that nonsense about the election results not being completely released. How many people do you think voted for the goat in the other party? They think it's their God-given right to lord it over us. Dress a goat in agbada, and we will vote for him."

"But you insist that if the same goat was dressed in babariga we should vote for him?" Omogui said.

"I mean . . . did you watch the debate? The presidential debate? When they asked the Republican Party candidate what he would do about desertification and droughts in the north, he said he would build rainwater receptacles. Rainwater receptacles! He actually said he would run drains from their roofs to gutters built around them for his people to drink from!"

"Wouldn't it have worked?" I think Omogui argued more to annoy than to inform. I felt sorry for Ejiro. He looked ready to burst. He was sweating. He still paced around the room, although he had stopped kicking at the table's legs. He looked as though he was preparing to kick Omogui.

Ejiro said, "Tofa didn't even know the price of fuel."

"Did you vote?" Omogui knew the question always upset Ejiro. He had turned eighteen a month too late to take part in the voter-registration exercise that preceded the election. Besides, his father would never have allowed him to go outside on election day, saying, "It's a very dangerous time." Ejiro always had the carpet pulled from under him by this question when he was in the flow of his argument. He hated it.

"When I say you be idiot, you go dey follow me drag," Ejiro muttered.

I started laughing. Kayoh and Omogui joined in, and soon Ejiro's face was cracked by a wide smile that became noisy laughter.

We ignored the scream from the next room that filtered rather too easily through the paper-thin walls, "People are trying to sleep here! Shut the fuck up!"

WE STARTED going to lectures more regularly after the strike: zoology, botany, organic chemistry, and physics. Dreaded subjects. We also came upon the lecturers who spent all the allocated time talking about the handouts they were selling. With these, we were promised that we would pass. Without, we were told to make sure we read hard, really hard. The most expensive handout was for ZOO 101, the easiest course.

I remember ZOO 101 for two things. It was during its classes that I experienced the most embarrassing and exhilarating moments of my first year in university. First, the embarrassing one: We had eaten a treat prepared for us that morning by Wilhelm. He had spent the night in A109 and promised he was going to make one of his mom's special German omelets with fried plantain. It tasted good, but, guy, was it in a hurry to get digested. It was less than forty-five minutes after breakfast, and I had broken out in this goose-pimpled, shivering cold sweat. The short female lecturer always started each class with an admonition for those who wanted midclass breaks: there would be none. And if anyone dared her, she would take the person's particulars and fail them. I sat through the class sweating and shivering at the same time. The eggs were peeking out of my yansh. Anyone who has seen a National Geographic special about meerkats will have a graphic picture of what I am trying to explain—bobbing out, slipping back in. Wilhelm sat beside me, and instead of apologizing, he spent the remainder of the lecture laughing his head off. And if you had seen the small thing that came out when I made it back to the hostel . . . one small squirt, and I was done. My experience was the topic at that night's car park parliament.

The second episode was the exhilarating one. I saw her walking in with Omogui and one other girl, Janet. Janet was Omogui's girlfriend—Janet Bytheway, but everyone called her Janet By-the-way. Janet's friend was fair, wore glasses, and was dressed in a floral-patterned white-and-pink dress. So this was Tseye. Omogui had spoken about her. He hated her. He said she was always around when he needed to get Janet alone. Anytime he wanted a stroll with Janet to some dark corner around school, she always insisted that she could not leave Tseye alone in the room. Omogui was always looking for a double date to escort him to their room. He was always refused. Nobody wanted to hang out with a geek. But Omogui was wrong. Seeing her in person . . . she was an angel. She had the kindest eyes, and the glimmer in them when she smiled? Heaven. The seats beside me were empty that day. It was between lectures, and my friends and I, always late for class, sat in the only seats that were always empty—those in the back. I struggled to catch Omogui's eye, and when I succeeded, motioned them to the free seats. It was as though he read my mind. He sat in the penultimate seat to mine and pulled Janet down into the seat on the other side of him. Tseye smiled at yours truly—oh, that smile—and sat down beside me. We did not talk much that afternoon. All I found out, after we were introduced, was that she was in medicine and she lived in Lagos. The others then settled down to listen to the zoology lecturer who had just come in. I didn't. I was intoxicated by the smell of her— like soap with a hint of an aroma that I imagined an LSD trip would interpret as blue. I could not understand what was happening to me. My mouth felt like I was chewing a concrete-and-custard mix. My heart was doing the Atilogwu dance, and my pen slipped through my fingers. I stayed beside Tseye until the lecture ended. I knew as I watched them leave that I would be escorting Omogui on his next visit to the girls' room.

8

I LOST my virginity a few months after I finished secondary school, when I still did the school run, when I still worked in Dad's company, buying materials for the builders at the head office. That morning—it was October 14, 1992, a Wednesday—I was driving back from FGC Warri along the Ogunu expressway. I had just turned off the flyover near the Chevron complex and had dodged that treacherous pothole whose victims were abandoned on either side of the road—trucks, a few saloons, one station wagon—when I saw her standing under the shade of a dangerously leaning trailer, its left back tires bent like soggy prawn crackers, another victim of the pothole. She was tall for a woman—5'10"—which was about my height. Her hair was blowing in the wind—probably not her hair; it was probably an unfortunate yak's from the Russian steppes, but it was still striking. She seemed a picture from a clichéd Hollywood scene: her skirt was pulled tight to her right, accentuating the left curve of her hips; blown by the breeze, the edges of it flapped in time with her hair. She had her hand stretched out, palm down.

Why did I stop? Why did I, almost too late, stamp on my brakes and screech in a cloud of early Harmattan dust a few meters from where she stood? I had endured another argument between my brother and sister that morning about who I should have dropped off first at school. I had dreamt the night before of Onome, my puppy love from secondary school. While doing my best to ignore the twins during the drive, I had let my mind drift to Entertainment Night in secondary school. The last Saturday of the month, funk, R & B, and hip-hop played until 10 p.m., when the announcement "Junior students, vacate the dance floor, and go to sleep" signaled the beginning of the slow ballads. Slow dance—we called it blues. We were teenagers with our hips and knees slightly flexed, keeping our groins from making contact, ashamed of our arousal. Furtive kisses that began as lips accidently brushed against a cheek, searching, hoping, and ending the night with blue balls, a handkerchief wrapped around ice cubes wedged against your crotch, jealous of the junior students already asleep. That morning in October of '92, on the way back from dropping Osaze and Eniye, I stopped and offered this stranger a lift. I looked in the mirror. I saw her wave to someone behind her, someone in the isolated three-story building behind the damaged Mack truck in whose shade she stood.

When she came to my window, she said, "Are you going towards DSC cross-and-stop?"

Was I going to the cross-and-stop junction? No.

"Yes."

She opened the car door and entered. It was her hair. Permed, shoulder-length with honey-blonde highlights in a halo extending from ear to ear. She was fair, with small tribal marks, vertical lines, two on each cheek. I did not say a word to her for several minutes, my mind instead on what Wilhelm and Kpobo would say. She spoke first.

"My name is Tessa. What's yours?"

"Em, Ewaen, Ewaensigha Omorogbe," I stammered.

Tessa smiled—I think it was a see-this-shy-young-man-o smile—and said, "So, 'Ewaen, Ewaensigha Omorogbe,' where are you coming from this morning?"

"I just dropped my younger ones at school."

"Ha. It's eight thirty already. They must have been late. What school?"

"THS and FGC," I said.

"Eeyah . . . do-o. That must be long trip o." She used a soothing tone. Her accent was Warri, sing-song, the last words of almost every sentence ending with "o," the *l*'s and *n*'s indistinguishable.

"Yes, it is."

We stopped speaking. I wished I had taken Kpobo's advice and installed a radio. The squeak-squeak of the long-overdue fan belt was a poor substitute for music.

I kept my eyes on the road, ignoring the imposing gas flare of the Warri refinery as we passed. The steel-and-chrome complex on the Ekpan part of the expressway was burned into my memory. I did not need to stare out of the driver's side window to locate every tower, every steel stilt. The refinery was just restarting production, and the long queues at the fuel stations had not yet cleared.

I looked down, pretending to change gears, and glanced at her thighs. She had on a brown knee-length skirt. The golden skin of her knees bore no scars, no blemish. I looked back up when I saw her hand reach down to pull the skirt over her knees. She had caught me looking. I snuck a glance at her face and saw that she was smiling.

When we got to cross-and-stop ten minutes later, I asked, "Are you dropping here?"

"Are you going further?" she asked me back.

"I'm going into town. I have some time on my hands. Where exactly are you going?"

Some time on my hands? That was a lie, but I knew I was already committed when she said, "Well . . . I'm going to the market at Orhuworhun—"

I dove in. "I'll take you there, and from there I'll take you and your stuff to your place."

See me o. The boldness. Where did it come from? Why did it feel deliciously decadent? Without any trepidation whatsoever, I gunned the car down the expressway towards the market, not actually hearing her say, "Okay."

We spent about an hour in the market and another at the home of an equally attractive friend of hers to whom she introduced me as her new friend. Using her friend as a proxy questioner, we got to know ourselves better. She was in her mid-twenties—she refused to tell me her exact age—and was a businesswoman and hairdresser. What had she been doing alone on the express road at eight thirty in the morning? Her boyfriend, an oyibo oil worker, lived there. Was I jealous? No.

"And you, Ewaenshigha, what do you do?"

I was a twenty-year-old undergraduate studying medicine at the University of Benin—not sixteen, not fresh out of secondary school, not awaiting results.

I drove her home. She lived in Sedeco, a suburb named for a local oil company. Sedeco had potholed roads along which children, naked or in pants only, played in the late morning sun.

Some time on my hands? What was I doing? I was supposed to be at work. Was I thinking straight? My mind was on other things. For one, the backside I followed up the two-tiered staircase in the single-story building where Tessa lived. The fantasies, the dreamtime sequences—I had pictured this. It felt right.

Daddy would wait.

One day off-duty would not kill the company. After all, the day before, I had bought a surplus of nails and roofing sheets and concrete blocks.

I wish I could seem wise and honestly report that all these thoughts ran through my mind as I walked behind the beauty whom I had just met. My real thoughts were more immediate: Where would I sit when we entered the house? What would make a good vantage point from which to launch a pass? She was turning the key in the lock. What would I say? Where would I start? The flirting in the market and at her friend's place had been suggestive, or had it? I was sixteen. What did I know about women and their hints? I stopped thinking: all die na die. We were at her door now. I placed my hands on her hips. My fingers rested on the light leather belt on the waistband of her jeans. She stopped moving, the keys clinking in the quiet of the moment. I let my hands move forward; they crept forward slowly at first, then hurried to greet themselves as I cupped the slight bulge at the bottom of her tummy. I didn't flex my knees, didn't flex my hips. I smelled her hair; it was a sickly-sweet smell of burnt sugar, of old sweat.

She placed her palms on my interlocked hands. I was going to receive a slap and a thorough scolding for being so forward. Instead, I heard a soft purring from deep in her throat as she turned and kissed me. We kept on kissing as we stumbled and half-crawled to her bedroom. We kept kissing as we shook off our clothes, our shoes—miraculous, as I was wearing my lace-up joggers.

We did it. It was okay. Where were the electric shocks, the little explosions that were supposed to start at the feet and course throughout the body? Where was the warmth that enveloped you while waves and waves of heat crashed against you as though you were a beachhead at the start of high tide? My mom's romance novels that I stole to flip through backwards to the naughty bits promised "an explosion of passion" and "spasms of delight." The dirty video cassettes that my friends and I watched—dirty in all ramifications of the word, they even damaged video recorder play-heads—were filled with contortionists, screamers, and music that sped up and slowed down at just the right moment. Instead, all I felt now was an intense need to take a piss. So this was what writers and historians and romance novelists and porn stars claimed had brought empires down? What was all the fuss about? We did it three times, though—my count.

I turned to my left and stared at Tessa. She was wrapped in a glow, the sheen of sweat on her rapidly rising and falling breasts flattering her fair complexion. I confessed that this had been my first time and that I was sixteen, really.

"You too lie!" Her eyes were still closed, a small smile played at the corner of her lips; a small flicker of motion, incipient amusement, passed over her closed eyelids. If she was really in her twenties, then she had premature crow's feet.

"Na true. I am sixteen."

"Not that, my darling. I know say you be small boy. Before you even talk, I had already reached that conclusion. But you don spoil tay. Tay-tay. Virgin no dey fuck like you just fuck. You be expert o."

She rolled on top of me and rested her left hand on my chest. If I had chest hair, she would have picked at it just like they did in Sean Connery films. My head swelled. I was an expert; I was James Bond. For the first time, I looked around. The ceiling was finished in asbestos, gray sheets painted white. There was a ceiling fan that tried its best to blow cool air, failing and instead showering us with the smell of our sex. Once every few seconds, a draft would hit us from the open window beside Tessa's bed, its wooden shutter straining against the length of string that kept it ajar. Intertwined between us was a blanket, soft, almost satiny. I could lie here forever basking in the feel of the blanket, the hot air from the fan, and the softness of her bare chest on my belly. This was what sex was really about: the after, the later.

Then I noticed the time on the clock that hung on the wall above the bed's headboard. I had to look at it upside down so that it looked like it was seven o'clock on the numberless face. One thirty p.m. Federal Government College would close in thirty minutes. I had to hurry and start the afternoon school run. I rolled off the bed, kissing her on the forehead before I did so, wrapped the cotton-wax cover-cloth around myself, and started to dress up.

"I have to go," I said. "My brother and sister have closed from school."

"See this boy o. Won't you baff first?"

This was true. They always did that in the movies—a bath afterwards.

The after, the later.

THAT WAS why I always laughed when my friends teased me about my supposed virginity; there was no inexperience here. But Tessa, my first, my only so far, had been an older woman, a stranger who wanted me as much as I did her, who told me she would never meet my friends, never be seen with me in public. I enjoyed the mornings after the school run, sweaty in her bed, the after, the later, the afternoons under Dad's withering stare, him shouting, "Where have you been, you, this boy? Fucking around town on company time, are we?" If only he knew.

But I was now in university. I was seventeen, and I had no girlfriend, no real love. My experience in matters of the heart would have difficulty filling up the back of a five-kobo postage stamp. And Omogui was taking me to see Tseye tonight. I felt like a completely clueless mugu. It was a mid-September night. The mid–wet season's sunny break had come late that year, so the nights were still hot and humid. Omogui and I meandered through the shortcut connecting Halls Three and Two. The blocks closest to the wall separating our Hall Three from the coed hostel were occupied by the male students. These blocks boomed with the sounds of Mad Cobra and Shabba Ranks and

Maxi Priest. They were smelly affairs—of shit and stale urine. We passed the busy hallways, dodged wet laundry and boiling pots of beans and soup, and came upon the corridor connecting the boys' side with the girls' side. The stifling heat I felt on the walk through the boys' corridor was not all down to the weather. Part of it was the environment—the smelly pots of beans, dirty, stale boxer shorts, and busy hallways. There was something about the girls' half of the hostel. It was better lit, neater, smelled better, and dare I say, cooler. The slightly cold sensation I was getting was actually my shirt cooling on my back.

"SO YOU stay in Warri?" Tseye asked. We sat alone in her corner. The door had just been shut by one of her roommates, grumbling about why Omogui and By-the-way had left it open when they went out. They had gone for a stroll and had promised to get us ice cream from Six Candles on their way back. The quiet they left behind had just been broken by Tseye's question.

"Yeah," I replied. She had gone into the next corner to change into her nightie just before our friends left. I was trying not to stare at the sheer fabric, not that it revealed much. She had on a sleeveless top underneath.

She was determined to get me to gist more. "That jaguda town. And you grew up there? The gist we hear in Lagos is that every Warri boy is a ruffian."

"I'm not," I said, "and besides, it's not like I grew up in Warri-Warri; we live on the outskirts. I think the first time I ever took a taxi alone was, what, two years ago."

"Ah, you can't even defend your hometown?"

"No, really. I don't go out at all."

"Oh, you have a curfew?"

"Something like that." We both laughed. I tried to explain, "It's not really a curfew. It's just that where I stay is very far from town and coming back late through our lonely road isn't very wise."

"So, you have a curfew."

"So, you can say the curfew is more self-imposed."

Tseye laughed again. She had small "open teeth." It should not have looked as attractive as it did at that moment. I joined her, hearing how odd I sounded and not caring.

WE TALKED a great deal that first night. I found out a lot about her and she about me. Her father was an inspector in the Federal Ministry of Finance. Her mom was just thirty-six—sixteen years older than Tseye. I blurted out—before I could stop myself—that her father must have been a cradle snatcher, but she laughed it off. She said it was something she heard all the time.

We found out we had a lot in common. It started with my using that ever-reliable gist starter, the zodiac. Her star sign was Scorpio, her birthday was late October, and I was a Taurus. When I pointed out the fact that our stars were compatible, she said it meant we were destined to be very close friends. Other things seemed to prove her right. She had scored 237 on the matriculation exams, same as me. They were three children in her family, two boys and a girl. Same here. She was the eldest. She went to a federal school, albeit Federal Government Girls College (FGGC), in Benin. She had fallen very ill just after her junior secondary exams. I had spent two weeks in the hospital for typhoid after mine. She had a protruding navel and—she laughed out loud when I confirmed this—so did I. The coincidences came hard and fast. Our gasps of delight and surprise were barely over before the next anecdote shared drew a parallel from the other. We were exactly what we were: a pair of giggling teenagers, obstinate in our insistence on discovering everything we could about ourselves in a single conversation. When Omogui came back with a slightly disheveled Janet—I could have sworn she had worn lipstick on her way out earlier—he literally had to drag me away from the room. I dashed the ice cream they had bought for me to Janet. I skipped all the way back to our room, pausing along the corridors to spin around a pillar here and there and declare to my incredulous friend that I was in love. I was in love. *I am in love.*

EVERY EVENING was a blessing. The twilight was like a new experience. The reddish sunsets, the lone evenstar, and the emergence of a blanket of twinkling sisters to keep her company. I noticed things I had taken for granted, things that fake boys noticed, things that I was ashamed to say I did. Everything was gorgeous. Everything was different. I barely had time for my guys and our evening sessions in the car park. My entire psyche was concentrated on getting to that room in Hall Two. Even the excuse of escorting Omogui to Tseye's room was discarded. I started going to school. I started paying attention in class, if only to impress my new girl-bestfriend.

Brenda was very upset with the new situation. She did not see me anymore. I gave many excuses, but none of them stood well with her. When she found out how close Tseye and I had become, she was extremely displeased, not because I was spending time with Tseye, no. She was upset that I "tried to hide it."

"Why would you hide this from me?" she asked.

I did not know. Why did I feel the need to hide anything from Brenda? I told her everything. I told her about the butterflies in my stomach. Then she asked what talking to Tseye was like. How could I describe talking to someone who finished your sentences for you? How could I describe the experience of only having to look in someone's eyes and knowing immediately what she was thinking? How could I describe a conversation without words?

Slowly, I noticed something else about this new experience: the pain. When I did not see her, I was in agony. When I saw her, it was worse. I spoke to her about everything, everything but the new experience I was having. It was not like with Tessa. Being with Tessa was like eating iced fish compared to Tseye's beluga caviar. I had never had caviar, but that was how I pictured it. Teenagers—we spent every waking moment together, but we did not talk about the things that adults found so easy. Oh, at times we allowed ourselves the occasional daydream: What kind of person would the other like to be married to? But in the answers, satisfying as they seemed, I noticed an effort to dodge what I was sure we both felt. There was also her religiosity. Tseye was Pentecostal. She was a member of the Agape Addiction.

The AA was the place to find the finest, *goodest* Christian girls. It was a new-wave students' fellowship. Its members were filled with that fire that only the young can muster, and the young male preachers seemed to have picked up their oyibo accents somewhere in the mid-Atlantic. Tseye had been drawn to them immediately after she entered the school. Their message of God's unconditional love was, to her, irresistible. They said God did not place importance on what you wore—not that you could come to fellowship naked. What God cared about, they said, was your heart. All you had to do was give your life to Christ. Tseye seemed to grow two shades brighter when she talked about her fellowship, although she never preached to me. From our small-small discussions, she knew about my almost-agnostic background. I told her about how my mother was stopped from receiving communion in the Catholic Church for marrying outside the one true faith.

Tseye did invite me to fellowship once or twice but stopped after she noticed how uncomfortable I was with altar call. Altar call was when newcomers and those who had decided to "give their lives to Christ" walked down the long aisle in the Main Café lecture hall, where the fellowships were held. One had to walk to the makeshift altar and wait until the end of the Wednesday service for the outreach people who came and took addresses. These outreach guys and, might I add, very attractive girls, then became pests for the next few weeks—always visiting, always asking why I missed last week's fellowship. It was as if I had not had this experience before. I went to FGC Warri. We had a vibrant Christian Union. But I had not seen anything so extreme. Tseye understood and laughed at my discomfort. But behind the laugh was that reserve—that reserve that I knew would one day blow up in our faces.

So there it was. I was in love with a good, born-again girl. Dare I tell her? No. This was the timidity of a seventeen-year-old. I made myself content with just spending time with this kind angel—that, and enduring very excruciating teasing from my guys.

I LEARNED to smoke in October of that year. It was a month to exams, and reading had begun in earnest. No excuses though: I knew they were bad for you. It just happened. It was night in the car park. I was being teased about how cheap it was to entertain me. Omogui was there and so were Tuoyo, Kayoh, Harry, and his best friend Chunky.

"When men are drinking, when men are burning the hair on their chests with hard liquor, what do you do? Sit down there and drink Fanta," Kayoh said. He was making mouth because he had just come back from raiding his father's petrol station in Lagos, and his pockets were full. He had, as he said, opened fire; in front of us were bottles of beer and a Fanta. Everyone but me had a stick of cigarette in his lips.

"Instead of you being happy that Ewaen saves you money," Tuoyo said. He had been back since they called off the strike. Tuoyo still had the cast on and struggled to write with it and to hold on to "cigar" with it. He said he could manage to handle bottles of beer with his left hand, but writing and smoking needed his right. His formerly white POP cast had a flap-covered window in it. This, Tuoyo lifted every morning to dress the still-open wound beneath. We had redesigned the fenestration with a garish car motif; the window looked like the half-wound-down window of a blue-red-and-black Toyota. Our signatures were all on the cast: Kayoh's, Omogui's, Wilhelm's, Oliver Tambo's, and mine.

"Forget! There is money. I need my guys to drink," Kayoh said, laughing.

Everyone but me joined him.

"Wetin even dey this cigar?" I was irritated. "It's not as if it makes you guys manlier." I reached for Tuoyo's lips and pulled the stick out of his mouth. "How them dey drag am?" I asked.

Tuoyo smiled and told me to place it between my lips, take a drag and hold it in my mouth, and then inhale with my lips open. I did exactly as he said, expecting to break out in a sputtering cough. I did not cough or choke. But I felt dizzy after the first hit. I took two more drags and passed the stick back to Tuoyo. Everyone started clapping.

Tuoyo joined in the chorus by saying, "Ah, Ewaen. You're a natural. Remaining only marijuana for you to jump into." He paused; the twinkle, the slight light in his eyes told me he was being silly. "Abeg, don't try it o. Weed no good o!" What he did not say, or perhaps even know, was that you never picked up a cigarette. Once you did, you were done. You were hooked.

9

BY EARLY '94, Wilhelm, perpetual virgin, four eyes, dedicated arse, and, oddly enough, very correct guy, had been my close friend for seven years and counting. We first met during the interviews into Federal Government College around mid-1986. It was a few years after his family returned from Germany, six years after his father had left earlier to begin work at the steel company in Aladja. Wilhelm still spoke with an accent then, with pip-squeak, guttural *r*'s and confused *v*'s and *w*'s.

The children who qualified for the interviews were those who had passed the common entrance exams held in December of '85. I had topped my primary school. I was a local champion, I soon found out, because everyone who sat around me that day did very well in their respective schools. I remember that the examiners soon took us away from our parents. Only my mother and the twins had come with me. Daddy was busy in the creeks laying pipes. I remember seeing this tall—yes, he was taller even then—oyibo boy with his blonde mother and baby sister. He wore an A-Team necktie on top of a gray short-sleeved shirt: Face, Hannibal, and Mr. T posed in a line, one on top of the next, standing at ease in the middle of his chest; Murdock stood beneath them, but he was bigger, his big crazy hands spread out, embracing Mr. T's black bus. I felt awkward in my DSC Primary School III uniform as I shifted seats to allow him space. He wore trousers, a little too short, his white socks showing above his Cortina sandals. I pulled at my shorts to cover my knees. We sat together on small plastic chairs that faced benches where our parents, a few winking, raising fists, thumbs up, cheering their champions, their local champions, sat looking at us across a lawn. I tried not to stare at the oyibo boy beside me. Wilhelm didn't use glasses then, and I noticed his eyes were very light, like Malta sweets. Films like *Mary Poppins* and *Oliver!* had prepared me for one type of oyibo accent in children—the mid-Atlantic one with the oddly pronounced words, with "nothing, something, everything" sounding like "nofink, somefink, everifink." But, no, this boy sounded different.

"Hello? My name is *Vilhelm?*"

I thought he had asked me a question. Then I understood. "Sorry," I said. "My name is Ewaen." I was taken aback by the way he pronounced my name, "Evahen." Wilhelm told me that he went to the steel company's Primary School I. I told him I went to School III, immediately ashamed when he looked at my starched uniform, his eyes saying, *I know*. He had come second in the common entrance exams at his primary school. I trumped him there: I had come first in mine.

"Vhat kind of questions do you suppose they ask in this interview?" Will asked. A few minutes into our friendship and he had already insisted I call him Will. *Vill*.

"Why do you speak funny?" I asked Will, my new friend.

"I'm sorry. I grew up in Germany. I . . . we came back two years ago. My father works in the steel company."

"So you speak German?"

"Ja." It sounded like he said *yah*.

"But you do not speak pidgin."

"I am learning," he replied, every syllable carefully enunciated.

"I dey learn," I said. When I saw that he looked at me oddly, I explained, "That is what you're supposed to say in Pidgin English—I dey learn. Get it?"

"I dey learn," my new friend said carefully.

And that was it. Wilhelm took it from there and ran with it. Over the years, his nicknames had matched his pidgin knowledge: Will in junior secondary, Don Willy in the silliness of early SS1, and finally, Baba-Willy, the don dada, the crazy, half-caste, self-proclaimed bane of the ladies. I still could not match him for verbal dexterity, for sheer vocabulary, for syntax, for old and new words and phrases in the pidgin lexicon. At times, Wilhelm still blamed me for being the first to corrupt him, for being the first to spoil him, to stain his oyibo.

I had left him for DSC's Technical High School in SS1 after my bullying incident. But since he lived in his family's flat in the staff quarters of the steel company as a day student, we had not lost touch. I introduced him to my new friend, Kpobo, and three of us became fast friends.

ON THE night the wahala that would define year one for me in Uniben happened, I was supposed to sleep in Wilhelm's prof's house. We smoked cigarettes, sitting on stools by the well-trimmed hedge in front of Willy's room. The other room had been converted into a store by the madam of the house, a European member of Willy's mother's Niger Wives club. I had spied through the curtainless louvres and seen that it contained the flotsam and jetsam of a life lived in the plenty of the seventies—old, discarded toys, Mecanno and Lego cartons, Barbie and Sindy dolls, an old gas cooker—and with the detritus of the deprivations of the eighties—an old kerosene stove, an iron suitcase spilling over with faded Ankara and lace, and saved egg cartons stacked about a foot high.

Earlier that evening, while we read, Wilhelm had mentioned to me that there would be a party in the boys' quarters of the staff quarters later that night. The deprivations of the last decade had forced many of the university's teachers to rent their servants' quarters (the boys' quarters, BQs) out to students willing to pay the exorbitant prices they went for. After all, the BQs were empty. Which lecturer could afford domestic staff? Every year saw amateur estate brokers springing up in school. These included the good, the bad, and the ugly. One had to be careful. Chaps claiming they knew this prof or that doctor who had a room to let in quarters were already visiting rooms in the hostels. What was curious was that most of these brokers lived with us in the hostels—why didn't they live in the rooms they had to let? Swindlers.

Wilhelm kept disturbing me about this party, and I found myself reading and rereading the same heading—"Tricarboxylic Acids and the Thermodynamics of the Kreb's Cycle in Living Systems"—from the biochemistry textbook in front of me. When he finally stopped describing how hot the party would be, how the girls from social science would all be there, how we had to go there since we could not hope to be cool year-one boys, fine boys, by missing the hot party, he asked what I thought.

"Well," I said, "I like this sentence I am reading." The sarcasm was almost wasted on Willy.

"Ewaen, get out," he said. "You wan' go the BQ party?"

We sat in the pharmacy lecture hall. Five seats behind me sat Omogui, By-the-way, and Tseye. I had told Willy about Tseye, about how I was in love. "Who dey follow us go?" I asked.

"Wetin you mean?" He followed my eyes. "No. No. You no fit carry your girlfriend come o. She will disturb our enjoyment of the girls there. Na wa for you o. Na so the love do you?"

"Not them, my guy. We tell no one in the room? Ejiro, Omogui, Kayode?"

"Why?"

"Why what? Na only you wan' go?"

"Ewaen, this is a special party. Invite only. If you like, you fit tell them, but you'll have to manufacture these for them." Willy brought out two small cards from his pocket. The IVs.

"Party till mama comes knocking," I read the last line of the invite aloud. "Where did you get these? Who invited you?"

"See this fake guy. You think your best friend came to this school to suffer and die? Haba, we have endured enough in this year one. We have been dodging confra boys since we got here. We have been dodging mosquitoes. No girls, no nacking. Abeg, make we enjoy ourselves. It's the end of first semester."

"Who dey do the party?"

"Na one guy for science. I no know am, sha, but my neighbor here in quarters invited me. He said I could bring a friend."

"Just like that?"

"Just like what? If you see the wahala I gave him. I told him I had to bring my best friend along. He finally agreed after I told him what a correct guy you were."

"Okay."

"Okay, you'll go?"

"Okay, I'll go."

The fellow reading in front of us turned, put his finger to his lips, and shushed us.

We had left class together for Hall Three so I could change. I put on my Carrera flared jeans that I had stolen from the bottom of my father's box. Willy was decked out in a stonewash gray denim shirt, white inner T-shirt, and blue jeans. I sprayed on some of his perfume, put a couple of breath mints in my shirt pocket, and we were ready to go.

WHEN WE got to the bungalow, it became obvious why the invitations ended with the words "party till mama comes knocking." Mama wasn't home; the home was empty. No lights shone out its windows. From the street, down its short driveway, students milled around, dressed in all that was reigning—leg warmers and transparent rubber shoes for most of the girls; stonewash jeans and plain blue jeans were just beginning to make a comeback then, and a few of the guys wore these with lumberjack shirts open in front and plain white T-shirts underneath with Timberland boots or Chelsea boots. There were many boys, a few girls, and lots of posing and ignoring. Willy and I walked through the loiterers down the driveway to the back of the bungalow where the sounds of Biggie's "Juicy" boomed out of the loudspeakers. Willy knew the lyrics to the thing and rapped along as we passed a couple kissing near a fragrant Queen of the Night hedge.

Both rooms in the boys' quarters were lit with shaded lamps—hued streams of light made possible by the multicolored tissue paper wrapped around each bulb. The music thumped now, having switched to the West Coast. I was a West Coast guy, and I hummed under my breath when Dr. Dre and Snoop came on. Willy introduced me to the guy who invited him. I smiled when I saw whom he was standing with. Willy's neighbor stood with a girl on his arm and was gisting with Lorenchi—the Cosa Nostra goon I liked, TJ's guy. I said hi to Willy's guy and greeted Lorenchi.

"Fanta-boy," Lorenchi said. "How na?"

"I'm fine."

Willy's friend turned to us. "Willy, Ewaen, you guys should feel free. Go in. Dance. The drinks are over there."

I did not have the liver to ask any girl at the party to dance. Willy, being oyibo and all, had no problems. He danced with jambites, and he danced with staylites. I stood in a corner, smoked my menthols, drank my Fanta, and watched my guy rock the party.

When I went out for fresh air, I saw Oliver Tambo. He hadn't seen me and was talking to a girl I recognized from 500

LT. I snuck up behind him and saw the look of boredom on the girl's face change to one of mild interest when she saw what I was about to do. I clamped my palms over Tambo's eyes.

"Who be that?" Tambo tried to turn. I turned with him. "Okay, I give up."

"Tambo." I could have sworn I felt him stiffen when he heard my voice. "So you were coming to this party and you did not invite any of your guys?"

The girl Tambo had been gisting with took this as her cue to escape. Tambo spoke, "Ewaen."

"Yes?" I said, smug in the knowledge that I would tease him to death at the next plenary session of the car park committee.

"Who invite you? How you take come this party?"

"Abeg, gerrout, Clement," I said, half-smiling, using the name his father gave him. "You dey come party and you no tell anybody? That na real sheylaying o."

Tambo relaxed; he let his shoulders down half an inch. He exhaled. "Only you come?"

"No. Me and Willy. One of Willy's guys for quarters na 'im give am IV. Two IVs, and Willy gave me one."

"Ehen? At least you see say na invitation only."

"That na why you no tell anybody for hostel?"

"Exactly."

"Anyway, I told them, Ejiro and Tuoyo."

Tambo laughed, "Them no beg to follow you?"

"As in . . ." I stretched out the words.

We both laughed. Tambo copped a cigarette from me and said he was going inside to say hello to Willy. I followed him back in, took a chair, and sat down. By this time, I began to notice that there were fewer girls than when the party started. I looked for Willy and saw him in a circle with Lorenchi, his friend from quarters, and Tommy. Tommy with the armed-robber face.

Tambo appeared at my side and said, unnecessarily loudly, "Ewaen, abeg come give me cigar."

I was about to reply to him in an equally loud voice that I had just given him a cigarette when I felt him pinch me. I looked at his eyes.

"Escort me outside. Pretend like say we dey go buy cigar. Quick, follow me, follow me."

Tambo walked ahead. The music had changed again; now it was blues time. "Walk On By," the Sinead O'Connor version, played. As I walked out the door, I looked at Willy. My friend shouted a tipsy greeting to me. The three guys that stood in the circle with Wilhelm all turned. I remember that scene like a polaroid. Willy, with his fair face and light hair changing colors with the stream from the wrapped-up light bulbs, his glasses a shade of pink, then blue, then purple; friend-from-quarters standing there filmy eyed, his arm around the last girl in the party; Tommy, still looking like a thief, only his eyes had a hungrier look in them that night; and Lorenchi, still goofy, still play-play, still scary.

TAMBO HURRIED along the driveway. I struggled to keep up, asking, "What's the matter? What's the matter?"

He stopped when we reached the street, the one that led to Ekosodin Gate. We stood in an island of darkness under an unlit streetlight, away from the glow of the other too-far-apart dull streetlights.

"Ewaen, na injuns' groove be that."

"Injuns' wetin?"

"Confra party. Ewaen, that was a Mafia recruitment party."

He had started moving again but stopped when he saw that I wasn't following him. I turned back. Tambo dragged my arm. He spoke, "Where you dey go? Ewaen, I put myself on the line to get you out of that place. Where you dey go?"

"Wilhelm. Wilhelm dey inside. We have to go and get him."

"No we do not. About you, I am sure. But Willy? You said Willy invited you. He might know what the party is about."

"No, he doesn't," I said. "Na my friend. I no fit leave am, Tambo."

"Ewaen, if you go back, you no go fit leave."

"Why?" My chest ached. My throat felt as if a heavy chunk of yam was stuck in it. Everything was happening too fast. Everything was becoming too clear, too quickly. A confra party. A fucking confra party? Oh God. Fucking Willy. Stupid fucking Willy.

"Did you notice the fence between the BQ and Ekosodin?" Tambo asked me, his grip on my right arm strong, vice-like. "It's wire mesh; it is broken. They go soon close the party, and everybody go pass there enter bush for the initiation. If you are there when that happens, it means you want to blend."

"But time still dey, Tambo. Let me go and call Willy. Willy doesn't know it is a confra groove. Let me go and call him."

"Ewaen, what can I say to make you understand? See, I owe you; you give me room sleep when we first enter school. I know say you no wan' join injuns. That na why I dey do this thing wey fit put me for trouble."

"I hear you, Tambo," I said. "But Willy. Let me just go and call him. Let me go and ask him for cigar, just like you did with me."

Tambo shook his head, not briskly, not sadly, somewhere in between.

"You believe I didn't think of that? Did you see the guy that Tommy and Lorenchi were gisting with? The guy that Willy was standing with? The one with the fine girl?"

"That is the neighbor who invited Willy."

"See, it is worse than I thought. That na Frank, TJ's second-in-command, our caporegime. Guy, you get to go now. I promise I go try take Willy comot for that place."

Oh God, oh God, oh God.

Oliver Tambo led me along. I stumbled on a loose piece of gravel by the roadside. He told me he had a bike waiting for me at Ekosodin Gate, he had already paid the fare to hostel, and he would see me later. And yes, that he would try to get Willy out, but, but, but he couldn't promise anything.

10

EJIRO, TUOYO, and I sat very quietly, legs dangling, along the edge of the corridor outside our room. It was 2 a.m.

"Confra party?" Ejiro asked.

"Confra party," I said.

Tuoyo passed me his cigarette. I had to pull it from where it was wedged deep between the fingers in his cast. He had wet the filter again. I dragged deeply, pulling on the hot air, drying Tuoyo's spit.

It was a warm, balmy night. Moonless. We sat under a fluorescent light. My lap ached from my restless legs. I had been shaking them ever since we sat down. Tuoyo laid his left hand on my lap and stilled me.

Ejiro said, "Well if we needed any proof that Oliver Tambo was a confra boy, we have it now."

I grunted. I took another pull on the cigarette.

"Ewaen, stop worrying. Tambo is there with him; he will look after Willy," Tuoyo said.

"How can he do that? Tambo was even scared of Frank."

"Kai, Willy get bad luck, sha," Ejiro said, laughing, his eyes almost closed in a sardonic squint. "Of all the people to invite him to a confra party, of all the people who could toast him, he gets invited by the second-in-command of a confra."

"Na because he be oyibo," Tuoyo said.

"What are we going to do?" I asked.

"First of all, we are not going to tell anybody. Four of us now know. We keep it quiet. And we wait for Tambo to come back with or without Willy." Tuoyo scratched at his cast. He took the cigarette back.

"Make we tell Yibril?" I asked.

"Are you crazy? You wan' start confra war?" Tuoyo whispered the questions as though he was afraid that the night would carry the gist.

"But he is Willy's cousin. Surely—" I stopped speaking because Tuoyo shook his head vehemently. He was right. Yibril would be the last resort.

Ejiro said, "What of TJ?"

"He wasn't there. If he was there, I would have gone to meet him," I said. Tuoyo looked at me quizzically when I spoke. I said, "He was the person who helped us recover our things when you were in hospital. He's my cousin's friend. I'll explain later."

"So we wait for Tambo," Ejiro said.

If I had my way, we would have sat outside all night. I did not care if the next day was lectures. But Ejiro started yawning. I had nodded off when Tuoyo tapped me on the arm and said we should go inside.

I MADE up my mind the next morning to go to Ekosodin and look for TJ. Ejiro and Tuoyo were already dressed to follow me when Tambo showed up at the door. He called me outside; he wanted to speak to me alone. I told him Ejiro and Tuoyo already knew.

"Wilhelm is in Ekosodin. He is all right."

"You were able to get him away?" I asked. I hoped.

"No," Tambo said.

"He don blend?" Tuoyo took control. I could hardly think. How would I look at my friend again? Of all of us, Willy was most vehement about not joining any bloody, dirty confra. He would die. They would beat him, and he would fight. But Tambo just said he was okay. That was hope.

"No, they never blend. The procedure never complete. Willy and the other potentials are in a flat in Ekosodin, naked and blindfolded. The ceremony—"

I interrupted him. "So they never blend. Thank God. Clement, sorry, Tambo, we dey go Green House. We dey go see TJ."

"Are you guys mad? Go see who? And there is nobody at Green House."

"Where they dey?"

"Where who dey?" Tambo replied with the same question. His eyes said that one question he would answer; the other he wouldn't.

Tuoyo knew which to ask. "Where TJ dey?"

Clement "Oliver Tambo" Unegbu relaxed. "TJ dey class, for my department. I can't escort you there."

"We understand," Ejiro said. He and Tambo had never settled their quarrel after our things were stolen, not really.

"Thank you, Tambo," Ejiro said. And they were settled.

AS I SPOKE, I noticed TJ smile, then frown, then smirk, and smile again. It was not enjoyment I saw on his face, I suppose. It was bewilderment and anger. We sat under an ebelebo tree in front of the faculty of agricultural sciences. I had gone into TJ's faculty alone; I mentioned to Ejiro and Tuoyo that it would be a good idea if TJ assumed that not many people knew about Willy's wahala. I had called him out of the lecture theater where a lecturer was talking about "the economics of peasant subsistence farming in the early Soviet Republics."

Sitting under the early morning vitamin D sun, we talked.

"You do not understand what you ask of me," TJ said.

"I know."

"Do you?"

I decided to risk saying a little of what Tambo had told me. It wouldn't be dangerous; TJ would assume I heard it from somewhere else. "But the procedure isn't complete. You can still help. TJ, what can be more dangerous than someone who doesn't want to join your group being forced to do so?"

It seemed he didn't hear the first part of my statement. The second part struck a nerve though. TJ smiled again. I thought I understood why he did not speak. What could he say to me? That as head of an organization, his subordinates had taken decisions without his knowledge? That he was ashamed that boys had to be tricked into joining his confra? I almost mentioned Yibril; I almost told TJ that Wilhelm's cousin was a major guy in the Black Axe. It was on the tip of my tongue.

But I kept on talking. "And you promised me. You told me if I had any problem, I could come see you."

"Ewaen, it's enough. Give me a few hours. Go to your room and wait. I'll see what I can do. I make no promises, guy, but I'll see what I can do."

WILLY WALKED into A109 at six that evening. He was dirty. A few buttons from his jean shirt were missing; I could see smudged fingerprints where someone had held his shirt. His shoes and the bottom part of his trousers were muddy. He still had on his glasses, and when he smiled, I saw his eyes light up in part amusement and part embarrassment. Part amusement because he knew that we—Tuoyo, Ejiro, and me—had been waiting for him. Part embarrassment because, I suppose, he suspected what had been going through our minds all day.

We shook hands when he walked in. The room smelled of beans from the pot of one of the roommates, and we had to walk outside to rid ourselves of the stench. No one spoke; no one tried to say anything apt. There was nothing to say, nothing to do that would not have seemed melodramatic. Willy was safe. My friend was safe. He told us what happened.

When I saw him in a circle with Frank, his neighbor from quarters, Lorenchi, and Tommy, they had been talking about chicks. Chicks—not confra, not blending. Willy didn't even know when I left; he had been very tipsy. What he noticed was that there were no girls left in the party. He noticed that, though slow music played, no couples were on the dance floor. By then the gist had—in that interminable way that discussions have of moving—shifted to fine boys and the Cosa Nostra. That was when he began to suspect that Frank was a Mafia boy. Willy still assumed that this was the typical front and that all he had to do was let them down gently and then he would look for me, gist me, and we would have a laugh about it.

"I looked around for you, Ewaen."

"I know."

"I saw Oliver Tambo, and he told me that you had left. He was so cold, not typical Tambo. I didn't understand what was happening."

And then the party ended. Willy told us that Tommy walked over to the deck and switched off the music. He announced that they would all be leaving for Ekosodin through a breach in the fence at the back of the BQ. That he was happy that so many nice gentlemen wanted to become Made Men of the Cosa Nostra. Willy told us that when he tried to leave, one tall guy blocked him. When he tried to push his way through, they started fighting. There was a big argument with Lorenchi on one side, Tommy and Frank on the other, about whether they should allow him to leave. By then he was sitting on the ground, his glasses with one of the boys—so they would not break, they said. From what Willy gathered, Lorenchi had assumed that he wanted to blend Cosa Nostra and was very upset when he found out that Frank had tricked him into attending the party.

The day had gone dark by the time Willy reached the last part of his gist. The hustle of late evening in the hostel had begun; we could see students sitting in the common room watching the seven o'clock news. The efficos—efficient readers—walked past us in the corridors, their books in their hands or slung over their backs in knapsacks. Willy told us that his stubbornness had not helped him and that if we had seen how humble he was, we'd know how he begged while everyone laughed at him, laughed at the scared oyibo with the thick glasses. He seemed the only one who didn't know what the party was about. The other year-one boys—there were six other potentials—smiled and laughed and teased him. Oliver Tambo had walked beside him into the bush. Tambo reassured him that it wouldn't be so bad.

Tuoyo left us and went back into the room to get his cigarettes. He came back with Tambo, Omogui, and Kayode. Omogui and Kayode had no idea what had happened. They would find out later, but at that moment, everyone reached an unspoken agreement not to say anything. Willy and Tambo exchanged a look, and Willy stopped talking. Tambo thanked me and insisted that Willy do the same. That was when Willy's stubbornness came back.

"Tambo, not you go tell me who I go thank."

I started laughing when I noticed that this was the first time he had spoken in Pidgin English since he came back from the bush; he was back to his unserious self. Our friends didn't know what I was laughing at, but they joined in.

Willy caught my eye and winked, *I'll gist you later.*

WILLY TOLD me the reason he had come first to A109 and not gone directly to his room in quarters was that he needed to change his shirt and trousers. He could not risk walking past his guardian's house looking the way he did. I took a pair of trousers from Tuoyo, who was closest in size to Willy, and gave him one of my shirts. I escorted him to take a bike back to hostel, and he told me the rest of the story.

"Ewaen, I fear, ehn! I was so afraid when they took us to a flat in Ekosodin and told us to remove our clothes. Some other guys, people I had not seen before in this school, they walked in and blindfolded us. I recognized Frank's voice. He told us that we would be kept in a state of omertà."

"What?"

"Omertà. Some mafia film shit. We had to stay in this room, blind and quiet, for the entire day. I wondered about that, Ewaen. I wondered if I spoke, whether they would kick me out of the ceremony. But somehow, I knew it would not work.

"Later in the afternoon, some girls came in and spoon-fed us rice and beans."

"I can't imagine you quiet for twenty minutes, talk less of an entire day."

"Abi," Willy laughed. "I do not know what you did, but Tambo said I owed you a lot. Thank you, Ewaen." He stopped and held my arm.

"I spoke to my cousin's guy," I explained. And I told him. Willy already knew of my "relationship" with TJ. He was surprised that it was worth so much, that it could work such magic. He wondered aloud about his own cousin Yibril.

"If they had blended me, I would have gone straight to Yibril," he said.

"You would have caused a confra war?"

"Fuck that, Ewaen! Those fuckers be wan' blend me. God forbid, Ewaen. I go do them back, I swear. I go do them back."

"Guy, stop making mouth. I'm just happy that it ended. I couldn't sleep all night."

Willy told me as we walked to the bike stand at Hostel Gate about how he had heard a ruckus in the adjoining room to the one in which he sat blindfolded—a big argument with raised voices. After this quieted down, someone had walked in and tapped him on the shoulder. This person helped him up and escorted him outside. Willy felt his feet on soft earth and knew he was standing outside the flat. The person who removed his blindfold was Lorenchi. Lorenchi told him to leave Ekosodin; that just at the next junction there was a bike stand. Lorenchi gave Wilhelm back his glasses, his shoes, and bike fare, and he came to hostel.

"Lorenchi apologized for everything. But first he threatened me, told me not to tell anybody about what had happened, that the only reason I was allowed to leave was because very few people knew what had happened."

"So they do not have to save face. They would just keep it quiet."

"Yes, they plan to keep it quiet. Do you know that the Mobile policemen at Ekosodin Gate stopped me?"

"Why?"

"I had to lie that I just had a bike accident."

"Because of your clothes?"

"I am telling you. They even laughed when they saw I was going to enter another okada."

The last thing he told me before he hopped on the bike that would take him to quarters was this: "You know, Ewaen, I almost told them that I was already a confra boy. I almost told them that Yibril was my cousin, that I was his main man."

"Do you think it would have worked?"

"I do not know, Ewaen. I got scared—scared that they would just kill me to cover their tracks. Would it have worked? Maybe?"

"I guess we will never know now," I said, hoping that he understood how close he had come to doing something he would have regretted. The way things stood, he was a protected Ju-man. Nobody in the Mafia would touch him. If he had said he was an Ah-kay boy, God knows what would have happened.

"Follow me go my place na, make we gist?"

"Dude, you dey fear?"

He was, but he wouldn't admit it.

"Me, fear? For what? Where are you going to tonight?"

Ignoring the fact that he spoke to me in good English, that he wanted someone to talk to, I said, "I will go and see Tseye. She will be worried that I didn't walk her back to her room the other night after reading."

"No wahala, we will see later."

"No wahala," I said.

"Thank you, Ewaen."

"Stop it, Wilhelm. You would have done the same for me."

11

THE RESULTS for the first-semester exams came out two days to Valentine's. Crowds of excited students gathered around the faculty notice boards all around school. In Tseye's room, where I had spent the afternoon, we listened to worried roommates snapping and shouting at each other.

"If this is how they take it, I wonder what will happen when the results finally come out," Tseye said.

I was helping her stir a pot of stew and sneezed, my eyes watering from the excess pepper she had put in. "I don't know . . . maybe it will get them to keep quiet."

"You're not worried, are you?"

"Pass me that glass of water." I stared at her. Sweaty, with strands of her brown hair lying in wisps on either side of her steamed-up spectacles, she was beautiful, sha. She had asked why I did not look worried. All worries were banished in the presence of such peace. But like a slow flame, something was eating into our relationship, into our friendship. Tseye had once told me that born-agains found it tricky preaching the gospel to loved ones. Instead of hearing what she was trying to say, all I heard that day was that she hinted that I was a loved one.

She pushed the spectacles up the bridge of her nose, sniffed, and held the cup just out of reach. "Answer me, now. Me, I am worried o. I don't know what to expect. But you . . . you act as though nothing is happening."

"Tseye, pass me the water." I took a sip and cleared my throat. I said, "Of course I worry. But how's that going to help? And you of all people shouldn't be bothered. I saw how prepared you were. You did not even have my time throughout the exams. I had to wait in line to see you."

"Get out," she laughed. "You nko. Did we see you?"

"My point exactly. You were too busy to have the time for us mortals." We had been repeating this conversation for days now and finished off each afternoon with a stroll to the teaching hospital to see if there was any gist about when the results would come out. In a day or two, was the answer.

When Janet rushed in around two, she almost knocked over the pot in her excitement. She said, between gasps, catching her breath, "The results are out. They pasted the year-one results in front of medical hostel."

Tseye blew out the kerosene stove while I pulled my button-down shirt over my BYC inner shirt. We reached the medical hostel in record time, outrunning, I think, motorcycles on the road beside the school library. Rushing there wasn't any help. The place was crowded. I noticed Wilhelm and a family friend from Warri dancing just outside the hostels' brown gate. They had passed. When I asked why they had not checked my result, they asked me if I did not know that results were not placed with any names. Only matriculation numbers were put beside the As, Bs, and Ds.

I joined Tseye at the line. Janet stood aside—she had checked her results before coming to the room. Tseye saw her results first and suppressed a shout of happiness. She turned and hugged me. Determined not to be swamped by the niceness of having her in my arms for the first time, I kept on looking. Ha, there it was. PHY 101, pass; PHY 103, CHEM 101, BOT 102, CHEM 103, pass, pass, pass, pass. Then, *kai!* ZOO 101, fail. That lecturer had been serious about her handout: if you buy it, you will pass my exam. At least I was not repeating. At least, not yet.

WHEN I told Tseye I was going to carry over zoology, she laughed.

"I'm carrying over botany. Why was I so happy? Because I did not fail. I am not repeating. We are not repeating. Do you know how many people failed? They say that a third of the class is repeating already. And second-semester exams are just weeks away."

"But zoology was the easiest course. I am sure I passed it."

"Look at the blessing in this thing. It means you know you have no blanket anymore. Think about it like a thief in the night. God's given you a glimpse. Now we can pass the second semester by focusing."

We ate the rice she had boiled and the stew. I left her room for the car park where the party had started.

WILHELM SWIRLED the dark liquid in his bottle of Guinness. He sat beside me in the gutter and spoke, "Thank God o!"

I nodded and put the cigarette back between my lips.

He continued, "Ewaen, don't be fooled. Do you know how many of our guys failed? Oh, they won't be repeating. No. They will enter year two and year three. And," he said, "they will still be here in year fifteen. We in medicine are lucky in a way. The department puts you on your toes early." Wilhelm had become a quieter person for a few days after the Mafia kidnapping incident. But days before the exams began, he reassured me that everything had been taken care of, that he was okay now. I tried to press for details, but he was not forthcoming. I guessed that he had told his cousin, and some arrangement had been reached above our heads. He said he was okay now.

I stared past him. Omogui was doing a jig, laughing and spilling drink from his bottle in libation to imaginary drunken ancestors. The light from a passing car caught the sneer on Wilhelm's face. "See that idiot? He has four carry-overs. You know how many courses they have in year-one history? Seven. Tell me though—how did Brenda do?"

I laughed and smiled at Omogui when he paused in the middle of a eulogy to his ancestors to stare at me. "She passed."

Wilhelm nodded and flipped to the subject closest to his heart. "So how Val's Day wan' be?"

"I no know o."

"Hurry up and know o. I am taking this girl, Weyinmi, to dinner at UPH."

Was the University Palace Hotel not fully booked already? From the gist I had heard, everyone was going there. "Who's Weyinmi?" I asked.

"Na one girl wey dey stay close to me for quarters. She lives with a politician uncle in Lagos."

"Hey! Cool. Have you guys done it?"

"That's why this Valentine's Day's important, isn't it?"

I WENT with Wilhelm to town on the thirteenth. It was a Sunday in name only. The streets looked as busy as they would on a Monday morning. Benin was painted over in red. Not the hue of its muddy, notoriously difficult-to-wash-off earth. It was the color of lovers' day. The tuke-tukes, boisterously painted shuttle buses, blasted the area around Main Gate with love songs—dancehall versions though. Ugbowo, Uselu, Wire Road, and Ring Road— all the way to the gift shop at Phil-Hallmark's, we could not get away from the infectiousness of it. I quickly picked up two cards, the first with a fat cartoon character cracking a joke about what he wanted for his Valentine, and the second, more muted, with a greeting to a close friend at Val's Day. Nothing too loud.

We left for school after Wilhelm had picked up a small statuette of an angel, which he complemented with two very showy cards.

TSEYE HAD promised we would spend the evening together. Her fellowship was holding a counter to the pagan festival, a Christian one of crosses and Bibles instead of heart-shaped balloons and candy. Tseye and I would attend together and maybe, I hoped, go for ice cream afterwards. I had seen the awkwardness with which she asked me to the fellowship. In our silent way of talking, I imagined she was asking me out for a date.

That night in Tseye's room, Janet bothered me with questions about what Omogui was getting her. I tried my best at a noncommittal answer and turned back to my girl-bestfriend. Tseye and I would get off class early, maybe around two, and hook up. Then we would go to the Real Lovers' Day with Agape Addiction, which was starting at three thirty. I hoped she had bought me a card and flippantly asked the question. She *hooked* and was rescued by Janet who told me that I would have to wait until tomorrow. And then Janet asked me again what Omogui got her.

Later, back in A109, we had a roll call of the daters and the roasters. Wilhelm, who had lied to his professor uncle about reading with friends again, was there and fully in the dating camp. With him were Omogui, Ejiro, Harry, who was spending tomorrow with Brenda, and Kayoh. On the roasting side stood Tuoyo, Tambo—who insisted he had a babe until we asked him if she was aware, if she knew she was his girlfriend—and Chunky, Harry's best friend. I was unanimously declared a "maybe roaster."

I DID not spend Valentine's Day with Tseye. We did not meet in class as planned, and she was not in her room when I went there to check later that afternoon. I met Omogui and Janet in their corner. Janet had a look of pity mixed with compassion on her—I hated it—when she told me that a friend from fellowship had come to take Tseye away that morning. It seemed the friend—a girl, of course I asked—had a crisis of sorts and needed a shoulder to cry on. Tseye had dropped a message with Janet for me. I could go to the fellowship alone. She would see me tomorrow. I felt stupid standing there at the door, shifting at times to give passersby room and holding a paper bag with the Valentine cards in them. I gave these to Janet, murmured a greeting to Omogui, and left.

Now with no doubt as to where I belonged in the caste system we had drawn up the previous night, Tuoyo was not going to allow us a moment's peace to contemplate why we were alone. There was a bar in the Osasogie side of the university's off-campus suburbs called Jowitz. Harry and Brenda were on a date there, and we would go and make a general nuisance of ourselves. I also promised to wipe the morose look off my face. That and I would be having my first whole bottle of beer. My friends confirmed that it was very good at drowning sorrows, at rinsing away worries.

THIS WAS my first time in Osasogie Stores. The two-story building for which this side of school was named used to be a large warehouse and supermarket, but the landlady, since the eighties, had divided it into rooms for off-campus girls. The bar, Jowitz, was nestled in the left-hand corner of its ground floor. Just beside it was a snooker hall with a single snooker table. Boys in jeans and girls in cut-off tops hung around both joints. Five of us sat in a circle outside. The stinging tobacco smoke inside Jowitz and Brenda's insistent coughing had made us move here. Harmattan was still in the air, and beside the brown wooden doors of Jowitz, just under the "Established since 1987" sign, stood a poster from two weeks before congrat-ulating the Super Eagles for winning the African Cup of Na-tions. I was convinced to have a large bottle of Guinness Stout, a very auspicious start to a drinking career, and sipped from it and smoked my stick of St. Moritz while Brenda frowned at me from behind Harry's shoulder. I ignored her, and soon the gist shifted to tales of woe from each of the roasters as to why they were alone today. I looked around and noticed everyone was laughing at a joke Tuoyo was just ending—something about a girl named Nkechi, a toilet bowl, and her boyfriend's mischie-vous parrot.

The time was past seven, NEPA had taken the light, and since Osasogie stores had no generator, the snooker patrons had all deserted the place, leaving only Jowitz's customers in forced candlelit dinners on this night of romance. I went into the deserted snooker hall, climbed on top of the empty table, and drifted off into a Guinness-induced doze. The vertiginous feeling of sinking into the hard green upholstery morphed into a dream in which I was falling. I was about to hit the ground when Tuoyo woke me up. The Blackky show at the Main Au-ditorium was going to start at nine, and it was eight thirty al-ready. What? I had slept for an hour and a half?

I almost ended my night with what I hoped was a very discreet retch behind a hibiscus hedge between Chunky and Tuoyo, who covered me. It was then I understood why drink-ing was so attractive to the heartbroken. I had not thought of Tseye throughout the time I spent with my friends. It wasn't the alcohol. It was the camaraderie. The shouting and teasing and laughing.

My eyes became clear after I threw up. So here was the se-cret of drinkers. When the fire was too hot, the way out of the kitchen was to get sick. And there was a reason it was done at night. I was already having my first hangover. A splitting headache seemed to have a vice-like grip on my forehead. I looked at my wristwatch. It was only an hour after midnight. Surely, this must be a record. I had gotten drunk, slept, vomited, and was having a hangover; I had done all these in half a night.

SOMEHOW TUOYO still managed to convince me to go to the show at the auditorium. Tuoyo and I slid across the faux leather seats and, leaving Chunky, Brenda, and Harry behind to watch our spaces, walked between the aisles up to the easiest exit for a smoke. Behind us, Uniben's Celine Dion—a rotund, dreadlocked girl who maybe sounded like the original if the listener squinted hard—performed her version of an old classic that was not even a Celine Dion song. When we reached the landing at the top of the steps, I saw Tommy, TJ's armed-robber-looking guy, standing alone. The confra boys always provided security at these events. As we passed him, he beckoned to me. I excused myself and went to speak to him, not missing the disapproving look on Tuoyo's face.

"Ewaen, long time, no see." Tommy with the armed-robber face tried hard at familiarity.

I replied, "True. How you dey?" I looked towards where my friend stood, waiting by a door to our right. I waved him off. Tuoyo understood that I would be with him soon.

Tommy stared down towards the stage at the singer who had finished her first routine and was introducing a new song. She started singing a slow ballad. It filtered up to us, the lyrics a sharp contrast to the direction our conversation would take. I turned with him and faced the stage, listening to what he said.

"Ewaen, you dey fuck up."

Well, he did not waste any time, did he? Was he talking about my meeting his capo, TJ? Was he talking about the fact that he tried to kidnap my friend? Wilhelm had threatened to take the matter up with his cousin Yibril—was that it?

I glanced sideways at him and asked, "How?"

"You dey waka with Black Axe boys."

What? He was talking about Yibril. "Who?"

"You know who."

I knew this much: of the friends in my room, the friends I walked with and played with, I only suspected one of being an Ah-kay boy, and that was Omogui. So if Tommy was talking about mixing with Ah-kay boys, it must be because Wilhelm had spoken to his cousin, and the cousin had made a complaint to the Cosa Nostra.

"I am speaking about your friend. The oyibo boy, Wilhelm."

He turned to look at me. I am sure he saw the look of shock on my face. My lips trembled, and my eyes widened like big frying pans. I couldn't think.

"How can you say that, Tommy?" I said. "You know what you did to my friend. Why come to me, small boy like me, to say that he is a confra boy."

What Tommy did next shocked me. He reached for me slowly. I thought he wanted to pat me on the back, maybe affect some crude parody of brotherly concern. Instead, he pulled my T-shirt up with his left hand and rubbed my back with his right.

I lurched away, shocked. "What's wrong with you?" I asked.

"Just checking to see if you have any lash marks. To see if you had gone to the bush to blend with those ruffians." His manner was bold. "You know that you are a potential." He spoke as if he owned me. I did not ask, *Potential for what?*

"See, we can't have you running around with Black Axe boys. You must choose your friends carefully. If he is worrying you, tell me, and I'll take care of you, hmm?"

"Worrying me? What are you talking about?"

"You must be a real mugu, Ewaen. I almost want to take back that compliment about you having potential. Stop sounding like a zombie. Your friend, your so-called close friend, your oyibo, blended Black Axe the week before resumption."

"No." Yes. Wilhelm had left Warri early. No. No.

"This is why you have to choose your friends carefully. Hang with us. We will protect you from all these dangerous elements." He spoke with a completely crippled sense of irony.

My eyes were red. What gall? I was not thinking when I said, "You can't choose my friends for me. I don't know you." I did not look at him. I stared at the stage. My voice was slow and quiet in tandem with the singer downstairs as I continued. "Don't ever presume you know me. Don't ever touch me again." I walked away.

I could feel his eyes burning holes into the back of my shirt as I opened the door and walked down the steps towards the cigarette light I saw blinking by the concrete stools of the auditorium's back lawn.

"GUY, NO rush the cigar. You'll get dizzy," Tuoyo said with concern. He tapped his foot on the grass, counting off the beats from a local rap group that was performing inside. We had been outside for close to ten minutes and were sharing the last stick. Tuoyo asked again, "What were you and that guy talking about? E be like he vex you."

"Oh?"

"Yes, oh," Tuoyo said as he reached awkwardly with his left hand and dragged the stick from my lips. "Oh," he complained. "See how hot it is. You drag too deep." He spat out the smoke. "Tell me, now. Wetin he ask you?"

"Nothing," I replied. "Na all the routine about fine boys. He say make I join him confra."

We went in to enjoy the rest of the show. A small incident involving some Cosa Nostra boys and the Black Axe almost brewed into something nasty until leaders from either side came and separated the warring parties. TJ was there talking to a light-skinned Ah-kay boy. Yibril, Wilhelm's short cousin, was in the center of the crowd of boys talking and cajoling. I saw the bump at the back of his trousers. He was packing a weapon. So were these Wilhelm's new friends?

Tambo filled us in on the details the next day. Some wahala over a girl. The caporegime of the Mafia confraternity and one of the Ah-kay boys had been in a fight. Guns were drawn. But it was more than that. "Guys, I dey tell una. This school go soon explode. The wahala that's coming, eh. Cosa Nostra boys and the Ah-kay guys are clashing too frequently. La Cosa Nostra dey try prove say because them be the smallest and newest confra no mean say they cannot protect themselves. And Ah-kay dey threaten to deal with them, just like they did with that Yoruba confra in '91."

12

I HAD just passed half a cigarette to Tambo when I heard my name whispered at the door to A109. A familiar voice.

Oh my.

It was Tseye. She came to my room. I jumped over sweaty, smelly bodies to reach her and Omogui at the door. "What are you doing here?" I asked.

"Didn't Janet tell you? I said I was going to see you today."

Behind me, Tambo, Tuoyo, and Kayoh begged me to let her in. "Come, let's go to the common room," I said, pulling my sweatshirt over my head.

Did I say she was beautiful? She wore a light cream blouse, linen, and matching trousers. She drew close to me. I could not see her; I was halfway through wearing my shirt, but I felt the difficulty with which she said, "Don't worry. Go and get ready. I'll wait for you here. We can talk later."

From inside the room Kayoh shouted, "Ha, Ewaen. Let her in now. Tseye, welcome o. We have heard so much about you. Please come in. Let's shake hands."

I took off the shirt and saw that she was smiling. While I went to the wardrobe to get my toilet things, Kayoh and the boys surrounded her with gist. They were on their best behavior.

WE RODE okadas to the staff quarters. On the walk to the hostel gate where the bikes waited, Tseye told me where she had been the day before. Margaret, an old friend from the government estate where she lived in Lagos, had quarreled with her boyfriend a day to Valentine's Day. She came to their room brokenhearted and begged Tseye to spend the night with her in her room, a BQ, in quarters. The night had turned into day and into the next night. Tseye said she had just seen her off at the Lagos taxi park at Main Gate. She asked again if Janet did not give me her message. I wanted to tell her that I did not listen to what Janet was saying. Instead, I asked her if she got my cards. She showed them to me, smiling.

Our bikes stopped at A56, a nice semidetached bungalow with a cute garden up front bordered with red, yellow, and purple hibiscus hedges. My mind went to Wilhelm, whom I knew would still be asleep in a suite at UPH with his Valentine date in his arms. I remembered the last time I was in quarters. I remembered what Tommy had said last night. A lump rose in my throat, and I banished all the thoughts, all the negative vibes. Tseye said she wanted us to spend the day in Margaret's room. She still had the keys and only had to return them when her friend returned from Lagos.

Would we get a chance to come to grips with our relationship? Tseye could not say she did not know the way I felt about her. She could not say she did not feel something. I crossed the lawn behind her. The BQ had two rooms. Tseye told me both tenants were girls and that Margaret's neighbor had gone to be with her boyfriend. We had the entire place to ourselves. I stood behind her as she turned the key in the lock. The first time with Tessa, I had made my move at this point. But not with Tseye. Tseye was special. Tseye was good.

"So this is the place o."

I looked in past her shoulder as she kicked her shoes off. The light that seeped in through the sheer curtains bathed everything in a blue translucence that made the room look like one of those Igbo Market shops where the most awful pair of jeans miraculously became a pair of Versace specials. The room was spare and beautiful. A fridge was on the right just beside a reading table and chair. On the opposite side at the foot of the bed stood a small stool with a TV and video cassette player. Tseye entered, and I followed. She pulled the curtains after turning on the air conditioner, and I saw the room proper. It was as beautiful in the light as it was with the curtains drawn.

I said, "So, what are we going to do with the day?"

"We eat. I'll cook you breakfast, and then we will watch films. No disturbance." She went to a corner of the room, put some eggs and half a yam in a basket, and skipped out of the room. "The films are by the bed o," she shouted from the kitchen.

We ate. We watched two films, *House Party* and *Tango & Cash*. I was so happy . . . happy and confused. In later years, I would ask myself why I did not make a move that day. But as I looked at Tseye's face—she had taken off her glasses—I was scared to spoil a beautiful thing. There were times when our fingers touched, sharing a piece of yam, reaching for the remote at the same time. But we laughed off each almost-uncomfortable moment. I sensed some of the discomfort I was feeling in her, in her smile, in a caught glance. But I was too scared to spoil the moment, the happiness. Or maybe I was just a scared seventeen-year-old mugu who did not know when it was handed to him on a platter. It was the last time Tseye and I would be that happy together.

WE WROTE our second-semester exams a month later. They went well. I shared my reading time between Tseye and Wilhelm.

Wilhelm and I talked about what Tommy said. It was a cold conversation, awkward. Yes, my friend was now a con-fra boy.

"How could you do this? After everything we talked about, after all we promised ourselves?" I asked.

"What did you expect, Ewaen?" Willy countered.

"Not this. You said you would speak to your cousin, that he would square things up with these Cosa Nostra boys." We sat in a beer parlor. The tension that had started the conversation had been slightly broken when Wilhelm heard what I ordered. A beer.

"And how do you think that would have gone, guy? Look, I became a target. Every Mafia boy looked at me funny. They would have come after me again."

"But I had spoken to TJ. He said—"

Willy interrupted me. "TJ is graduating this year. That bastard Tommy threatened me with this fact."

We kept our noses in our beer glasses for a few minutes. Finally, Wilhelm spoke.

"Ewaen, I did what I had to do. In the Black Axe, I have a relative. And they are not pretentious sissies who prance about in movie clothes and speak funny. Ewaen, these are real guys, real and hard bastards, who would die for a friend."

I looked at my oyibo friend speaking good English. My oyibo friend who always said I was the first to spoil him. I watched him defend confra. God forbid bad thing.

THE RIOTS broke out two weeks into the end-of-session exams. We had suspected it was going to happen soon, but the final trigger came unexpectedly. People had been complaining about the anti-riot policemen. The gist spread throughout the school that the police detail posted at the main gate had descended on and beaten the shit out of a group of students who were coming back late from an off-campus party. The next morning, the student leaders, TT and Nna Ojukwu, paraded the bloodied clothes of the victims before the impromptu gathering at the hostel car park. They linked the incident to the attacks on our democracy, to the annulment of June 12. I did not stay to listen to them, hurrying instead to the pharmacy lecture halls where Tseye and I were supposed to revise PHY 124. They came to the night prep too. Politely asking for ten minutes of our time, they repeated their litany in every lecture hall in every department that night in school. They requested a gathering of students the next morning at the hostel car park. They were going to march to the vice-chancellor's lodge and then to the main gate.

I smelled tear gas for the first time the next morning. The university authorities had heard that we were going to riot. Defying the police at the hostel gate, the crowd of students surged on through to the VC's lodge. The ringleaders marched in front, holding blown-up pictures of the bleeding students. Everyone in A109 went along to see this first riot. We sang solidarity songs and marched. I stood, arms locked, with Ejiro on my right and Wilhelm on my left. We sang lustily, spraying droplets of saliva on the backs of those who marched in front of us. We breathed in the dust from the march; we sweated in the heat of bodies, in the glory of the fight. We were young; we were young.

The policemen, most of whom had been posted to school for more than a few months and had made friends, or at least learned to respect our single-minded and naïve sense of right and wrong, lost their nerve after firing a few canisters of tear gas and let us pass. Tear gas dey pain o. Do not answer anybody who tells you otherwise. My nose ran like a tap, and I wept like a baby. My eyes stung. We had been told to carry handkerchiefs and bottles of water, but the wet rags did not help.

The demonstration turned ugly when we got to the main gate. There was a small argument between the student leaders about whether to march into town or confine the demonstration to the school premises. They reached a compromise. We would slow down traffic at the expressway and make sure the drivers going to Lagos knew that the general's troops were not going to cow the vibrant and astute Uniben students. That was when the trouble started. A new group of police officers met us at the gate. We did not know these ones. They came from the governor's special guard. They showed us pepper.

The authorities did not close down the school. The VC shifted the exams by two days and made threats that the ringleaders of Tuesday's disturbances would be punished when school resumed. But we knew he was just blowing hot air. The mood of the country said it all. The liberal university community, although scared shitless of Abacha, wanted something to happen. The only organized group still untouched by the general's goons was the National Association of Nigerian Students, NANS. The VC just wanted us to get on with our exams. Nothing was going to happen to the student union leaders.

I RAN into Tommy the night before my last paper. He should not have been in school. Sophomores finished their papers two days before jambites began theirs. I was walking with Tseye along the corridors of the science faculty. We were looking for a class to read in.

Tommy ignored Tseye and spoke to me.

"TJ tell me say he follow you talk."

"Yeah, we discussed," I replied.

"Just remember say your guy no go dey this school forever o."

YEAR TWO

March 1994–March 1995

13

I DO not know anyone in A109 who did not move off campus at the end of the Harmattan of '94. Harry moved with his siblings to an estate near the Osasogie gate; Tuoyo and Wilhelm moved into a series of face-me-I-face-yous in Osasogie—Willy said he was tired of living with the prof, that he needed freedom; and Tambo was trying to get into Bulgaria—not some exotically named hostel, no, the real Bulgaria, in Europe. The last weeks of the previous semester had seen new alliances— people moved in pairs or threes looking for accommodation off campus. Kayoh spoke to me about this guy, Efe, who was looking for quiet roommates to share his flat with. After our experiences in year one, none of the A109 boys were going to move to Ekosodin on the other side of school.

HARRY AND his siblings lived in a flat in Ekosodin in Aiwerioba Estate. No. 42 FGGC Road was a single compound of twenty-six flats. Students who could afford the high rent lived in most of the flats, marked by the letters A through Z. Aiwerioba shone with the shimmering reflections of recently waxed cars, and the half-sand, half-grass lawn in its center, surrounded by twelve of the flats designated with the middle letters of the alphabet, was used as a football field for Sunday matches between competing flats. Flat 42R, where Harry lived, were the current champions.

Harry was never in class. He lived with his younger brother, who was in my class, and sister, a year-one student in Brenda's department. We joked that his father was training three professionals—an engineer, a doctor, and a lawyer and was most likely going to get two, which wasn't a bad return on investment. Tuoyo and Wilhelm, who lived nearby, were usually in Harry's room in the mornings, and on weekends they took part in the football matches. When I got to Harry's flat, we would spend the entire day sitting on their veranda, gisting and bird-watching the fine girls who lived on the estate. We skipped lunch and ate dinner in Jowitz before retiring to our residences.

If the day was an anatomy day—the course I loved most because I loved the cadavers—the routine was slightly different. I still got up at nine, late enough to miss the crowded early-morning lecture, hooked up with Wilhelm at Osasogie Gate, and headed for classes. Dissections began at ten, so the thirty or so redundant minutes waiting for them to begin were spent in the Tea House.

"DON'T PUT that in your mouth," Oluchi said. Thirty of us stood around a skinny cadaver laid out on the slab in the dissection room. Oluchi had just slapped my pen from my right hand. It had been on an absentminded journey from the skinned, thin forearm of the cadaver to my mouth. As it clattered to the floor, I looked up from it at her and said *Thank you* with my eyes. Was I really going to put it in my mouth?

She smiled back, flipping a page on the anatomy manual in her lap. Around us, other groups worked; the gatherings of ten to fifteen in their robes of white surrounding supine naked bodies, and with the open manuals in their hands, looked like worshippers at a Wiccan conference. The bulbs that swung above each slab shone with incandescent brilliance, reflecting off the short-sleeved lab coats that everyone wore. The click-clack of cock shoes and high heels added to the atmosphere of business-like religion. Oluchi directed the designated dissector today, a chap named Ayo, to "lift the ventral patch of skin medially, expose the forearm wrist flexors, and trace the median nerve distally to the carpal tunnel."

We watched and took notes. The first thing you noticed in anatomy class—after the smell of formalin, the green, dry, gray state of the corpses, the bright surreal lighting, and the sound of the shoes on the slippery, tiled floor—was that most of the textbooks got it wrong. In them the nerves were always yellow, the arteries red, the veins blue, and the muscles a reddish shade of brown. But in the formalin-preserved cadavers we worked with, everything was on a spectrum between green and brown. Our minders told us that when we started work as doctors, we would note that the inside of a *living* human body was a metallic-smelling, sticky, red mass of intertwining strands of flesh—no yellow or blue.

We nicknamed the cadaver Thrilla. He was going to be with us for the next two years. Our anatomy professor, Dr. Okocha, balding, gifted, a sketch of the archetypical distracted genius, told us to make friends with our cadavers. He called them our wards. We were to take good care of them and make sure nothing happened to them like the misplaced penis of group G1's that ended up in the handbag of that girl seven years ago. A classmate whose attentions the girl had rebuffed put it there, the professor told us, and the culprit was discovered and promptly kicked out of medicine. We were to respect these men and women who had made the ultimate sacrifice, who became tools for the education of a gaggle of mindless, giggling teenagers.

I felt the speech was better suited to a European anatomy lab where idealists had actually donated their cadavers in their wills. None of the people on our slabs had donated their remains.

The bullet holes on Thrilla suggested how he came to be there, even if his actual profession was in doubt, which was debated over glasses of beer in the evenings by his team of dissectors. I was convinced that Thrilla had been an armed robber who met his end at the hands of policemen, the Mobile units ever brave, ever resourceful in their drive to rid our cities of crime. Oluchi felt he was probably a victim of "accidental discharge"—the ubiquitous police excuse that hung over anyone stopped at a checkpoint and asked for his or her papers.

But I think Fra had the most accurate answer. He reminded us of the reason we had given Thrilla his nickname. Thrilla was skinny. Our futile attempts at separating his hopelessly atrophied muscles should tell us his real fate, Fra said. He had probably been awaiting trial, arrested for stealing yam or wandering, and executed in lieu of a guiltier culprit, a murderer with connections and money. The excuse then would be that he had been shot while trying to escape. Or maybe he was "cleaned up" in a sanitation exercise before a big man's visit to "inspect" some prison.

I had seen some of these visits broadcast on TV with the caption, "Compassionate Chief/JP/Judge 'this or that' presents inmates with gifts." There was always something of the primordial serpent in the smiles of the visiting dignitaries. The prisoners were made to sit in the dust and listen to the prison choir, clad in striped colonial-era shorts and threadbare jerseys, sing for the visitors. When the visitor was a member of the judiciary come to free those awaiting trial who had served more time than they could possibly have been jailed for, the prisoners could be seen out of focus in the background, on the seven o'clock news, pleading with the guards to give them a chance to present their cases to the big man. The successful petitioners then knelt in the dirt, in the sun, in front of the group of judges, while they pontificated on the dignity of man.

The charade always brought a lump of impotent anger to my throat. I skipped the evening news at home and watched UK Gold instead. *Some Mothers Do Have 'Em* was more interesting and at least more honest in its portrayal of idiocy.

After classes, we usually ended the afternoons at C6. The occupants of this single story in the doctors' quarters had converted their garage into a beer parlor. Surrounded by our future colleagues, we sat and eavesdropped as the surgeons and physicians discussed this iniquitous boss or an intriguing case.

Fra had a crush on Oluchi, yet always sat farthest from her. He posed the more serious questions and offered the enviously deep insights. He tried very hard to impress her. Oluchi, who had grown up the youngest child and only girl in a family of five, humored Fra and teased him ruthlessly about girls in class she thought he liked.

"Hey. See, Preppa," I said, interrupting a pointed discussion between the potential lovebirds about who Oluchi fancied in class. Ikechukwu "Fra Divialo" Azanobi and Fidelis "Preppa" Okodua were very close friends since attending Federal Government College Warri.

We named Fra for his playful vengefulness. The "brotha devil" ended any joke cracked at his expense with the words "I will revenge." And he always did. Always. Preppa's nickname had been borne by four others before him in FGC Warri. It meant one who could read all night, a preppa. Only the first of the siblings had earned it. Now Fidelis, he was no preppa. He played and laughed his way through class and exams, but always seemed to pass. He was brilliant. Like Einstein. They made quite a pair: Fra, tall and lanky with an impossibly long head (though he had the gall to call me Bighead), and Preppa, chubby and taller than he looked.

Preppa was walking towards us, smiling painfully in the heat, his lab coat serving as a makeshift parasol. He greeted some doctors and then shifted and squirmed his weight between the tightly packed plastic chairs towards where we sat.

"Wetin una dey talk about?" Preppa asked.

Fra briefed him. "Oluchi and Ewaen were complaining about their cadaver, Thrilla. He is too lean."

"They are lucky. Ours died of cancer. A fifty-something-year-old woman. There is a big lump on her belly. I'm dreading the day we get to the abdomen in dissection."

"Preppa!" Oluchi and I chorused.

"Sorry o. I'm just nervous, that's all. Forget what I said."

After drinking half a pint of lager in record time, he belched loudly and spoke at the same time. "Una don see the list?"

"Which list?" Oluchi asked.

A few weeks ago, the notice boards in school had been pasted with lists of students who were ordered to present themselves before the university senate panels for trial. As the university bylaws said, quoted with admirable succinctness on the foolscap mimeographs, any student suspected of a misdemeanor had one chance before a panel of his peers and his teachers to make his defense. As with most end-of-session notices, these were filled with students accused of exam malpractices. TJ's name was there. There were rumors that this was because of the almost-fight at the Main Auditorium last session—the Valentine's Day fracas. His was the only name I recognized from Tambo's gist about that night's wahala.

"The Senate's list," Fra said helpfully.

Oluchi huffed, waving impatiently with her left hand for Preppa to complete his report.

"They've made their decision?" I asked.

"O' boy, they rusticated like fifteen students. There was even one guy who's supposed to be in year-five medicine, and they gave him five years for cheating."

"Five years," I said. "If na me, I go just die. I can't tell my father that kind of gist: Daddy, em, they said I should resume school in five years' time. He will kill me."

"At least they no expel am. If he is sensible, he will go and write JAMB again and maybe finish a degree before he comes back to read this stupid course," Preppa said.

"Why, you hate medicine like that?" I asked him.

Preppa reached for his glass of beer and held it to his lips. Before he drank, he said, "What are we suffering for? Of all the professionals in this country, after teachers and lawyers, na we poor pass."

We all laughed at his frustration and Fra said, "Lawyers poor, sha." His folks lived behind the high court complex in town. "You should see some of their wigs. They even stop at our neighbor's to buy fifty kobo pure water."

"Pure water don reach fifty kobo? Things are getting cost-lier," Oluchi said.

"And making change is getting more difficult for the sell-ers," I added. "Remember in year one when a five-naira note could get you a cigarette and a Fanta?"

"Yeah, round figure," Fra said. "Now that combination is seven naira."

Preppa nodded. "Maybe by the time that medical student comes back to Uniben, a bottle of beer will be one hundred naira."

"Impossible," we shouted. "Never."

"But he is still lucky, considering what one guy got."

"What happened?" Fra asked him.

"They expelled one chap. A final-year agric econs student. And to believe he just wrote his final exams last month. Sad."

How many agric econs final-year students had been on that list?

"What was his name?" I asked.

"Toju something. One Itsekiri-oyibo hybrid name like that. They say it was for cult activities."

THAT NIGHT, while we played *Street Fighter* in my room, I told Ejiro about TJ. He had already seen the list and was planning to gist with me about it. I voiced my worries.

"My problem is with that Tommy guy. The guy threatened me last semester. Shebi, I told you about his pulling my shirt at the Blackky show?"

"Yes."

"I was so mad."

"You told me everything. But why you dey worry? You dey year two. Nobody go harass you to join confra."

"No be everything I tell you. Towards the end of exams, he saw me and asked if I was aware that TJ would not be in school forever. Ejiro, I no like the boy at all."

"So wetin you wan' do? You want to join Black Axe like Willy did?"

"Of course not. Why would you think that?"

Ejiro glanced from the TV and looked at me. "I feel you concerning this Tommy guy. I no like am too. I just wish Tambo was around to give us in-house gist."

"Because he is a Cosa Nostra boy? Don't forget that his primary allegiance is to them and not us."

"No, I no agree. Tambo is our friend," Ejiro said.

"Forget. Trust no one. You no dey watch mafia films?" I paused to concentrate on a Guile hurricane kick that I executed to perfection. "How the idiot sef?"

"Omogui told me he called from Sofia. He said Tambo was arrested at the airport for having a fake visa on his passport but was moved to halfway lodgings for asylum seekers after he claimed he was from Rwanda."

"Haba! Oyibo, sha. Do they really think we all look alike? So Tambo is Tutsi now?"

"Hutu. Omogui said Tambo was busy speaking Bini to the oyibos until a fellow 'Rwandan' welcomed him with 'Obokian' at the refugee center. It seems they are all Bini boys there."

"That part na lie. Omogui too lie?" I said, and Ejiro did not disagree. "How you see next month?" May was almost ending and June hung above us all like the sword of Damocles.

"The June 12 anniversary? School go hot o. I'm planning to travel on the tenth."

"Make that earlier. You don't want to be on the road that weekend. Police will be harassing people at checkpoints. If you are going to travel at all, which I don't advise, make it earlier."

"You nko? Are you going to be in school?"

"Yep. Tops, I'll just stay indoors for the entire weekend. Maybe find a girl to spend it with."

"Dreamer."

"But seriously, the safest place to be will be off campus. Any wahala will be in school. Meanwhile, the twins dey write JAMB next week. Tuoyo say some waka go dey for exam expo. He said I should follow him. They might need a car for their waka."

"Just be careful sha. Exam malpractice is not the same as inside school o. If police catch una them go flog una o. When are you planning on traveling?"

"Next week."

14

I HAD no idea what the Joint Admissions and Matriculation Board exam, the University Matriculation Examination, was until I filled out the forms. The UME, which everyone just called JAMB, after the organization, was one of those things that had no meaning, was of no concern, until it was almost upon you, until it was your turn. Or maybe it was the first-born thing again. The ignorance of our parents for the perils we faced was endless.

Now it was Eniye's and Osaze's turns to write this JAMB. I remembered what Kpobo went through the year we wrote ours—arriving early only to fail an exam because a civil servant somewhere forgot to present his exam papers properly, in the right order. I would be damned if I allowed some snafu, unforeseen by my siblings, or some misplaced quota system that claimed to protect the educational disadvantaged result in the twins failing this exam. This was why I left school, why I was home this weekend. This was going to be my own small rebellion against the system.

I GOT home from school to find the twins locked up in Dad's room, reading. This was something that I had also experienced, and since it seemed to work for me—after all, I was in university—the twins were condemned to this tried-and-tested method. The idea had come to my father when we were in primary school. When I was preparing for my common entrance exams into FGC Warri, Dad said he had found a solution to the distractions that ten-year-old boys faced when reading. This solution, attractive only because of its simplicity, was to lock me up in his room with the TV and video unplugged from their sockets, the circuit breakers turned off, and the refrigerator stocked to the brim. He said that when he was preparing for his A-levels, he had done the same thing voluntarily. When I passed, of course, this was the reason. Then he tried it with the twins, and they passed.

My parents were happy that I had come all the way from school to help Osaze and Eniye with their JAMB. Would I drive one of the twins to a center tomorrow? Yes, I said. Good. Good.

Mom and Dad seemed distant at dinner. Speaking through one of their children but never directly to each other, they sat on opposite sides of the dining table while Sharon, our house girl, passed around steaming bowls of rice and stew. Mom looked thinner, and when I asked about Nene, she was succinct in her reply. We were all worried about Nene's health. Mom said that Nene was fine and by God's grace they would be traveling to Enugu next week for her pacemaker surgery.

"This is good, Ewaen. It is good that you are around. At least you can speak to them about working hard. They have not been reading," Dad said, pulling the gist back to why I had come home.

Osaze smiled sheepishly. Eniye frowned at her plate.

Mom agreed and said to me, "Your father's right. We don't know how Osaze's SSCE is going to be. He has to pass tomorrow's exams. And I have told Eniye, Daddy is not going to beg for any child to enter university and I don't have the energy to start pursuing lecturers around school."

We went to bed early. Mom and Dad never let us read beyond 10 p.m. on the night before exams. They said there was nothing new to learn and that exams required a fresh and well-rested brain. Lying in the dark, I spoke to the twins.

Eniye's matter was more straightforward. She was going to write her exams at her alma mater, FGC Warri. The letter from JAMB detailing where Osaze was supposed to sit for his exams had not come. We would have to be in the special center at Hussey College very early the next morning. Tuoyo was supposed to meet us there. Once Osaze found his center, Tuoyo and I would leave him and try and hook up with the guys who supplied the expo.

"When you guys are done, you'll come to my center first o," Eniye said.

"It depends on how the waka is," I replied.

"No. No waka. My center first. Look, it's simple. Osaze will be getting settled in because he will most likely be writing in a special center."

"It makes sense, Ewaen," Osaze said. "While I'm getting settled in, you can rush to the expo guys, collect the thing, and branch Eniye's center first."

"Okay."

I asked my brother if he had raised the cash. He said he had made the withdrawals from Dad's trousers and had raised a considerable sum—about six thousand naira. I decided that was enough.

"MAKE THIS boy do quick now. What's the delay?"

Tuoyo sat in the car beside me, chewing on an egg roll. He had been annoying me all morning by farting and playing with the hand brake between us. I had slapped off his left hand at least twice. It was past eight and Osaze was still in with the mob. A JAMB invigilator, probably a state schoolteacher "volunteering" for the extra cash, was surrounded by a hundred screaming students and was passing out exam-center slips. We had been here since six in the morning, first waiting for the people to resume, and then watching as Osaze joined in the initial rush of the students to be accredited and recognized as genuine JAMB applicants. This was the last stage, in which the students found out where they would write their exams. It was eight thirty already. Michael should have dropped off Eniye at FGC Warri.

What if Osaze's center came back as somewhere in Sapele or Ughelli? Tuoyo told me that this was okay, better even, as the village teachers and principals were sometimes easier to bribe since the opportunity to make money only came once a year.

I looked at him. Tuoyo was a real thief. The dashing, chivalrous kind. He was from an old Itsekiri family. Tuoyo's house was just down the road from Hussey College. He had walked to the school and had been waiting for us when we arrived. While Osaze had gone in to register his name, we had strolled to the house so I could know it. It was a monolith of cement—a two-story building meant to house the chief's platoon of children. Tuoyo was the eldest of his mother's five. I was introduced to his mom and some of his younger sisters. The family lived upstairs. The flats downstairs were for tenants, mostly distant cousins who did not pay any rent. One of these was our point man, Ese. Ese had left earlier for Ughelli. He said that some people there were going to get the papers out and start solving them. These were all specialists: English, physics, chemistry, biology, and economics undergraduates. No matter where Osaze's center eventually was, one of us was to wait here for him.

Osaze came out. He looked puzzled. "Any of una know where Unity Commercial College dey?"

"UCC? It's not far. Ewaen start motor make we dey go." Tuoyo slammed the passenger front door and let go of the hand brake before I had time to slap his hand off again.

"Who go wait for Ese?" I asked.

"No worry, we go come back for am."

We drove away. Tuoyo told us that Osaze's center was a state school situated between Igbudu Market and God's Kingdom Society's Salem City. Because neither Osaze nor I knew where the school was, he offered to risk missing Ese and directed us there. The plan was that as soon as we arrived, Tuoyo would take a bike back and continue his wait. The school was not between the market and anywhere; it was inside the market. We jostled for parking space with mammy wagons laden with tomatoes and yams. The traffic jam even affected people. Many stood in one spot, shuffling, cursing, some bending over to price foodstuff spread along the small streets that wound through the market. The unwashed smell of bodies and rotten fruit wafted into the car and stung our eyes. Tuoyo pointed out the school's gate and jumped out of the car with Osaze. It was ten minutes to nine. Eniye would be getting ready to write at her center. I looked for a place to park and found it beside a fresh fish stall. I waited.

When Tuoyo came back to the car, he was laughing. "They have not even begun. The question papers are late. They just sat Osaze down and distributed answer sheets. No worry. Everything will be fine."

"So you are going back to Hussey College now?"

"Yes o. Osaze said the money is with you."

"How much you need?"

"See your eye. No worry. It won't be more than three thousand."

I handed the money to him. "Make your man do quick o. We still have to reach Eniye's center."

"No worry. Worse comes to worst, I go take bike reach there myself. No worry." He would soon be back, he promised.

I strolled out of the car, dodged a bucket of fish entrails thrown by the daughter of the fish seller, and went to buy cigarettes. I thanked the man selling the cigarettes and soft drinks and sat down in his stall. I looked across the street at the secondary school where my brother was supposed to be writing his entrance exams into university. Rundown, ramshackle. It was a symbol of everything wrong with the system. Its gatehouse had been converted into a market stall; it sold provisions and electric bulbs. The rusty gate hung on only one of its hinges. The buildings beyond were light blue streaked with gray and black stains. The ancient asbestos roof was melting in the heat and hung almost halfway down the sides of the walls like rags on a market lunatic. Around the outer perimeter fence, children stood beside wheelbarrows singing, "Ten naira for your wheelbarrow." We were going to be here for just a day. What of the kids who came to learn every day in this filth? UCC was the kind of school we joked about, where the teacher came into class with melon seeds from her kitchen and, as a class assignment, distributed these to the children to sift for her husband's pot of soup.

But like the sharp intake of air—life-giving, life-affirming—after a dunk in a cold bath, behind this depressing swamp of lost dreams lay the serene Salem City. This commune was built in the late forties by adherents of the God's Kingdom Society. The GKS had completed one of those places that marked out the old town of any growing metropolis from any new pretenders. The tall palm trees along its wire-mesh back fence towered and bent over the buildings of the secondary school. Salem City's grounds were well-kept sun-bleached sand almost devoid of grass, well-trimmed ixora and hibiscus hedges that lined the brushed, sandy streets of the commune, flagpoles that flew scenes from the Bible, the Fall from Eden, Cain killing Abel, the Great Flood, the Annunciation, and the Crucifixion with Christ on a pole, not a cross. Salem City was self-sufficient. It housed its own schools, clinics, and a pharmacy.

The GKS members had until the mid-seventies been very strict about contact with the outside world. But with the death of the founding father, the elders relaxed certain rules.

Someone tapped me on my shoulder. I turned to see Osaze. "Wetin happen? Why are you outside? They have not brought the question papers yet?"

"No o," Osaze said. He sat beside me and ordered a Fanta. "You won't believe it, and it's almost ten. When is Tuoyo coming back?"

"Soon. How did you leave the class? They are not supposed to let anyone in or out after nine forty-five."

"I saw one boy paying the invigilator cash to allow him use the toilet, so I got up and said I wanted to see my brother outside to collect pencils. It cost me about—" Osaze reached into his pocket and brought out a mashed-up bundle of notes. Counting backwards, he said, "Three hundred." He was looking at my cigarette, and I saw him scratch his right middle finger with his thumb.

"Why you dey look my cigar like that?"

Osaze shrugged and stared into space, smiling at himself and taking a sip of the drink.

"You've started smoking."

He nodded.

"When?"

Before he could start telling me, we heard Tuoyo hailing us from a bike coming to a stop.

Tuoyo had already sent Ese on to Eniye's center. He had rushed down to UCC because the time had gone. He was very surprised to see Osaze sitting with me outside. Osaze took the tiny strips of paper from Tuoyo and walked back into UCC.

The question papers didn't arrive from JAMB until around twelve thirty. By then, the school gate was filled with students from other centers—everywhere else in Nigeria the exams had ended at twelve—trying to sell their marked-up question papers. To prevent a riot, the invigilators were reinforced with police officers from the local station. We were lucky that we got to Osaze when we did.

AFTER THE exam, the four of us went to see Nene. The twins spent the drive asking Tuoyo and me where we had found the idiots who solved the math and physics questions. "They got a lot of the answers wrong!" they chorused.

"You're both welcome. Tuoyo, see the thanks I get?"

At the hospital, we sat with Mom in the waiting room. The nurse eventually told us we could go in; the children, yes, but only ten minutes o, only ten minutes. Nene had lost weight and was in the hospital bed with a maze of tubes dancing everywhere. She smiled at us, a painful effort judging from the wince immediately afterwards. When Osaze, Eniye, and I left her, we met Tuoyo and Mom gisting. Tuoyo was trying to speak to her in Itsekiri. She smiled quietly, ashamed to tell him that all the Itsekiri she understood could be written on the back of a five-kobo stamp with space to spare. I told Tuoyo this fact.

He laughed. "No wonder. Ewaen is worse."

We all laughed.

15

THE FIRST June 12 anniversary came and went very quietly. The World Cup distracted the rest of the civilized world while the Americans, who hosted the competition, changed their TV channels en masse to catch OJ Simpson trying to outrun the police at forty kilometers per hour. We kept busy watching football, not paying attention to the pressing issues that our country faced. Ken Saro Wiwa had just been arrested.

Who heard? Who cared?

In Nigeria's first match on the world stage, we trashed the Bulgarians 3–0. A wonderful day it was. No one, not even those who maintained a fashionable aloofness when it came to football, could resist the euphoria. Banners of green-white-green, made with bed sheets or cheap plastic, flapped from the doors, boots, and bonnets of cars. We spent the evenings, as we waited for the games to air, playing matchups between that night's contenders on our video game consoles or on the small pitch in the middle of Estate. It was the first World Cup I actually watched.

Bloody Americans, being six hours behind us, made the match times particularly horrendous. Bleary-eyed from an evening of drinking, we would stay awake until two in the morning. Thank God the Nigerian team was based in Boston. Eastern Standard Time was easier to deal with.

All the while, armored personnel carriers stood at the junctions in school. The student leaders still ranted and raved.

Nobody paid much attention. Democracy was having a hard time competing with football.

The days before Nigeria played Italy were fun. There was a real sense of "yes-we've-arrived" in the air. Did they not see Finidi and his doggy-style celebration in the Greece match? Or Amokachi and his funky groove matched only by his funkier goal?

Tambo came back. He had been thrown out of Bulgaria, and we added a short-lived suffix to his already long nickname. He was now Clement "Oliver Tambo" Unegbu *of Sofia, Bulgaria.* Considering the fact that he had spent his time there in and out of sleeping bags, he looked quite good. He smelled of Jand: that supermarket/new/hotel-room smell of Johnny-just-comes. And Tambo milked this for every kobo. At the late-night drinking sessions before watching matches in which the Nigerians impressed and the Cameroonians embarrassed themselves, Tambo would be seen with two girls on either arm, his pockmarked face grinning ear to ear as he told them how clean Sofia was and how lovely the streets were—streets that he had only glimpsed from behind wire-mesh fences. But he was allowed to get away with it. After all, Nigeria was in the World Cup. Everything was forgiven, wasn't it?

I ran into Tommy just before Nigeria versus Argentina. NEPA had taken light and we had gone to Jowitz to watch the match at around two that morning. As Maradona and his compatriots stretched the limits of fair play at the expense of the Super Eagles, Tommy came up to me and asked how I was doing. I said fine. Then, just as Siasia scored, he said he wanted to talk to me about something. During the halftime break, we strolled outside.

"Your father owns a bureau de change?"

Well, as in the past, he had proven that he did not waste time. "Hmm," I replied. I knew where he was going.

"I get this guy. Very cool chap. But his father is such an arsehole. I was wondering if you could do him a favor. For me. You see, the guy papa has this bag of hundred-pound sterling notes that the boy can have access to—" He paused when he saw the smile on my face—one of disgust, of sadness.

"Tommy, stop. Why do you do this to me? I have always respected you, haven't I?"

"What are you talking about?"

"Tommy, there is nothing like a one-hundred-pound note. And even if there was, I wouldn't switch anything with the real stuff in my father's office. Just take am say I no fit."

"You never even hear wetin I wan' talk."

"I no go ever fit, Tommy."

He walked silently away, murmuring something about my not appreciating everything that his friendship could do for me. I thought nothing more of it and went back to watch Nigeria lose to two quick goals from the Argentines.

We still qualified for the second stage, though. And everywhere in school, the tension was palpable. We were going to play the Italians. Dirty sons-of-bitches who thought nothing of the odd dive here, the dirty tackle there. We knew that at the end of everything, like that British commentator said in the '82 World Cup, "Skill will always prevail."

At times, my mind went to the country itself. Nothing was happening. No strikes, no student riots, nothing. Ejiro, complaining of the boredom, had come back to school after less than a week at home. They said that the winner of last year's election had been abandoned by his friends. His running mate was serving in the junta as the foreign affairs minister. Governors, recently stripped of their offices, and from both political parties, were busy hustling for contracts outside the offices of the military administrators of the states. One little-heard and even-less-listened-to rumor said that MKO was back from exile and that he was going to declare himself president of the republic the day before Nigeria played Italy. Talk about poor timing.

Nigeria played Italy, and we lost. Nobody knew that MKO had been arrested and thrown into detention a day before. That morning the rumors began filtering in—not about MKO, no. They said that seven—I remember the number—Italians were drug cheats. Italy had been disqualified; Nigeria was going to meet Spain in the quarterfinals.

Yes! Good news!

But it was a fib. The euphoria disappeared quickly. We passed the student union leaders shouting from podiums at the school junctions beside the military vans and finally stopped to listen.

What! They arrested MKO? For what?

I dodged the demonstrations when they began. They lasted for two days, and the only hint of them in our flat was the smell of tear gas filtering in through the windows. At night, when the students had been chaperoned back to the hostels and the town was quiet, my flatmates and I strolled to Estate, to Harry's room, and listened to gist about the wahala.

"Oboy, if you'd seen what Soalim did. That guy is a mad man," Ejiro said. Soalim was a lunatic who passed for normal because he was so articulate and always impeccably dressed. He went to FGC Owerri and was currently a year-two law student.

"What did he do?"

"If I did not see it, I would have thought it was a lie," Ejiro answered. "I'm telling you, when the tear gas canister landed right beside us, I thought I was dead. If you *hear* the odor. But Soalim, with a kerchief over his nose, just picked it up, danced around in front of the shocked policemen, and threw it back. If you see how the police pick race helter-skelter. It was so funny."

But it had been hopeless. The *nice* officers were replaced by korofos from the army barracks and these fired shots in the air. The students remembered that they had mothers waiting at home praying for their safe return and ran. The mothers' prayers were answered. No one was hurt.

I SAT on our veranda beside Kayoh, looked at the blank night sky, and thought about Warri. How was Nene? Dad and Mom had traveled to Enugu with her for the surgery. Hopefully, it went well. I also thought about Brenda and hoped she was okay in the hostel. The soldiers had not come into school, Harry had said; therefore, she was safe.

"But una hear say school go close?"

Yes, we had heard the news. The universities were going to be closed for preventive security. The announcement was made that evening by our darkly bespectacled dictator on Nigerian Television Authority. It was to prevent the peace of the nation from being shattered by disgruntled elements "who would deceive our children into misguided actions." They would not be allowed to disturb the direction of the nation's ship of destiny, he said.

Because we lived off campus, we were asked by students who lived in the schools' hostels for places to crash. I already had a roommate for that evening—Amide, a classmate. She was going to spend the night in my room. I had a stupendous crush on her and had bought a bottle of wine and potato chips from the supermarket at Osasogie. And condoms. I walked back home from the supermarket in darkness. The moon was new. The darkness was helped occasionally by flickers of light from trucks on the expressway. I passed students in pairs, boys and girls, huddled so close together you would think they were a new species of four-legged hominid. Across the street, I could see that the school generators were not turned on. I remembered my lantern from year one and how it had lain broken on the floor after the robbery. I remembered Lorenchi joking that I only drank Fanta.

When I got to my flat, I met a party. Efe had invited his former flatmates for a candlelit gathering. Amide had let Kayoh into my room and my deck, battery powered today, was blasting out hip-hop from the radio. I joined in with a glass of fresh palm wine mixed with beer. I stole a cigarette from Amide and sat beside her, watching Efe and Kayoh lead the others in a line dance. We sweated in the heat of the rainy season and did not give a damn. We were young; we would live forever.

"What's on your mind?" Amide asked. Her face was lit up in profile by the candle.

I had no idea that it showed. "It's my granny. She's sick and has just had an operation."

"Her heart?"

"How do you know?"

"It's always the heart. When my gran had her bypass last year, it was the same. We were lucky. But she's back to her old ways again, always eating fatty food and eba."

"I know what you mean. I just wish we could get this thing over with. I'm going to be the first doctor in the family."

"Me too."

Amide was cute—that kind of Hallmark-card puppy cuteness that cried out for love. In year one I had not known she existed, blinded as I was by Tseye. But since year two and dissection class, we had become close. She lived in Benin and had no business being here with us out-of-towners, stranded by the school's closure.

We had exchanged glances and notebooks in class and not much else during the past month, but I knew there was a spark there. I liked Amide. I liked the way she could disarm me with only the hint of a smile. When I had asked her, during biochemistry practical yesterday, if she had a place to stay in case they closed the hostels, she had hesitated only for a moment, then asked me if I minded if she smoked in my room. I did not know she smoked. Her lips, kind and harmless as they seemed, did not quite fit around a cigarette in my mind's eye. I was blown away when she said she would stay in my flat. And we shared brands.

Amide leaned against me, and I sniffed her hair. We were in that position when Kayoh turned off the music. He suggested that we play truth-or-dare. We did. The girls took control; they banned the "truth" part of the game outright and said only dares would be allowed. Cowards drank large shots of alcohol that night instead of kissing or taking off shirts or showing bra straps. When the spun bottle settled on Amide and someone dared her to kiss me, I knew she would.

I WOKE up the next morning with a headache. Amide was naked, face down on my left, snoring softly with her arm draped over my chest. She groaned when I lifted her arm. I crawled out of bed, pulled on my boxer shorts, and walked out to the furnitureless sitting room. I sat alone on a discarded pillow and lit a cigarette. I stared at the smoke as it curled up around my outstretched fingers. I did not take a drag.

There was something wrong. I could feel it. What was I doing with my life? Why was I smoking? I was not reading, content instead with the illusion that since there were no exams to write I would have all the time in the world to catch up before the Second MB exams next year. Next year? With the way things were going, I did not know when I would get to year three. I put the stick in my mouth and dragged long and deep. A flash of dizziness hit me as I blew out the smoke, brown now from mixing up in my lungs. I watched as the exhaled swirl mixed with the bluer and deceptively cleaner one dancing out of the stick. I rolled my tongue around the menthol taste of the next few drags and thought, *Abeg, make them leave me, jo.*

What if I was now a smoker and a drinker? What if I was sleeping with my very beautiful classmate? I had never failed my parents. I had never called them out to a police station to bail me. I was fulfilling all my duties as a good son. I just wished they would fulfill theirs and be a happy couple.

Nene was going to survive this thing. She had to. Somehow, perversely, she was the only thing holding my parents together. The other, Dad's father, had died in '87. If Nene, whom Dad feared and respected, died, what would happen the next time he and Mom fought? I choked on the smoke and, sputtering, smiled to myself. Somehow, I did not see Dad going to any of Mom's sisters to beg forgiveness for beating up his wife.

IT WAS one of those things that when they happened you thought, oh, it can't get much worse. We were wrong. When Harry's flat was robbed the day after the university was closed, we did not recognize the event as only the latest in a series that began back in first year and that it would snowball to affect everyone that gathered around.

We found out about it when we went to visit after escorting the girls who had spent the night. It was a typical late June morning, wet and damp, the mist rising out of the grass as Kayoh took a piss beside the road. Rain had fallen during our truth-or-dare game the previous night, and the sleep that followed had been to the soundtrack of thunder and wind. The girls climbed bikes under the watchful eyes of an army detail that had set up a checkpoint at our junction and rode on to the parks at the university's main gate, where they would get vehicles to take them home: Warri, Lagos, and Port Harcourt. I hugged Amide and kissed her on the cheek. She waved back from the moving bike until she was out of sight. We thought, okay, let's branch Harry's house and see if his sister and Brenda have prepared breakfast. That was when we found out they had been robbed.

They were all gathered around their veranda. Harry's sister was rubbing her brow where a purple welt, barely visible on her dark skin, slowly rose. Brenda looked lost, holding the tattered remains of her traveling bag. Harry was walking up and down outside the flat and picking up stuff scattered in the grass: a handbag, ripped to shreds, here, a broken wristwatch there. Neighbors, oohing and aahing, murmured about how lucky my friends were that they only lost belongings and not life and limb. Remembering my experience from year one, I knew that they had been robbed.

Brenda told me that I had just missed the thieves yesterday. In fact, she said, when they heard the low growl threatening them through the open window, they thought it was me fooling around and they told the person to piss off. But it was not me. The thieves had been quick. So quick that there was nothing much to tell. They had robbed my friends and, in the process, slapped Phoebe, who had been loudest in telling "me" to piss off. They had taken Harry's stereo and, as if they had been told where to look, the two hundred dollars that he was hoarding to swap for transport money home for himself and his siblings. None of the victims could tell us anything about what the robbers looked like. They were masked and very wicked was all. Slowly, all the old friends from year one heard about the robbery and gathered around: Tuoyo, Wilhelm, Omogui, Kayoh, and Ejiro.

Harry shifted about. He looked distracted and answered questions in monosyllables.

He pulled me aside. "Ewaen, I don't trust anyone here. The guys that came here last night were confra boys. Na only you I trust say never blend. But I feel that they were either Black

Axe or Cosa Nostra boys. I hope to God that they are Cosa Nostra. I'm going to meet my brother's guy, Frank. He is the new don. He fit find out who did this."

"Harry, wait—"

"Why? They slapped my sister." Then he whispered, "I thought they were going to rape the girls. One of them was even feeling Brenda up. But then NEPA brought light. Only for four minutes o, but that was enough. The bastards panicked and left. God! I no fit vex. Why didn't I join confra?"

16

NENE DIED in July at the teaching hospital in Enugu from what the doctor said was a *successful* surgery to install a pacemaker in her heart. The family held her funeral a month later in Okpara Waterside. The entire community turned out for the celebrations, and as we turned in from the interstate expressway in a convoy of cars, we saw the colorful canopies that surrounded the new bungalow that Nene's children, my aunties and uncles, had built for her. The canopies were assigned to each child of the deceased and their spouse. They stood in a semicircle just to the side of the new building. In front of them was a bandstand with bandmembers still setting up their equipment. We all wore white.

The funeral was the first time in a long time that all the cousins were gathered in one place. My older cousin Justin had driven our aunty from Lagos. He brought Tuoyo, the recently expelled Uniben Mafia capo, along. It was true; TJ and Justin were close friends. Ayo was the closest in age to me; we were so close as babies that people thought we were twins. We even took our mothers' respective complexions and looked just like them when they were children, everyone said. As soon as I could get away, I left my father's canopy and joined Justin and his friends with Osaze, Tuoyo, Ayo, and Wilhelm. Justin was an Ah-kay boy in Unilag, and most of his friends were confra boys.

"How is that your weak confra?" someone asked TJ.

"Guy, no make me cry now. You know I'm not in school anymore," replied TJ. His tipsy right hand held the bottle of Gulder at a precarious angle, and he spilled some of its contents in an unintended libation to Nene.

"But even when you start the acting, you're sure you won't go looking for Godfather parts to play? You don get enough experience."

TJ was done with higher education. He had registered with a modeling agency in Lagos and told me that, apart from the toothpaste and soap adverts that we would soon see him in, he had been approached by producers from Surulere, the capital of Nigeria's burgeoning film industry, soon to be named Nollywood. They said he had a new face, full of character and angst. He had taken a break from shooting, in front of the camera that is, to follow Justin and his Ah-kay friends down from Lagos.

"No worry. When I famous, I go employ you as my bodyguard. With your ugly face, nobody go fit try me."

"Or me," one of my cousins joined in. He did not know the kind of guys he was drinking with. Dangerous boys, dons, and hit men. The black T-shirts they wore were apt for what they became back on campus. But now they were just having fun. Not all the boys who came with Justin were Black Axe boys. There was a Seadog among them who smiled—a short, swift smile, gone before it even registered—when my cousin blurted out that if he ever entered a Nigerian university, he would join the National Association of Seadogs.

"How?" Justin asked. "Them no dey university again. Only graduates are allowed in."

Everyone laughed at this myth perpetrated by the first Nigerian university confraternity. The Seadogs, in the eighties when the violence in university gangland was spiraling out of control, had self-proscribed themselves out of existence. They would henceforth remain a sociopolitical club open only to graduates. Their spokesman and patron, a Nobel laureate, had run a lecture circuit denouncing the violence and said that it was not what they had in mind when they formed the club in 1958 at the University College, Ibadan. But they were still in the universities, Uniben at least, just a lot quieter.

"No worry," the Seadog friend said. "Whenever you enter school, the Seadogs will still be here."

Justin shouted from across the table at him, "Hey, stop that. You no go toast my cousin to join your confra in my presence."

Wilhelm watched with his jaw held open and slack. I took notice and quickly closed mine. I felt the same thing Wilhelm did. In school, these guys would not be caught in the same hundred-foot square—talk less of drinking together and laughing at jokes made at the expense of their respective gangs. Wilhelm, now a Black Axe boy, could not believe what he saw. I did not feel sorry for him; yes, he should feel like a fool for blending, for putting himself in something that made no sense. In Uniben, Justin and TJ would be implacable enemies. But here, they sang off-key versions of their bush songs.

While the older chaps sang, Tuoyo told me about school. He had stayed behind for three weeks and had the latest gist.

"So continue now," I begged. "How them take know say na Yibril rob Harry?"

"Lorenchi. TJ's guy. Lorenchi was playing cards with Yibril and some other guys in Ekosodin. They say that Yibril lost heavily and, after borrowing money from Lorenchi, he lost some more.

"When the card game ended, Lorenchi escorted Yibril to his room to collect what he was owed and heard music. He noticed Harry's CD player—you know say Harry's school father na their new don, so them dey follow him visit Harry room well-well—and asked Yibril where he got money to afford such a fine piece of equipment. Yibril tell am to take 'im money and fuck off. Lorenchi comot there and immediately go report to Frank."

"Harry's brother's friend?" Frank. Of Willy's confra party. Of the girlfriend and almost-confra-fracas at the school show. The new Mafia don.

"Ehen now. Guy, no interrupt my gist. I go stop o."

"Abeg no mind am," Wilhelm joined in. I thought he had been asleep, what with his head lolling about at an extended angle. He wiped spit from his cheek, and in the moonlit darkness of a two o'clock morning, voice barely heard above the din of Uncle's band, he urged Tuoyo on.

"Continue. What now happened?"

"You heard what your cousin did to Harry?" I interrupted.

"First of all, Yibril no be my cousin like that, you know this already. Na just my village neighbor. Second, everyone in school has already heard. You weren't around. What I want to hear is what Frank did." Willy nodded at Tuoyo. "Guy, continue."

"Frank called Harry and told him that they were going to the police; that they had found his things and would get the thieves arrested. Na so they put Yibril inside cell for three weeks. Last I heard, he had been released after refunding the two hundred dollars and was promising hell and brimstone to Lorenchi and Frank."

I shook my head and said, half to myself, "This na unnecessary wahala. If TJ still be don, if they no expel am, he for collect Harry stuff, even maybe the dollars without any such stress."

Tuoyo agreed. "Exactly what Tambo said. When he was giving me the gist, he said that Frank watched too many mafia films and was showing symptoms of what he called 'the Marlon Brando syndrome.'"

"Wetin be that?"

"Tambo said that ever since Frank became don, he has changed the way he speaks. The new don barely talks above a whisper and is always rubbing his chin and talking about offers impossible to refuse."

Wilhelm said, "Abeg, make them gerrout! All these fake Cosa Nostra boys."

"My friend, keep your voice down. Which of the confra boys be correct boys? No lose your focus because you dey inside o," I said.

Wilhelm calmed down. "Yeah, Ewaen. I hear you. Meanwhile, you don hear from Kpobo since he travel?"

"How? Is your telephone working? Ours isn't."

"Where Kpobo travel go?" Tuoyo had not heard. Kpobo had left for the UK. His mother could not bear the thought of her son wasting ten years for a four-year course and had forced his father to keep his promise. We had not heard from him for the three weeks he had been gone.

Tuoyo asked that we stroll into the village for cigarettes. I hesitated because I never smoked during the short holidays. But all the drink and gist had given me itchy fingers, and I needed a smoke.

17

WE WROTE our first assessment tests in October of '94. My classmates had been kept deceptively idle for weeks while the rest of the school struggled through the first-semester exams. As for me, I had to write the repeat exams for ZOO 101. The paper was as easy as it had been the year before, and I was more sure of passing this time. I bought the handout, twice.

Medical students did not write exams in year two. So you can understand the surprise with which we—Wilhelm, Fra, Preppa, and I, unserious bastards all—viewed the energy some of our classmates put into reading for the test.

Haba, it was a test! A test. The way they hoarded seats at night prep, the way they huddled around the lecturer during tutorials—I thought we had been deceived and would be writing the actual Second MB exams months early.

I tried to read but found it very difficult without notes. The first department to announce a date for its test was biochemistry. This would be fun. I took some of my mom's old biochemistry books—having chopped the money meant for mine—and dusted them off. Ester bonds. Nucleic acids. Nerve transmitters. I wrote the test. I scored thirty-nine. Not over forty. Not over fifty percent. Thirty-nine percent.

Wake-up call? Of course not.

Fra's result soothed me. He had scored eleven percent and was laughing and waving the result sheet, which he tore down from the board, around C6, our beer parlor. So I did not do too badly. After all, this test only accounted for part of the thirty percent allocated to assessment tests in the final reckoning in six months' time. The other test results came out too. Forty-two percent, anatomy, my best course. Thirty-six percent, physiology. While I laughed with Fra at the ridiculous results, deep down I was losing my confidence.

I no know book again?

The rest of school finished exams and left the medical students alone on campus.

The school was empty apart from the medical students. Wilhelm moved in with me; he took Kayoh's room. I wanted Amide to move in too, but she refused, saying that we would tire of each other too quickly. I said I did not know we would tire of each other at all, not to talk of too quickly.

"You know what your problem is?"

Amide looked at me and smiled indulgently. "Tell me."

I was escorting her to Osasogie Gate on a dusty Saturday morning. Harmattan had come early this year, and already the leaves were browning in the dust and dryness. A breeze caught her skirt, and she let it twirl around her knees, dangerously close to indecently exposing her. Wilhelm had been away on one of his recent absences last night, absences that I was getting used to and had learned not to pry into, even though they left a knot of concern in my belly. Amide had spent the night in my room, and we were talking about the tests. She scored fifty-nine percent in biochemistry, and she had been gloating when I changed the subject.

I told her what her problem was. "You like me. A lot. You love me, don't you?"

She laughed. She was still laughing when we stopped the bike. She leaned into me for a kiss, and I teased, "Say it. See if it feels right."

I had found one of the only things that could make Amide uncomfortable. She was like a gruff and quick-witted forties' film noir girl. Underneath the cool facade, I could see she was fidgeting. It was in the quick drop of her shoulders and rise again and the way she stared at the spot between my eyes and right shoulder, a barely imperceptible quivering of her upper lip. She finally whispered, "I love you."

"I love you too."

I bypassed the flat on the way back and took a shortcut to Fra and Preppa's place. The walk took me through the hamlets behind Ugbowo. Children played in front of old-style Bini compounds with the steeply sloping mud walls and central atrium and the ubiquitous hand-painted signs that said, "THIS HOUSE IS NOT FOR SALE. BY ORDER, FAMILY." Pant-wearing, snot-nosed kids danced around on dirt-floored, chalk-drawn hopscotch rectangles while their mothers fried akara for sale. I stopped to buy some Akara under a sign that said, "FUL-CANISA, REPARE YOUR TIRE HIA," and smiled to myself at the vocabulary—I would file it away for a joke, although I soon discarded it when I saw another that said, "OGHE-NOVO, CORFINS & UNDERTAKERS. AMBRANCE SER-VICES ALSO AVALEBLE." I ignored the hand the woman used in serving me. I could have sworn that, as I came around the bend, I had seen her wipe her toddler's bottom with it. I took the curve into Nova Hotel Road.

"TRY THIS one: four-letter word, acidic."

"What does it start with?"

Ejiro took his time. We sat on the waist-high fence in front of his new flat. He had taken over Kpobo's room after the latter left for London. The rest of Ejiro's new roommates played football on the grass and concrete lawn in front of us. Monkey post. Fra manned the goal and was sweating profusely, shouting and delivering tackles that would make an Italian cringe. The other players waxed and waned across the field, all in a crowd around the ball with no regard for positions or roles. Everyone, apart from Fra, was an attacker, then a defender, and then a midfielder. Preppa scored, his fourth for the morning, and we, the supporters, cheered. The clapping detail had a total population of two—Ejiro and me. We sat on the fence, occasionally cheered, and played crosswords on the back of a newspaper.

"Let me see," Ejiro said, "Thirteen across . . . it starts with a *t*."

"Tart."

"Oboy! You dey try o. And you say you don't play crosswords?"

I nodded and murmured to myself that I did not. I lacked the attention span and always felt the puzzle designers were idiots. I did not tell Ejiro what I thought of those who had the time to solve the puzzles. I looked away from the paper and stared at the football game. I stopped seeing it and let my mind travel. It was November already. Just like in my case, the twins would not be entering school the year they were supposed to. The last time we spoke, my brother had told me he wanted to leave Warri. He had taken over my job as purchasing clerk; the stress and the driving and Dad's screaming were not the only reasons for wanting to escape. Eniye worked in the bank as an office clerk. She too had learned how to drive and spent afternoons supervising Mom's supermarket; the deal had been reached where she would work in both companies. They were both bored senseless. I wanted them to leave Warri too; Osaze would enter Uniben for engineering while Eniye had applied to study computer science at the University of Lagos.

Mom and Dad's truce had lasted only a month after my grandmother's funeral. The cold war quickly turned hot, and most evenings at home began with us looking at an exasperated Dad pacing around the sitting room and a screeching Mom accusing him of every sin under the sun.

"Yes! Say it! You don't love me!"

"What kind of nonsense talk is that, Omasan?"

"Don't touch me! Why can't I go to law school? Yes! If it is to go around town with your nonsense girlfriends . . . even when my mother died, where were you? You abandoned me."

"Darling, watch what you say o. You can't take it back."

"Don't *darling* me! Even at her burial—even at her burial you could not stay awake."

"Haba!"

"Yes! I was alone. I was alone. I'm still alone. What I want from you is support. Have I not tried? I gave you children. When I was supposed to be doing my master's, my doctorate, I was here in Warri cleaning up after you. Now you have money, and you want to enjoy it with your rubbish small girls. I want to go to law school, to have something for myself, and you are telling me of family time. Family time, my foot. What of my time?"

We watched and kept quiet. The only time I intervened was when, after a thorough verbal lashing from Mom, Dad chased her around the house determined to beat his point of view into her. He caught up with her in the kiddies' parlor and was bent over her crouched form in a corner when I entered the room and said, "Don't touch my mother."

It worked.

Dad's shoulders deflated, and he turned away from her. He refused to meet my eyes as he shoved past and then shuffled to his bedroom. I did not go to Mom. Instead, I waited and looked at her. She got up, dusted herself, and said to the twins and me, "I'm sorry."

She won the battle. Following her graduation from the part-time university program, she would begin law school in January. But the fights continued. After each, Mom would kneel in her room, from where we could hear her praying loudly for forgiveness. She typically stayed in there for hours, appeared to prepare food, eyes swollen and bloodshot, and quickly re-treated into the room. Family dinners stopped, and both of my parents began eating in their rooms. Dad still called me into his to complain. I began to listen. I tried not to, and my heart broke when Dad's words made me ask my own questions. Why was Mom so angry? Why did she complain about having all her options taken away from her because of marriage and children? Were we a mistake? Would she have made professor if she had not had us?

I was so happy when the general reopened the universities in late September. I noticed the envy on Osaze's face, in his voice, when he escorted me on the drive back to school.

"This one, nko: twenty-one across, four-letter word, inter?"

"Bury."

MY FRIENDS finished their game of monkey post and we set-tled down to eat the akara I bought with soaked garri and salt. Preppa and Ejiro, the plumpest in the group, ate the slowest. They complained of our speed and had to have their portions divided out and separated. While we ate, Wilhelm turned up with more akara. He was looking fresh and had been to the house to have a bath and change. He asked me when I left, and I told him I had escorted Amide at around nine.

"No wonder I did not see you. How is she?" The bag of food had been dragged from him and was being devoured, bit by little bit, slowly, by Ejiro and Preppa.

"She's fine. Where you sleep?"

"You know . . . around," he said. I did not push further.

Ejiro smiled through a mouthful of akara and garri and said, "Did you hear that Harry and Brenda broke up?"

"My friend, boys don't gossip," admonished Wilhelm as he slapped the remaining akara from the plump boy's hands.

I had heard. Brenda had told me herself. She had finally moved out of the hostels and was staying at what used to be a hospital at Adolor junction, opposite the teaching hospital. I helped her move in when we resumed from the strike. The split had been amicable; they lived too far apart, Harry in Port Harcourt, she in Warri, and both decided that they should explore other possibilities. I was relieved that she took it well. It had been a long time since I had done the shoulder-to-cry-on thing, and I was rusty. I would not have been very *there* if Brenda had needed the shoulder.

Fra produced a bottle of cheap rum. He said the drink was for special guests only, but since Wilhelm and I had been so gracious as to provide the breakfast, all he could do in revenge was to get us drunk. We did not get drunk before the bottle finished, only tipsy and very animated. Wilhelm's tongue loosened.

"I'm telling you, my friends. The Neo-black Movement stands for the emancipation of the black man. We are disciplined, and there's nothing secret about what we do."

"There's nothing secret all right," Preppa said with a smirk. "Did you guys hear about what Wilhelm's guys did to Lorenchi last week?"

Everyone nodded but me. I had not heard. "No," I said. "Tell me."

"It was the guy's fault. He should not have been in school. Not after what he did to them Yibril and his guys."

Preppa was not a confra boy but was close to them. He lived, he said, on a Black Axe street. Terminator X, one of the most notorious boys in Wilhelm's confra, who was expelled with TJ because of a less-celebrated incident involving a broken coke bottle and a student's buttocks, lived just beside Preppa's family compound off Sakponba. Preppa always had Black Axe gist and was not afraid, even in front of Wilhelm, to relate any juicy gossip he overheard.

"They hit Lorenchi's flat in Ekosodin last week," Preppa said. "He was about to sleep when they struck. They beat the guy, eh. They put am for hospital. I hear he was discharged on

Friday and has gone home to Warri. I am sure when he comes back next semester, he will pack out of Ekosodin. So Willy, what do you think? Should the Neo-black Movement be defending thieves?"

"Like I said. It is something we are working on. We are trying to weed out the bad eggs," he said with a mischievous glint in his eye.

I knew how to read my oyibo friend and when I thought about it, I suspected he had been on the hit squad that attacked Lorenchi. Wilhelm would not have been able to resist the wahala, the chance to revenge for the hurt in year one.

THE DAYS turned into weeks and then months. We waited and read and played. All the universities in the country were rushing towards second-semester exams so that the year could be salvaged—so that them Osaze could resume with the '94 set. There was a real risk that the session would be scrapped, and then they would have to wait for the end of '95. The thought was unbearable. A lost year in the nation's universities?

It seemed like everyone was a confra boy now or in a life-and-death struggle with one. I had been wrong about Omogui being in the Black Axe back in year one. He only blended confra in this second semester of year two. He was now an Ah-kay man. He and Tambo were not talking because Tambo felt he had betrayed him by joining the *wrong* confra. Kayoh was now an Eiye man, or so Tambo and Wilhelm said. He vehemently denied this, and I was wont to believe him. I had seen him diss quite high-ranking members of that confraternity. But Tambo believed the clashes were staged. If they were, that would be a new level of sophistication for Kayoh. Maybe he was; maybe he wasn't. Harry had returned to his old boisterous self after the breakup with Brenda. He hardly remembered he had been robbed, and was quite callous about what had happened to

Lorenchi, shrugging and saying they were not in the same confra anyhow, so why should he care?

Tambo was great friends with Wilhelm, which was odd to those who did not know their history, because of the way he treated other Black Axe boys.

We felt the tension in the air. The issues that had led to the schools' closure five months before had not yet been resolved. MKO, who won the annulled election, was still in jail. There were rumors of coups and countercoups. Bus rides to town had become cautious affairs—a 180-degree turn from the way we handled them before the strike—as opportunities for strangers to gist about how the country was spoiling, which politician was stealing money, or who had a big house in Scotland or a bank account in Switzerland. Everyone had heard rumors of state security personnel who rode on the shuttles and arrested students who were too opinionated at the bus stops. An unpleasant incident, weeks after the Christmas holidays, told us how far gone things were. Some soldiers had assaulted university girls for wearing trousers. The female students had been picked up at random at Ring Road because of a rumor that the dark-shaded general had banned women's trousers in a radio announcement. At first, the soldiers stuck to only undressing those who sported combat trousers and denim. But soon anything was game, and the girls were made to ride the bus back to school in their underwear or whatever else Good Samaritans, traders at the market, could lend them.

We discussed all these things in the new version of the Six Candles car park conference, even though we had to be more careful about our usually reckless teasing.

18

FOR THREE days in February, the nation's universities burned. Nothing plans chaos better than spontaneity. The first school to take to the streets was Unilag, then Uniben, then Unical, and so on. It spread like wildfire, this appetite for protest, for destruction. The days preceding the riots featured the routine speeches on the soapboxes, the Mobile Police units chasing the speakers down, and the spare detail of students who actually paid attention.

I remember something that questioned the spontaneity of the protests: On the evening before the riots, I strolled to the old car park with Tuoyo to reminisce. We went to see our old room and afterwards sat in our old places by the gutter, sharing a beer and laughing at how unexciting the new occupants of A109 were. It was just getting dark, and it seemed nothing had changed in the year and a half since we had lived here. The shiny cars still drove in and out. The girls still stood outside their hostel gates like loaves of bread at the bakery. Six Candles still woke up early at six thirty in the evening.

A limousine pulled into the car park, blinding us with its eager headlights. We expected it to let out a pimp, a young male student who had connections with the porters and knew which girls were available for a night out. Instead, TT and Nna Ojukwu, our firebrand student union leaders, hopped out. Tuoyo had his mouth open. Mine was covered with my right hand. Nna Ojukwu walked around to crouch beside TT at the open door of the owner's corner of the car. They were talking with an old man, fair, with slack jowls that hung almost to his collarbones. I recognized him from CNN. He was one of our nation's founders. He was the man who had raised the motion for independence from the British. They said he was the leader of the national democratic coalition. There was somebody beside him in the shadows. Our beers grew warm as we watched them talking, the student leaders nodding as the old man spoke. When we got back to Osasogie that night, all that was on our minds—apart from the looming second-semester exams—was that we had seen this person. Over the next few days, I would begin to suspect the real reason he came to our school.

When the riots started, I was in the anatomy lab. My group was taking a break from assaulting Thrilla, our cadaver. We gathered, twenty of us, around an old microscope, taking turns to look through its fogged lens and trying to decipher which cells were epithelial and which were connective tissue. We heard the noise first, the chanting, the protest songs from parched throats. A crowd of leafy-branch-waving students stormed into the lab. They drove us out and force marched those who could not get away to an impromptu rally at the hostel's car park. The police detail was absent, I heard later, and the students listened to speeches from the soapbox climbers. I pulled back from the march at the bend near the library and, holding Amide by the hand, watched from a distance. The bonfires started. Black smoke rose into the afternoon. We turned and went to my flat.

"I SHOULD have gone back for my things." Amide was lying on the mattress with me, her left arm under my shoulder and her right thigh across my lap. The candle flickered when she moved. Kayoh sat on the stool from the kitchen and Efe was standing with his back to us, staring out the window of our otherwise empty parlor. Amide had just interrupted Kayoh, who was complaining about the commotion in school.

"No, you shouldn't have," I said.

"I should have. I didn't bring anything to change into tomorrow. What am I going to go to class with? The same clothes I'll sleep in?"

"Trust me, you won't sleep in them," I said.

"Idiot." She laughed and blew a cloud of smoke in my face.

Efe brought the gist back to what Kayoh had been talking about. "No be only you, Kayoh," he said. "When I went back to Warri, that woman who sells sweets at our junction asked me when I was finishing. She did not understand that I didn't know—'96, '97? When?"

I saw him put a cigarette to his mouth and reach for his pocket. I whistled at him and, as he turned, tossed a lighter. He caught it and stared at it. "This is not my lighter."

"I know. Ejiro took yours to his place by mistake."

He smiled and lit his cigarette. Then he put my lighter in his pocket. Somehow, the moment did not seem right for us to go into one of our arguments. Efe had come in around two that afternoon, sweating and talking. He said that there was a standoff at Main Gate between the students and soldiers from the nearby S&T barracks. He had joined in when the students locked hands and, singing "We Shall Overcome," marched on the line of gun-wielding soldiers. The young army officer broke first and ordered the soldiers to stand down. The protesters marched on into town and had been on their way to the governor's office when they were stopped at Wire Road by a police detail that fired tear gas at them. The normal response would have been to turn back. At least Efe did. But the protesters broke into two groups and outflanked the police. Efe said this was not a normal protest—that it would get ugly. He had heard rumors that the town was burning and students were being shot at. I did not believe that last one.

Kayoh had come in about an hour later. He had been having a beer in Jowitz when somebody rushed into the bar and pulled the proprietor out. The owner of the bar came back in and announced that he was closing up. He advised everyone to go home because "Benin is burning." After he came in, Amide and I moved my mattress and my Nintendo to the parlor; Kayoh brought his TV and Efe his video player. We watched films until around six, when the electricity went out. After a few minutes watching the twilight, we lit the candles and sat in silence.

Amide got up and went to the kitchen to prepare food. Kayoh took her place on the mattress and told her, "What's that noise? Don't break anything in there o!" She shouted an insult back. We ate. In silence.

I saw the shadows moving with the macabre dance a flickering candle throws before I heard the knock on the door. It was Fra. He had Preppa and Ejiro with him.

"Wetin happen?" I asked as I opened the door for them. Each was holding a knapsack.

"Oboy. You guys are here enjoying, and town is burning," Preppa replied. He shook hands with Amide, Efe, and Kayoh and, smelling food, went to the kitchen.

"What happened? Why are you guys packed?" I pointed at their knapsacks. "Wetin happen for Nova Road?"

"They burnt Nova Hotel, and Palm Royal Motel, and that supermarket in town . . . I forget the name." Fra dropped his knapsack beside the mattress.

"They burnt? Who?" That was Amide, upright on her knees, nearly spilling the makeshift ashtray in her hands.

"Students. It was like a joke when they first came to our street. I saw TT leading the students. The next thing one guy threw . . . what's that thing with the strip of cloth and a bottle?"

"Molotov cocktail," Efe said.

"Yes. One guy threw a Molotov cocktail into the hotel. The wahala, ehn? Guests were running helter-skelter. We no wait for police to come pick people o. We picked up a few things and came here."

"You followed them from dissection to hostel this morning." Amide spoke the question as a statement.

"Yes. Me too," said Preppa, who was back from the kitchen. "We got away when they started moving."

"Why Nova? Because the owner be politician?"

"I'm sure. They burnt parts of Palm Royal Motel too. The mob is going after anything owned by former Social Democrats serving in this regime. Even that guy who owns that supermarket for town. He has only said MKO was not a saint. They looted his store."

We talked until three in the morning. The engineering lecturer in the flat downstairs came up and told us that there was nothing on the riots in the local evening news. The government-owned station was running a special report on water projects for the arid north. But, he said, the BBC was reporting disturbances across the country in Lagos, Port Harcourt, Ibadan, Benin, and Enugu. Everywhere was burning. While we talked on the balcony, I noticed that Benin's sky looked familiar. It was like Warri's, but this was not a city of gas flares. Where was the golden sheen coming from?

HARRY WOKE us up the next morning. He held his nose as Efe opened the door for him and complained that our parlor smelt of armpits. It was eight.

"Wake up! Una dey here, and guys are making money." He ran around the parlor turning over duvets and bed sheets. I looked around and noticed that Amide was already up and outside on the balcony having a smoke.

"Harry, what's up?" Ejiro asked.

"They are rioting near Ochuko's house o!" Ochuko was an old acquaintance of several of us. He had attended the steel company's secondary school and gained admission to university the year before we did. His father, one of the richest men in Warri, had spared no effort to make sure his son got the best while studying in Nigeria. Ochuko had a split-unit AC in his parlor and a sound system that was, I swear, a story tall. His house was permanently open to anyone with wit and an appetite for beer. We had the usual arguments about money, girls, and politics. Over beer and cigarettes, we waxed philosophical about everything and nothing. Why was the earth round? Which breed made the wickedest guard dog? What was the best way to cut eba? If the single continent of Pangaea had really existed, what had been on the opposite side of the earth, only water? Would it have made the earth lopsided, like a rotund face with a large boil?

"This morning?" I asked Harry as I stood up, shivering. Haba, how long would this Harmattan last? I wrapped my duvet around my shoulders and shuffled past him to the balcony.

Harry replied, half to me and half to the rest of us, "The students are looting Goldland. Goldland! Fridges, radios, everything is free."

"Talk true." Fra was up.

"Let's go there. What do you guys say?" Harry said, rubbing his palms together.

The boys all stood and rushed to get dressed. I stood beside Amide and watched her smoke. She knew I was itching to go. "I'll be going to the hostel to get dressed," she said.

I nodded. "Try and be careful."

"You too."

GOLDLAND INVESTMENT Ltd. was a pyramid scheme that had gone bust in early '94. Its warehouse on FGGC Road, about three electric poles from Ochuko's apartment building, had been locked up for months because Goldland's custom-ers, upset that their investments did not yield the promised fruit, took the company to court. The investment company did not dish out cash. What it had offered in exchange for a few months of cooking your *miniscule investment* were household items like refrigerators, microwave ovens, and stereos. A few friends had been burned by promises of cheap goods, and we heard that the operators had upped and left the country. The place, which we observed on Saturday evenings from Ochuko's balcony, was overgrown with weeds. A rusty "Do Not Trespass" sign hung skewed off its iron gate.

When we got to Goldland that morning, the warehouse was like a shopping mall from hell. Cars drove down the street, away from the compound, boots full, rear ends almost touch-ing the ground, laden with fridges, sewing machines, and gas cookers. We saw a girl with a freezer on her head. She had a determined frown on her face and ignored us when we greeted her with a joke. As we passed Ochuko's apartment building, we saw him on his first-story balcony sipping red wine from a glass as he watched the show.

He hailed us, "Efe! Kayoh! Una too like free things!"

"You nko? We are sure you've already been there," Harry shouted back. He had. Ochuko already had three fridges and a deep freezer upstairs in his apartment.

Someone started running. And by the time we knew it, we were sprinting headlong into the place of madness. Peo-ple were pulling down burglary-proofing with their bare hands, chanting, "Asheobey! Asheobey!" It was every man for him-self, a tacit agreement reached without words.

Kayoh leapt over the waist-high fence first; he walked to a couple of boys trying to load a fridge into the back seat of an impossibly small Datsun and asked them something. I caught up just as they were telling him that all the radios and other small stuff were already finished. They pointed to the first floor of the warehouse. I followed the directions and ran ahead of Kayoh to the stairs at the back of the building. There was heavy traffic on the steps; students and area boys helped each other down with loot. A dark boy, a student, stood beside me, and as we writhed up the steps, he asked that we cooperate so that he would help me with mine and I would help with his. I agreed as long as we got mine down first. Dark Boy and I followed the trail of polyurethane chippings and torn cartons to a room that was almost empty, apart from a few unopened cartons. Even the ceiling fan in the room had been ripped down. We walked to the padlocked door of another room. We were crowded on every side by other looters pushing, sweating, cursing. The place was unbearably hot. I, too, was sweating and cursing under my breath as I struck the padlock again and again with an iron bar that Dark Boy handed to me. With each clang, I asked myself questions.

Clang!

What was I doing here?

Clang!

Where the hell were the police? It was almost nine, three hours since Harry said the looting started. They will come; I know the police will come!

Clang!

What if I get caught? What if we all get caught?

Clang!

Oh, to get a brand-new fridge for our parlor. What about a lucky strike at a brand-new sound system?

Clang!

The padlock broke. The cacophony around me slowly receded and changed into Beethoven's Fifth Symphony. Da da da DA . . . da da da DUM!

Gold!

Dark Boy and I rushed in, followed by a thousand others. We loaded laundry irons, deep fryers, and boiling rings into a small freezer and headed for the fence. Back on the lawn, I saw Ejiro and Fra pushing a sewing machine with three electric stoves balanced on it down the street towards Ochuko's house. Preppa saw me and shouted that I should take my things there. He was bent double with a freezer on his back. Dark Boy and I put the stuff under Ochuko's staircase and ran back to the warehouse. A fight had broken out on the bushy lawn. Three guys were in a free-for-all. A small crowd of satisfied looters, not in the mood to brave the heat and darkness inside, sat on the fence and wagered on which of the three would cart away the freezer.

It was like a carnival, this place. Local women, mothers with children on their backs, fought over electric cookers and sewing machines; local men, chubby with singlets on and wrappers tied around their waists, haggled, naming ridiculous prices, with those who would sell the things they had just looted. Kayoh was coming down the steps with Efe. They had a freezer between them and were shouting at a hanger-on to leave them alone. They weren't sharing. As I followed Dark Boy past them, I patted Kayoh's back. He turned and smiled and said, "Hurry up o. Everything go soon finish."

We had just got out when I heard the first sirens. Luckily, Dark Boy's place was not far. A kid with a wheelbarrow offered to carry his fridge and sewing machine for thirty naira, and off they went.

WE WATCHED from Ochuko's balcony. Harry had jumped into the boot of a Peugeot with his new fridge and hitched a ride back to Estate. The first police pickup had appeared thirty minutes before, screeching to a halt in a cloud of dust. Out jumped its occupants: baton-wielding policemen in the regular uniform of black on black. These guys had proceeded to thrash everything and everyone in their path. They cut a wide swathe through the rapidly thinning crowd but, curiously, had not arrested anyone. We watched open-mouthed with the bravest of the stragglers. The policemen loaded their truck with goods. They went about coolly and were joined by two other vans. Those who could not fit into the full trucks mounted a guard. Some of the students and locals who were still around heckled and shouted abuses at the remaining officers. The policemen seemed unperturbed, and one of them popped a tear gas grenade and threw it. It bounced on the street, coming to rest just at Ochuko's fence. We ran into the apartment and, with the windows closed, continued gawking.

Thirty minutes later, the stinging gas had cleared, and we were back on the balcony. Ochuko served drinks as we watched an amazing thing. The looters and the police were working together to empty Goldland. I saw Dark Boy and hailed him from the balcony. He smiled and gave me the thumbs up. The vans came back and left again, not as full as before; thus, all the policemen were able to leave with them. Goldland became spirit land, quiet and empty. We started discussing what to do with our loot.

"But you guys know that as the owner of this de facto warehouse, I'm entitled to a fraction of what you collected," Ochuko said.

"My friend, stop that." Efe knew him best and handled the haggling well. "I plan to put that freezer in our parlor. What do you want more for? Look at your own parlor."

I sipped my beer and watched a few students, late to hear about the goldmine at Goldland, despondently turn over cartons and polyurethane bars. The place was empty. It seemed most of the good things were here in our friend's apartment. Ochuko's parlor had acquired a new stereo, recently defaced

with soup stains and a nail file, he said, to convince any inspector that he bought it months before. And his kitchen had
a microwave oven with a thawing bowl of soup from his filled-
to-the-brim second freezer. He bought all of them last month.
No, he had not heard the rioting and looting. Yes, he was a
heavy sleeper. They would believe him; he was the chief's son.

A police van came back. The looters ignored it at first,
thinking it was the same pillaging policemen. But this van
was driven by Mobile police officers sporting AK-47 rifles and
bad moods. These new policemen started chasing the loiterers. I rushed in from the balcony, closed the sliding windows,
and called out to my friends. Soon we were all standing at the
window, noses pressed against the tinted glass, watching the
spectacle outside. The policemen used gun butts, horsewhips,
belts, and sticks to beat the shit out of anyone they caught. I
saw Dark Boy sprinting away from the warehouse towards the
fence; what was the fool still doing here? A policeman reached
after the running boy and caught him by his trousers. Dark
Boy pulled away, swung free like a slippery fish, and picked
race again. The police officer threw his club, his mouth open
in a snarl. The club struck Dark Boy on the back of his head.
He had been in midstride, just gathering pace when the solid
three-foot-long two-by-four caught up with him. He fell down
awkwardly and lay still. Kayoh gasped beside me, his quick
breathing steaming up the window. I turned away from the
scene, and our eyes met. I looked back to see the Mobile policeman stroll towards where Dark Boy lay. He picked up the
stick and swung. Dark Boy jerked with each thwack on his
back and buttocks, not from a reaction to the pain, but from
the force of the strikes. After the fourth hit, I thought I saw
the policeman hesitate. Around him, other officers dragged
back protesting students, some of whom had stayed behind
to watch, some just passing by, some from flats nearby. The

Mobile policeman reached down and prodded Dark Boy with the stick; it was a light touch, tentative. Another walked over to him and, without speaking, they reached down and caught my new friend under his armpits and dragged the unconscious boy to the back of their van. They threw him in at the feet of crouching students the Mobile police officers had already nabbed, and drove away.

I barely remember Dark Boy's face now. I would wonder for years to come if he survived. I never caught his name.

We were sober for almost an hour after seeing this. We wandered around Ochuko's flat. Someone shouted for Ochuko to turn that shit down, the music was too bloody loud and it was making a fucking racket.

It had not been that loud.

I got tipsy, sitting silently on the settee, Ochuko's last bottle of brandy in front of Kayoh and me. We agreed to share some of our loot with Ochuko if he promised to keep it safe, and then we left for our flat. Fra and Preppa came with us. Ejiro remained behind and promised to keep an eye on our new property.

OUR FLAT got a new occupant later that morning. Omogui knocked on the door in only a shirt and boxers and, between laughs and retorts, told us the reason for walking around half-naked. The Mobile Police had raided Estate. They at first knocked on doors and politely asked for the Goldland loot to be returned. But after a while, they just kicked doors open and arrested anyone with a new fridge in his room. Omogui had been to Goldland and was in Harry's flat, staring at a brand-new gas cooker and counting unhatched chickens. Harry took off as soon as the first police van entered Estate. Omogui was not as fast; he was arrested and thrown in the back of a truck with other students.

At first Omogui had protested his innocence, but when he saw the first guy leap off the moving truck after passing money to the policeman guarding them, he searched his shirt pocket. Two hundred naira. He paid the MOPOL, a grinning boy with kola-stained teeth, asked that a girl beside him be let go too, and they were waved off. They jumped, rolled in the dust, and he left her at the junction and came here.

"They are taking the others to the Central Prisons on Sapele Road. Guys, I was so afraid. They flogged one guy, ehn! Nobody in the back of that truck could speak. If you could not pay, you didn't speak."

The light came on, and we sat around the TV. Efe did not grumble that the house was too full. He sat in the middle of the room and watched the news. Nobody suggested that we turn on the video game console or watch films. We waited for news. Any news. When Harry came, he had told us that very early that morning a detachment of students had set fire to a business owned by a politician. They had bypassed a police checkpoint by using side streets and appeared in the middle of town, surprising everyone. There had to be something on the news. An announcement. Anything.

Martial music came on. The first time I had heard martial music on the radio was when my father woke us up on New Year's Eve in '83 and dragged the twins and me to listen to a brigadier on the radio announcing the coup, "Fellow Nigerians—" But this was not a coup. The state's military administrator appeared on TV beneath our coat of arms. He announced that the university was closed. That all the universities in the country were closed.

"By six this evening, anyone found on the campus of the University of Benin will have themselves to blame. A battalion of policemen from the MOPOL 10 unit based in Bauchi is on the way to *help* anyone who hasn't packed out by six—"

He then went on about how miscreants would not be allowed to gain from the free-education policies of the government.

"Thank God that we live off campus," Kayoh said. I saw him look at his wristwatch. "Two p.m. Just imagine. How does he expect that to happen? 'Empty the hostels by six!'"

"How do they expect the girls to manage?" Fra asked.

"You're worried about them—Oluchi? Don't worry. They are medical students. I'm not sure the announcement applies to medical students. Medical students don't leave school. How are we going to attend clinics?"

"You don't attend clinics, Ewaen. You guys are in year two," Omogui said to me as he pulled on a pair of jeans I had lent him.

"But we will. Our seniors do. Medical students do not leave school. Nothing dey happen." But I was not sure. I was worried about Amide. I hoped she would be okay. She should have stayed. Old clothes, dirty laundry or not, she should have stayed.

We did not sleep that night. We were kept awake by the *pop-pop* of tear gas grenade launchers and the *rat-a-tat* of assault rifles. A light acrid taste was in the air. Tear gas. I thought of my family. They would be worried shitless. During the last strike, Dad and I had gotten into an argument. He said that his best friend in university, a fellow Scallop Oil scholar, had a daughter who was a scholar in King's College, London. Instead of worrying him for more pocket money, I should be reading so I could be like her. I replied that if he had thought of sending me abroad instead of cutting costs on his children's education, I would have been better than her. I knew her from primary school and FGC Warri. I beat her in every exam. I thought of what Dad would now make of his retort that I did not deserve overseas education. This was not a university. It was a jungle. We were all jungle rats huddled around a candle, watching it flicker and burn out slowly.

19

THE NEXT morning, Fra and Preppa went back to their place. We told them to be careful. Preppa said he would branch Ochuko's and check on our fridges and sewing machines and microwave ovens. I moved the mattress back to my room, helped Efe sweep the parlor, and washed dishes. The madness of yesterday seemed far away. This morning was almost routine. We bathed and squabbled over water. We behaved as if we had spent yesterday morning preparing for class, not looting. And, yes, Efe and I argued. Over who finished the meat in the pot of stew. But there would be no classes today; that much was clear as soon as Kayoh and I stepped out of the flat, off to nowhere in particular. We would check on Harry and see if he and his siblings were okay; and from there, I planned to see if I could reach the medical students' hostel to find out if Amide was still there or if she had found a way out of school the night before. Our small dirt street was filled with traffic. Students lugging suitcases and traveling bags groaned under the weight of their cargo and knocked on the doors of friends they had off campus. I saw one of my classmates and asked him what he was doing here. Medical students were supposed to be safe in the medical students' hostel. Why was he outside school?

He told me, "The MOPOL raided the hostels o. All the hostels."

"Medical students' hostel?"

"All of them. They came in around eight. There was no warning. They just rushed in, beating and screaming. See my back." He turned and pulled up his shirt. There were lines, purple, crisscrossing his back. One of them had split open and leaked clear fluid, which was drying, caked and moist. His voice shook with anger, "Ewaen. They raped many girls. They entered the girls' half of the hostel, and we heard the screams. I'm just coming from UBTH. We took some of the more serious victims there."

"What of Amide? You know her now . . . short girl, she dey our class. Dark. Always sits in the back."

"Na your girl?"

"Hmm. Did you see her?"

My classmate tried to tuck his shirt back in. He stopped halfway and pulled the shirt out again, shaking the loose ends, shaking his sleeves. His shoulders were slumped, as though from the weight of a heavy knapsack. He carried none; his holdall lay on the ground beside him. He spoke slowly, with anger, his eyes never meeting mine or Kayoh's. "Ewaen. If I had a gun, I would have shot the bastards. Or they for kill me. Idiots. Bastards. Cowards, the whole lot. Laughing and shooting their guns in the air. They should let us bear arms in this country. All this nonsense for no dey happen."

"Guy, wetin happen to my girlfriend?"

"I carry am go UBTH myself. She wound small."

I started shaking. Kayoh walked to me and put his hand on my back. "Was she raped?" I could barely bring myself to ask. A worm crawled up my belly and hit my throat with a bump. I tried to swallow spit but could not. I spat on the ground and looked at my classmate. He put his bag down on the dirt road and hesitated. It seemed he wanted to hug me. I shifted back, bumped into Kayoh, and said, "Tell me."

"No. But the policeman beat her up."

"She wound small or they beat her up really badly?"

He didn't reply. Kayoh didn't move either, didn't say anything. He tried once to speak, to ask for clarification, but stopped himself.

My head scattered. I walked away from them in a daze. Where was I when it was happening? I was sitting in my parlor enjoying the afterglow of the looting. And I was planning to call home this morning with the news that I was not hurt. Why did Amide not stay? I told her to. Did I? I could not remember. She had said to me, "Be careful." I had said, "You too."

I bumped shoulders with a couple of chaps who cursed at me after their luggage fell to the ground. I did not turn. I did not hear them.

Kayoh was soon beside me. I heard him say, "I asked your guy. She is in ward A3. That's where they put the female students."

"I'm not sure the guy's correct. You saw how hard I had to describe Amide before he knew whom I was talking about. He no know whom he carry."

Kayoh helped me sustain the delusion. "Yes. He made mistake. Short girls full una class."

THE TEACHING hospital was like a war zone. We entered through the side gate and were frisked by a policeman who said that students were not allowed in. I flashed him my *hospital pass* and claimed that Kayoh and I worked in the hospital. It was my medical student's ID. He grunted and waved us on. At that moment, I hated all policemen. The corridors were filled with injured students overflowing from the wards. The place smelled of blood, dreadful and metallic, and of disinfectant. Medical and nursing students hustled around, passing pills and applying bandages. There was palpable anger in the air. You could touch it. You saw it in the faces—the impotence. We could do nothing. We were sheep.

Kayoh was going to ask for directions to A3. I stopped him and climbed the stairs. It was the gynecological ward. Most of the curtains were drawn in the long open hall. The nurses were tough to get past and let only me in when I proved to them that I was a medical student, yes, preclinics, but please, ma, my friends, my friends, only a few minutes, ma. Kayoh waited outside.

I pulled the curtain on bed eight and saw her. She had her back to me and said she did not want any more pills; that she was okay.

"Amide, it's me," I said.

"Ewaen?" She turned and tried to smile.

I saw that it was painful. Her face was a mess. She had been slapped black and blue; she had a cut and swollen upper lip, and her left eye was shut. I cried. Silently, I allowed the lump in my throat to melt into tears that ran down my face.

"Come here," she said.

I hugged her, and when she grunted, I pulled back, shocked. She tapped her left shoulder. The bastards had sprained her shoulder.

"You should have seen the other guy," she said.

I laughed, sniffling. She was okay. They had not beaten her spirit.

"Kai," she started.

"What? You need anything? The pain? Make I call the nurses?"

"A smoke. Ewaen, when we graduate, we have to lobby for a cigar room in this hospital. I wan' die here. I have to get out of here."

"For a smoke?"

I should not have been angry. With her or myself. Why was she so stubborn? She lived in Benin. She could have gone straight home. She should have come back to my place. I should not have let her leave. It was as though nothing happened. She was as flippant as before. Her parents had heard. A classmate called them. They were on their way. Her things were safe. And yes, the other guy looked like shit. There was a lull in the gist, and I spoiled everything by saying, "I'm sorry."

"Don't," she said.

"I'm sorry." The second one was for my saying sorry in the first place.

She started crying. A shudder shook her and escaped from her lips in a whimper. I held her gently and let her cry. "Ewaen, I was so scared. I fought him. I fought him."

"Shh . . . it was my fault. I should not have let you go back to hostel. I should have followed you to make sure you got your things and came back. It's not your fault. Na God go punish them."

"Yeah," she said, "and may He shrivel their dicks to the size of pencils." She sniffed and pulled away.

Amide the Indestructible. We started laughing again and continued the nonsensical, useless gist.

I heard a throat clear behind me and saw recognition and gladness in Amide's eyes. When I turned, I saw a mature version of my Amide. Her mother. Behind her in the shadow of the curtain were Amide's father and Oluchi. I greeted the parents and left with Oluchi.

Oluchi offered to buy us drinks, and we strolled to the C6 beer parlor. We ran into Tuoyo near the hospital gate. He had a light bandage on his arm. The Mobile Police had raided his house. He cut himself on the fence when jumping over to escape them. As he followed us to C6, he said he had come to UBTH for treatment and a tetanus shot. While the others sat down at the beer parlor, I strolled to Osasogie Gate to make a call at our local phone booth. I got Dad in the office.

"Hello?"

"Daddy, it's me."

"My son. Are you okay? It was on the news, on the BBC. What happened?"

"I'm okay. It was dreadful. MOPOL entered the school premises. They even raided some places off campus."

"But not yours?"

"No o. My place is far, too far. They didn't come. I'm okay. Dad, I'm coming home today."

"About that, son . . . your mom and I discussed that this morning."

"She's around?"

"Yes. She's on court attachment from law school. She said that the situation would be like when she was in school during the '76 riots; that the fucking police will operate checkpoints along the road and harass any students they find. Stay put. Wait a week. I'll send some money to the Benin branch office."

"Thank you, sir." Dad always asked advice from Mom when it came to Nigerian universities. He was out of his depth with the violence, the corruption, and the stench. At times he talked about the demonstrations of '68, but he said these had not really hit England. He had no experience with the Nigerian equivalent of a students' demonstration or with what the police did.

"No problem. Take care, son."

I hung up and went back to join my friends in C6. I felt a little better after speaking to my father. I ordered a Gulder. We sat in a corner of the converted garage. The place was empty apart from us, and we spoke in quiet voices. Tuoyo had gist from the state university at Ekpoma.

"They had it worse over there. The students went to the neighboring town of Uromi and set the local government chairman's house on fire. The MOPOL, from the same unit that came to Uniben, raided the town. Everyone stays off campus in Ekpoma. They messed them up, eh. One Ekpoma boy that came into town this morning said that most of his house-mates had to run into the bush. He said they trekked a trail down through Ihumudumu village and came out at Iruekpen. The police pursued them. He said the bush there is full of dead bodies—students and townspeople."

"They were shot?"

Kayoh was a master of the obvious. But was our irritation at his shock a measure of his silliness or our callousness? Was our psyche so damaged that we had stopped being shocked by atrocities? Our people were being killed by those sworn to protect them. Being shot. Being raped. What was the crime? That we burned a few houses and wounded the ego of a few thieves? Bastards all. They deserved much worse.

Oluchi was speaking. "How can they do this? You guys were lucky in Osasogie. If you see what they did in Ekosodin."

"I heard," Tuoyo said.

I sipped my beer and listened to what had happened here in Benin. It was almost a facsimile of events in Ekpoma. The police had entered the village and had gone from house to house, thrashing, raping, and pushing the students out. Ekoso-din, the confra capital of Uniben, was raided and nothing happened. No gun fights between the armed gang members and the police—although Oluchi insisted that there were rumors that this had happened here and there. We laughed her down, and while she sulked, digging her face deeper into her glass of Guinness, Tuoyo told us something else he had heard. Yibril—Wilhelm's cousin—had jumped a fence with a bag of guns and ammunition when the police came to his house. That was not all. He had zigged and zagged, dodging bullets, and escaped into the bush. This guy's name always came up in Uniben gist. Yibril, the devil Black Axe boy; Yibril, the guy who robbed Harry and his siblings; Yibril, the boy who dodged bullets. People like him always survived. They lived, and the fools who followed them blindly died, always. I thought about Wilhelm. He had traveled; he did not tell me where, but he had missed this entire wahala. It would pain him, ehn.

"Did anyone die? Here in Uniben, did anyone die?" Oluchi asked no one in particular.

Kayoh looked at me. Dark Boy. Did Dark Boy die?

Tuoyo saved us two from thinking too much about that; he replied first, "The police shot a Uniben student at Main Gate yesterday morning. The guy had joined the students who stopped a Coca Cola truck. They were trying to commandeer it into school when the police opened fire."

"People can't forget this. People shouldn't forget this," Oluchi said.

"People will, Oluchi," I said. "People always do."

YEAR THREE

June 1995–Eternity

20

"WHAT ARE we going to do about these fucking boys?" Dad asked no one in particular.

We were in the air-conditioned trailer that I had called home for the last two weeks. He and Osaze sat on the pull-out seats by the door. I perched on the edge of the cot and listened to my father talk about the problems we were having with the youths. Polytech, our oil-servicing firm, won part of a contract to wrap the Scallop Oil pipeline that pumped crude from the fields at Osuben to the refinery in Warri. We oversaw the Sapele–Amukpe run and mobilized in late July, moving heavy equipment and men and materials to the swamps on the outskirts of Sapele. Early August was the best time for completing the contract because the August break gave us a window of a few weeks from the relentless rain that fell in the wet season. Dad reemployed me, this time as field supervisor, and I moved in with the workers. Osaze still had my old job as the firm's purchasing clerk and was based in Warri with Dad. He had come this morning because of the small crisis that we were having at the site. This was a board of directors' meeting.

"Tell me exactly what they did," Dad asked again. I had already explained over the radio, but he wanted to hear it again.

I obliged. "Remember we had refused to pay what you called extortion fees last week—"

He grunted, his eyes impatient. I had disagreed with him over that. When we arrived two weeks ago, we had gone to visit the local chief, who told us that we would have to employ some of the young men in the area if we wanted to work. Dad had been the only one speaking and agreed wholeheartedly. After all, he was used to this. He had been living and drinking the swamps since he was in his mid-twenties, when he was a young engineer with Scallop Oil. But a lot had changed since the late sixties. The youths were not the same.

While MKO was in jail, while the Italians were shaming Nigeria out of the World Cup, while the universities burned, while students sat idle at home, a paradigm was shifting in the delta. The local contracting community was abuzz with the gist, with rumors of unreasonable demands from communities that were formerly very cooperative. Just over a year ago, the arrest of Ken Saro Wiwa on allegations of incitement to murder had made him a cause célèbre for the aspirations of the people of the delta. There were rumors of harassment of oil workers, of threats, and of vandalization. But we did not expect any trouble. At least that was what Dad said. He had dealt with these touts all his life and was not expecting any wahala. We started work. About twelve indigenes, sixty percent of our staff strength, were under my supervision. But these guys were tardy, undisciplined, and lazy. They did not work. I had to shout, sounding so much like Dad, with his gruff voice, that I scared myself. But nothing moved them. Plus, they stole. Safety boots, cutlery, helmets, overalls. Anything they could get their hands on. And they expected to be paid. That was what got Dad angry.

Last week Friday, at the end of our second week, we were two miles of naked pipe behind schedule. Dad and Osaze had escorted the money van from Warri. Instead of just paying the boys and bearing their indiscipline, my father paid them off and fired them all. He told them not to bother coming back on Monday, that he did not need them. One of the ringleaders then tried to make trouble. He stood in front of the door and attempted to block Dad from leaving. My father punched the boy, hitting him so hard that the troublemaker fainted. The others collected their money and left.

On the way to my trailer that day, I told Dad what I felt: that he should have paid them their salaries, promised to keep on paying them so long as they did not set foot in the yard again, and then employed chaps who really wanted to work from Warri. I felt we could afford it. I had seen the contract summary. This would be just a fraction of the profits we expected. But Dad had not seen it my way, and now everything had come to this: ten thirty on a Monday morning, everybody with their pricks in their hands, and no one working.

"When you left, that chap you punched came to me and promised hell if we continued working. I think he's a cousin to the chief," I said.

"Talk true."

"Shut up, Osaze. Let your brother finish."

"Last night after we turned in, they came again."

"Around when, son?"

"At about eight thirty. They came with torches and clubs and cutlasses. They threatened to set the camp on fire. They wanted me, but the manager said they should take him instead. So they took him and the storekeeper, Anthony."

"These boys do not know who they are fucking with." Dad was suddenly livid.

I glanced at Osaze, feeling the satisfaction of this mother of I-told-you-sos and tried to hide the smile that threatened to spread across my face. He mouthed something back at me along the lines of leave him o.

"Fucking bastards try and kidnap my son. I'll show them that I am a Bini man." Dad called his driver. "Michael, I want you to drive to Sapele to the A-division there. Get me a squad of MOPOL and meet me at the chief's palace." Dad turned to me after passing a note to the driver, which he was to present to the divisional police officer. "Ewaen, get the Isuzu pickup and meet me out front. We are going to the palace."

"Alone? Now? Shouldn't we wait for the police?"

"My friend! Get the fucking pickup!"

Dad's show of strength worked. The manager and the store-keeper were released to the MOPOL detail, and the ringleaders of the pseudo-kidnapping were made to sign an undertaking that if anything happened to us—if lightning struck us, we got hit by a bus, or we grazed our knees in a pothole—they would be held responsible.

WE RESUMED work. The local boys stayed away initially, until about three weeks after the incident. They asked us to re-employ them and said they would behave well this time, but my father refused. The guy who had been punched self-appointed himself as guide to Dad whenever he visited for inspection, and they became inseparable. They made quite a pair: Dad in calf-high safety boots and low-waist trousers, Stephen in shorts and a singlet, both wearing safety helmets, strolling around the bush in front of us, the manager, Osaze, and me.

What melted the ice was when our Caterpillar sank in quicksand. It had been bulldozing a path on which we were to lay the recently coated pipes. The truck carrying the twenty-ton crane that should have helped in lifting the caterpillar sank too. The ground looked solid enough but had cracked, shifting three-inch-thick pieces of crust that both vehicles had broken through. Stephen performed a miracle that day. He organized the village boys, and to cries of "asheobey!" roaring engines, and the screech of tires and tracks looking for purchase in the muck, they pulled both vehicles out with a length of marine rope helped by the crane. Do not ask me how they did it. They just did.

Later, when I told Dad about it, he said that the boys were not bad. They were just aggrieved. And justifiably so, Dad thought. The country was jailing their leaders. They drank and fished in crude oil–polluted water. Dad said that in a few years no one would be able to bluff them with only four Mobile policemen. He said the boys would soon become militant and that the smiling ones like Stephen would be the most danger-ous. We reemployed them, and even though they stole and did not know squat about the job, we paid them well. And we kept the extra staff we had brought from Warri.

I completed my part of the contract in early September, and I left for Warri. I was a medical student, not an engineer. I did not think the experience was going to help me in any way.

SEPTEMBER '95.

The twins were supposed to have resumed university back in September '94. I was supposed to be finishing year three. So it was official. Nigerian universities had lost a year because the students had dared to oppose tyranny. Nobody else made a sound. There was even a lawyer, former attorney of the pro-democratic coalition, serving in the junta. Wilhelm said that someone should juxtapose this lawyer's statements just after June '93 with what he was saying now. He looked fatter, and his suits were better cut. His tongue cut deeper too. He blasted his former comrades on the other side of the fence. He signed warrants of arrest. The dude's conduct broke any hope I had in any of the noisemakers shouting for democracy. They were all thieves and if offered the chance to serve the general would jump at it. Everyone had a price.

But what was the matter with Nigeria? Why could we not get it right? One thing I had always hated to hear during arguments with my old roommates back in year one was when Omogui would shout out the cliché of how blessed we were. I watched the international news, and all I saw were thin Africans rushing for packets of relief food or Tutsi skulls lying in the dust of a half-burnt church. There was no sign of my Africa—my Africa of music and video games, of Generation X, of teenage angst, which was translatable anywhere in any medium, of funky guys and gals, of books and medical school, of difficult, hard-to-impress lecturers, and of arguing parents— our version of *Prozac Nation*.

What was the matter with our leaders? Did they have no shame? How could they stand smiling with the oyibos and stay in their hotels and have their pregnant wives spread their legs for oyibo doctors? No shame? How difficult could it be? The Asians had done it, and without losing their traditions—or at least the ones worth preserving. I watched disgusted as talking head after head on our local TV came up with the line: Nigerians have to develop their own brand of democracy. What the hell was that? Was homegrown democracy looking at your representatives being arrested and thrown in jail? Was homegrown democracy the police thrashing, shooting, and raping the nation's next generation of leaders? I was turning into an angry young man, but I was still too shy to do anything about it.

Wilhelm asked me a question once. He asked if I thought we would do any better when we grew up. After all, we had joined in the looting at Goldland, and that had nothing to do with the fight for democracy. I told him he was just jealous that he had not gotten anything that day. He laughed back and asked me if I thought I had gained anything. I did not, in fact, have anything to show for that morning of hard labor. Ochuko had swindled us out of our stuff. He claimed that the MOPOL had come to his house too and confiscated all the new stuff they found there. Ejiro, whom we had left behind, said when he went back to Nova Road that afternoon, the loot was still there. I had accused Ochuko directly and had gotten into an argument with Efe and Kayoh over the matter.

I decided that when school resumed that I would move out. I and a friend, Mesiri Barlow, the chap who had carried Amide to the hospital, were going to look for a new place together. There was a flat that we were interested in. It was a four-bedroom place near Ochuko's with a parlor big enough to partition into a fifth bedroom. Already, Mesiri was in Benin talking to the landlord, a chief who lived on the outskirts of town. Wilhelm, Tuoyo, and Tambo were interested. When I got back to school, I was going to live with my friends. There would be no big egos. We would live as brothers. Room A109 would be brought back to life. The fun, the jokes, the brotherhood. All that life had been about before confras and politics and other nonsense. I mean, look at the prospective roommates: a Black Axe boy, one Cosa Nostra gangsta, and three Ju-men. Tuoyo liked to look at the good side of things and reassured Mesiri that, with friends like Wilhelm and Tambo, no one would step on our toes.

I TOOK Wilhelm on a drive to see Brenda at her house the week before we resumed. We branched Tuoyo's place and picked him up too. I drove the Peugeot through the crowded Warri streets, and we gisted. I still had not put in a radio after all these years, so we crowded out the whine of the fan belt with inanities about school, life, and other gist.

"Ewaen, see that fine girl!" Wilhelm shouted from the back seat. "Stop now."

Tuoyo laughed. "Ewaen only has eyes for one chick."

"That's not it. He hasn't changed. Ewaen doesn't pick up girls," Wilhelm said, shaking his head sadly.

Some things never changed. Wilhelm continued describing the girl—her backside, her front side, her every side.

"Continue talking, and I will have to report you to Weyinmi," I said.

"Abeg, stop it. If na play, na dangerous play," Wilhelm said.

"You really like your girl o. Na so you dey fear am?" Tuoyo asked.

"Yes! Is that what you want to hear?"

"Yeah?" I laughed and almost missed the turn onto Brenda's street. I maneuvered the bumpy street and succeeded in somehow entering every single pothole. My teeth jangled with each clang of the broken suspension.

Tuoyo asked, "Ewaen, how's Amide?"

"Oh, she's fine. We get to talk on the phone when NITEL allows. I even saw her last week when I went with Mesiri to Benin to see that landlord."

"Una don settle with am?" Wilhelm asked.

"Yeah." Since the announcement that we were going to resume, I had been to Benin twice. The first time was when I escorted my mom and the twins to check their JAMB results— Osaze got in with the first batch and Eniye would be going to Unilag, computer science. The second time was with Mesiri, and I finally met the landlord. "We've settled."

"I'm happy for Osaze. His body has been itching to get into school. I hope you've talked to him about confra. My brother is entering Uniport. I've discussed my concerns with him, twice." Wilhelm had read my mind. He spoke without any irony about advising his brother not to join confra.

"That's true, Ewaen. Make sure say you tell am o. Osaze be like who wan' spoil. Tell him to hide himself. No smoking and drinking in anyhow place. Remember the stress we went through in year one. Remember the wahala Tambo saved you from last semester." As he finished speaking, Tuoyo reached for the hand brake between us—his fidgety bad habit. I slapped his hand away.

I remembered. Tambo had come into my room last semester, two nights after the riots, and he had told me to pack my things and leave for my uncle's place. I was supposed to be lying low until the express roads were clear before I would try to travel to Warri. But Tambo told me that Tommy had mentioned my name to Frank at a meeting the Cosa Nostra had to discuss the recruitment of new members. Tommy was still planning to lure me to the initiation ground in the bush. I ran to town and spent two weeks in Uncle Max's house before leaving for Warri. I remembered.

"What of Eniye? Una no get advice for me to give am?" I smiled as I asked.

"Na true o. I hear say girls don dey form cult for Unilag too," Wilhelm said. "Tell am to careful too. Tell her not to follow another girl boyfriend o."

We all laughed. Girls and secret cults? Ridiculous. But Wilhelm and Tuoyo were right. I had not talked with Osaze about the confra issue. My brother had grown, was sporting a wisp of a mustache, and could hold his liquor. But somehow, all Osaze and I talked about when we stopped at the beer parlor, Gusto's at PTI junction, was Dad and Mom's arguments and Eniye's new boyfriend—but never about school and confra. I made a mental note to mention it to him the next time we stopped for a drink. I told Tuoyo as we parked the Peugeot and got out at Brenda's gate, "I go follow Osaze talk."

21

DAD AND Mom had another argument the weekend before Osaze and I were to go to school. It began as a spat over where Osaze was going to stay. The week before, Osaze hooked up with a cousin of ours. They rented a room in Aiwerioba Estate, in 42S, the flat next to Harry's. Eniye's case was easier and cheaper because she would stay at Aunty Alero's. Dad had been complaining about the cost of educating us when Mom flared up and told him to shut it. Inexplicably, the quarrel jumped from Dad's oyibo education to my argument with him last year about going abroad because of the incessant strikes—a request he had refused.

"Come, this woman."

"Come what? I've been quiet too long. Not anymore."

They were in the upstairs parlor. Eniye, Osaze, and I were in the boys' room, lying in the dark as NEPA had taken light and the generator was out again. I sat on Osaze's bed and watched my parents' shadows play with the walls across the pigeon-holed screen of the dining room from our window. As they screeched, the wind blew. Was this going to be the last storm of the year? The whistling through the fronds of the skyscraper-high survivors of the palm oil plantation where my Dad had built his mansion screamed a resounding YES. A hopeful yes.

I heard a plate smash against a wall. Eniye left the room and Osaze followed. I remained on the bed. I was tired of this.

They could kill themselves for all I cared. Yes, Mommy, Daddy is tight with money. You must have known this before you married him. You must have. So bear it. Dad, I hope I grow up to be nothing like you, arguing with your wife, beating her up. I will never beat a woman. Never.

Osaze's and Eniye's voices soon joined the cacophony on the other side of the house. I watched the shadows and smiled. They looked like that Chinese shadow theater that Sergio Leone showcased in his masterpiece *Once Upon a Time in America*. I felt like Robert De Niro, smoking a hookah and drifting off, carried into oblivion by the hard-hitting opium mist.

The argument ended. Dad came to our room to talk. He had stopped the habit of calling only me into his room to blast Mom. I guess he figured that Osaze was old enough to hear poison. He talked forever until light came. He left for Eniye's room; she was due for an earful too. I jumped off the bed to blow out the lanterns we kept in strategic places in the house: the staircase, the cocktail terrace, and the upstairs sitting room. Haba, someone had left the upstairs TV on. Dad and Mom had been watching TV together when NEPA conspired to convince them to fill the subsequent silence with their racket.

"Ewaen. Ewaen!" Dad was shouting my name.

"What?" I shouted back.

"Come to my room immediately!"

I met Dad knocking on Mom's door. *Didn't they just quarrel?* That usually meant no speaking for at least twelve hours. This was a new record. Thirty minutes.

"What do you want?" Mom asked from behind her locked door.

Dad glanced at me as I turned into the corridor. There lay an overturned kerosene lantern at his feet, its flame mercifully out. Dad stood in the spreading stain of paraffin on the terrazzo floor and said to me, "Go to my room." I walked past him, stooped to set the lantern upright, and only then noticed two pairs of footprints leading from the spilled kerosene into his room. Dad was talking to Mom. "Omasan, please open the door. Eniye just tried to kill herself."

Eniye smiled sheepishly on the small sofa in Dad's room. Osaze was lying on the headrest of the chair I chose to sit in. I looked across the short marble-topped center table at my sister. I had just heard what Dad said.

"Wetin happen?" I asked her.

"I don't know," she replied. "I was throwing away some old tablets when Dad entered the room."

Mom ran into the room, guilt and worry on her face. She pulled Eniye up; they were now the same height. Eniye's chest was beginning to rival Mom's. They looked like negatives of each other—the same height, the same build, bowlegs and all—but Mom light complexioned and Eniye dark like our father. She hugged her. "I'm sorry. I'm sorry," Mom said over and over again.

This was all a big misunderstanding, I suspected. Suicide? Eniye? How? I looked from Osaze to Eniye, who was trying hard to breathe because of Mom's tight embrace. Dad stood at the door. He walked to his wife and daughter and patted their shoulders. He told them to sit down, that he wanted to say something.

He sniffed and spoke, his voice cracking and for once uncertain about what to say. After many false starts he said, "Do you know why I am so hard on you? Don't answer. It is not because I do not love you. I touched each of you the moment you were born. Your small fragile fingers clasped my fingers and you stared at me. I would die for you. All of you."

He glanced at Mom, who dug her chin deeper into the knot of the wrapper she had tied over her nightie and across her chest. "I grew up in my grandfather's house. My father—only you, Ewaen, will remember him—threw my mom, Uncle Max, and me out when I was still in my mother's womb. People had poisoned his mind. They said that his wife's womb was poisoned; how else could a woman have only miscarriages for twelve years? It was not natural. My mother was two-months pregnant when she went to live with her mother and father, your great-grandparents. I had to fight for my first breath. They said I was as gray as the husk of a two-month-old coconut when I was born. I hung on the threshold of this world for days. But I am a fighter. My mother, Iye, told me that I cried like an adult, dragging in every breath hungrily, suckling and biting at her breasts until they bled, even though I had no teeth."

My father's eyes glistened. Was he crying?

"None of what I try to provide for you was available to me. I had to learn to live. Uncle Max and I used to trek all the way from Sakponba to fetch water at Ikpoba River. My fingers bled. I was barely old enough to walk. And here I was fetching water with an iron bucket half as tall as I was.

"Your uncle, my older brother, left when I was seven. He left to pursue his future. The missionaries enrolled him in a City and Guilds College in Ghana. My mom remarried. I was left alone in that house with cousins and aunts who thought nothing of leaving me to starve. Did I give up? Did I try non-sense like this stupid girl here trying to kill herself?"

"I wasn't—" Eniye started.

"You are a fool. Have you seen life? What have you experienced, you silly girl?"

Still in shock at seeing my father cry, I was reassured by the flash of anger, of rage in his eyes at this last sentence. But his eyes watered again; a drop coalesced and dripped out of his right eye. His voice shook as he spoke. What memories could these be that would break down Dad? He sniffled and smiled, an awkward effort. Mom reached to him and patted his hand.

He looked at her. At that moment, I understood. They loved each other. Their love was like the cigarettes I smoked. They were bad for you. They caused you pain. But you could not live without them.

Eniye told me later that when Dad saw her with the sachets of tablets, he immediately assumed the worst. She decided not to say anything.

The arguments stopped, and I saw Dad kiss Mom full on the lips the next morning. Did they not know that seeing such things scarred a young mind forever?

MOM SAT with Osaze on the back seat of the 504 station wagon when the driver took us to school. I sat up front with Michael and rolled my eyes as Mom ran through a repeat of the lecture she had given me on that first drive to the University of Benin.

Mom did not shout, *Be careful.* None of us mentioned the brush with death. Instead, Mom continued speaking, segueing as abruptly as Michael the driver had swerved. "Never minding what you see; your father is a good man, and I love him very much," she said. "But one thing you must learn from us. Never hit a woman. Do not become one of those children who think that because of some worthless excuse that they witnessed in childhood, it is okay to fight with their wives. Use us as a bad example. A quarrel here or there is inevitable, but never sleep on an argument with your wives. Never. And never hit them. No matter what. Una hear?"

22

WILHELM WAS out on the veranda when our station wagon pulled up to the front of the new flat. The gate swung noisily on its hinges as Wilhelm pulled it open. The sound reminded me of my 505's fan belt.

Mom said, "Nice place."

It was—nice. Our new flat was located beside the University Palace Hotel and two NEPA poles after Goldland on Federal Government Girls College Road, the main thoroughfare that ran through the Osasogie axis of Uniben's off-campus residences. It was an old cream-painted flat with moth-eaten and lichen-riddled hibiscus and double ixora hedges lining its veranda. The compound was large and, because the flat lay deep in it, it had only a small sliver of a backyard that barely allowed enough space for the soakaway. Michael parked in front of the small waist-high gate that separated the frontage from the rest of the veranda. The luggage in the back of the station wagon tinkled and rumbled. Osaze was the first one out. It seemed he could not get away fast enough from Mom and her memories.

Wilhelm walked from the now-closed gate to Mom's side of the car and opened the door for her. He bowed, bending a little too low, and said, "Welcome, ma. How was your journey?"

"It was fine, my dear. Very respectful," Mom said. She spoke to Wilhelm, but she glanced at me. I rolled my eyes, opened the car door, and got out, walking into an exuberant handshake from Tuoyo. He had just walked down from the clothesline on the left side of the compound's front yard, where he had been hanging out the laundry. His hands were lathered and slimy. I wiped my wet hand on my jeans and asked, "Una quick o. When did you guys come in?"

"Yesterday," Wilhelm shouted from the other side of the car, where he was still charming the pants off Mom.

I pointed at the clothesline. "That means Tuoyo traveled with dirty clothes?"

"Yes, now. You don forget say he be pig? That's why he is washing now."

"What about Mesiri and Tambo?"

"Mesiri has already come, but he went to Stores to get brooms, a mop, and some toiletware. Tambo should enter this evening or tomorrow."

"Ha, Ewaen. These are good boys o. Thank God. I like this place. It is closer to school, not like that place you lived in before. I like this place."

"Yes, ma," I said, just as Osaze started shouting from inside the flat—when did he enter?—that I should come and show him my room and that his hands were getting tired because he was carrying my big suitcase.

"Come, ma," Wilhelm said. "Let me show you around."

"Thank you, my boy," Mom said. "How is your mother?"

While she and Wilhelm talked and walked around to the backyard, Michael and I went to the car boot, took down the rest of my luggage, and carried it in. Standing at the door, Michael shuffling past me, I looked around. I had been in the place twice already—both times to inspect with Mesiri and the estate agent in tow—but I was still pleasantly surprised by how big the parlor was. The last tenants were a lecturer's family who had left the country after the demonstrations earlier in the year. Even the engineer who lived downstairs in my former building left too, not for a job abroad, no. He had a job with an oil prospecting firm in the delta. Our new parlor was big, and I noted on the floor, carefully tucked into a corner by the wall, the sheets of plywood, nails, and lengths of two-by-four that Tambo planned to use in partitioning out his room from the dining room section. Mesiri had taken the guest room as his. It was separated from the rest of the bedroom wing and its door opened directly into the parlor. Smack in the middle of the wall, opposite the front door, was the corridor that led into the bedroom area. I pointed it out to Michael when he threatened that he was going to dump the load on the floor if I did not tell him where my room was. "Straight down," I said. "The last room on the left."

"Hmph," he grunted. I followed him. Osaze was already in the room. The flat had two master bedrooms that shared a toilet, which was where the corridor ended. I would be living in the one on the left while Wilhelm had already moved into the one on the right. Tuoyo was in the kiddies' room just beside mine on the left. We agreed that this made mine the mommy's room and Wilhelm's the actual master's bedroom. When I entered the room and dropped my bags, I saw that Wilhelm and Mom were at the window peering in.

I heard Wilhelm say, "This is Ewaen's room. He paid the largest sum of money, so he gets the best room."

"Don't mind him, Mom," I said. "We balloted for the rooms. Wilhelm got the best room. Tell him to show you. Oya, get away from my window; you're spoiling the view."

Mom laughed, and they continued on their tour. When I had almost finished unpacking, Mom finished with Wilhelm and prayed with Osaze, Michael, and me. She anointed the four corners of the room with olive oil. No evil would befall her son here. From this beautiful place, he would graduate a doctor. She surprised me with a new Bible and a prayer book and smeared my forehead with a cross-shaped dollop of oil.

I WALKED beside Mesiri on our way to old Jowitz to get some food. We did not have anything in the new flat to eat. Tambo, Tuoyo, and Wilhelm were in front of us. Motorcycles rumbled past us, their riders leaning laterally in precarious angles as they rode. The sound of passing cars rose in a crescendo and died in tandem with their now-bright-then-dim headlights. I caught Mesiri's face. Light reflected on his shiny skin. His complexion was almost a deep blue, and he had shifty eyes that perpetually darted from one thing to another, always looking suspicious. We nicknamed him Sinister because of the eyes and because he could give the strongest news in the calmest voice you ever heard. When we were in year one, he lived on the same floor as us in room A104. We barely spoke then even though we had been classmates from THS. He was always well-dressed, not expensively; his clothes were always clean and immaculately pressed. I remembered the kindness he had shown Amide on the night of the riot, and I smiled.

"I see that you've got new shoes," Tambo said to Mesiri. Tambo was walking backwards, taking steps in time with Tuoyo and Wilhelm on either side of him. They had not bothered to turn and were carrying on a conversation about Wilhelm's girl, Weyinmi.

I replied to Tambo's question, "You dey talk like say you no know Mesiri, the *Sinister*. He bought these shoes last year."

"But I've seen them. They are new," Tambo said.

"It's the way he walks. Softly-softly like an Indian mystic. Abi, Mesiri? No be so?"

"Ewaen, leave me alone."

"But it's true, Mesiri. You too neat; it's not healthy. Tambo, have you seen his room? Already it's looking like you could eat off the floor."

"I'm going to enjoy this new flat. It's already looking and sounding like A109."

Tuoyo joined in, "Except the bathrooms are cleaner."

"Ewaen, we suppose throw party," Wilhelm said. "I was thinking next tomorrow. Maybe you can invite Amide and her friends."

Wilhelm left us at Oba Ewuare junction. He walked on the dark street. His girlfriend lived just off the main road in a face-me-I-face-you that she shared with what seemed to be a battalion of beautiful chicks. Despite her Itsekiri name, Weyinmi was actually Urhobo. Her Urhobo name was Iroro. She had been brought up by her mother's brother, a wealthy and powerful Itsekiri chief who was always in the news as one of the patrons of the democratic coalition. The chief made headlines with his threats of organizing a civil disobedience campaign in the delta and elsewhere if the junta made good on the death sentence handed down by a military tribunal to Ken Saro Wiwa and eight others the week before. Weyinmi told us that his wife, her aunt, always nagged him about the ease with which people entered their mansion in Lagos to visit him despite the danger her uncle put himself in with his words. The chief always chastised his wife with words to the effect that she had married a man of the people and that since the people were his mistress, she had to make allowances for them. Wilhelm waved us on and said he might make it to the flat later that evening. He was having his dinner at his girlfriend's.

"But you said she traveled to Lagos."

Wilhelm shouted back from deep in the darkness, "I have the key. I for invite una but there's only food for one."

Tuoyo muttered, "Stingy bastard."

"I heard that."

JOWITZ WAS full of students back from six months in limbo and with cash to burn. The bar's patrons and matrons spilled into Stores's car park. Smoke hung like a low cloud above the heads of guys and girls. Glasses of beer clinked against each other like a West Indian drum band. And the bar's speakers blasted out sounds of fun, brotherhood, and mayhem. I sat at a table for four with Osaze, Edosa, and Mesiri. Edosa was our cousin from Benin, his dad was my father's older brother. He, like Osaze, had just gained admission into the university. He was Osaze's roommate and coursemate. Tuoyo pulled up a chair to a free corner of the table and sat down.

He said, "Tambo has found his friends. He is sitting at that table. No, don't stare."

I had already caught a glimpse and smiled indulgently at Osaze and Edosa, who were positively mortified by Tuoyo's warning not to stare. Tambo sat beside Tommy at a table on the right. In front of them was Frank, the Cosa Nostra don, with his girlfriend, the same girlfriend from the party in quarters in year one, from that night in the Main Auditorium.

"Who is that?" Osaze asked me.

"Oh, one of my roommates."

"No. I mean the other guys." He was whispering.

Tuoyo and Mesiri laughed.

I slapped my brother's shoulders and told him to sit up straight. "Why are you crouching as though we are in a film? You dey fuck up o. Sit up straight. Nothing dey happen."

Mesiri, the kinder of my friends, said, "Tambo na confra boy. I hope Ewaen has talked to you about confra." Mesiri looked from Osaze, who was nodding yes to Edosa, who still looked confused. He continued, "Tambo dey Mafia, Cosa Nostra. That's one of the university gangs. The guy beside him is Tommy. He is their enforcer. And the chap with the girl is Frank; he is their don."

"But I thought they were secret cults," Edosa said. "How do you guys know? And how can you just sit here and discuss them? What if they hear?"

"Maybe in a bush school like Ekpoma . . . but this is Uniben. Everyone knows where everyone belongs. Take for instance that guy." Tuoyo pointed as he spoke. The guy was smoking a cigarette and glanced at us as he took a seat at the table adjacent Frank and Tambo's. "That's Yibril. He is a Black Axe hit man."

I stared at Yibril. I had not seen him since year one. He still looked nothing like his reputation. He was still small and still had a shuffle when he walked. Wilhelm told me that they were not really speaking because of the robbery at Harry's flat. Yibril saw me staring and raised his right hand, the cigarette dangling between forefinger and index. I returned the wave and stared at the table, embarrassed. But what was he doing here? He was sitting on the table beside people who had him arrested for stealing Harry's things. I tried to see if any electricity coursed between the tables and caught it; Tommy leaned over the table to whisper in Frank's ear. The don turned in his chair and caught Yibril's grin. The Black Axe boy attempted a wave, but Frank turned away and caressed his girlfriend's shoulder.

"Hit man as in . . . hit man?" Osaze asked.

Tuoyo, Mesiri, and I chorused, "Yes, hit man."

We ordered the house special, a plate of rice and stew with dodo, and ate. Patrick, the owner of the bar, served us himself, hovering around the table and placing glasses of water at the precarious edges. He left us to serve Tambo and his friends, and I saw him returning.

"The bros for that table ask wetin una go drink," Patrick said. We ordered drinks and, when they came, toasted Frank, Tambo, and Tommy. We finished eating and lit up cigarettes, belching and feeling satisfied with ourselves. I leaned back in my seat and saw Tommy approaching.

"Hey, Ewaen. Long time, no see."

"Tommy, how now?" I replied.

"Tambo said that this is your brother. Una be carbon copy o. I hope you won't be a fake guy like your brother," he joked as he took Osaze's hand.

"No, he won't be," I said. I avoided Tommy's eyes.

WE HEARD the news when we were about to leave Jowitz. Someone rushed in and shouted, "They have killed the chief o! They have killed him."

Assassins had gunned down the head of the democratic coalition while he had Sunday brunch in his home. Weyinmi's uncle was dead. And she was in Lagos.

"Switch on the TV. Turn off the music. Turn off the music!" Patrick, the barman and owner of Jowitz, shouted.

We gathered round the TV on which we had watched the World Cup just last year. The NTA was showing the commissioning of water projects in the watery delta, so we switched to CNN. The scrolling lines beneath the main picture of the talking heads emblazoned the headline "Breaking News." Unknown gunmen had shot the chief on his bed this Sunday morning. Nothing more.

WILHELM WAS inconsolable. NEPA had taken light by the time we got back to the flat, and we met him alone in the sitting room staring at a flickering candle and smoking a cigarette. He had a half-empty bottle of gin beside him. We took mattresses from the rooms, opened the parlor windows to allow the cool October breeze in through the nylon mosquito nets, and sat around him, our faces lit up by the candle, our backs to the dark. It was an ill-omened way to resume in our new flat. We could not claim to understand what Wilhelm was feeling. He had not been able to call Weyinmi. He knew no more than we did. His girlfriend was in her uncle's house in Lagos. They had spoken that morning. She was rushing to church and had promised to call him later.

Wilhelm said, "The lines were engaged. When I tried to call from the payphone, the lines were engaged."

"They were most likely cut," Tambo said. "No worry. She will be okay."

I did not feel like saying anything. We slept with the candle still burning. Our own small vigil for the fallen democrat.

23

WILHELM DID not hear from Weyinmi for a week. It took that long before a mutual friend brought a handwritten note from Lagos. Wilhelm's face lit up when the girl, one of Weyinmi's flatmates, dropped it off. He read the note by the door while Tambo escorted the messenger back, propositioning her all the way to the okada that she kept waiting.

The note said that Weyinmi was okay. The chief's family had been bundled into a luggage room downstairs while the assassins—led by a man who, according to Weyinmi, spoke perfect Itsekiri—went upstairs and shot the chief twice, once in the head and once in the chest. She said they remained locked in the room for more than two hours before another visitor came and heard their cries. They were taken to the police station some days later to look at a lineup of suspects who the police said had confessed. She said her cousin, the chief's first son, had to shout before the family was allowed to leave the station. The police were pressuring the family to identify the men they had in custody as the assassins. Weyinmi was sure that these men did not kill her uncle.

Wilhelm's mood lifted after hearing from Weyinmi, and he became his cheerful self again. He had never really lost his wit, but his jokes had been strained, and any laugh he gave to one cracked by another seemed forced.

THAT NOVEMBER, we made the flat our own. We bought curtains. The kitchen came alive and was soon filled with the sounds of our girlfriends. Amide colonized a corner of the parlor, the far right, and sat there smoking whenever she came to cook. "Waiting for the rice to done," she always said. Tambo organized a television from his father's house in town, and with my Nintendo and Wilhelm's VCR we had a semifurnished parlor. The settee was a discarded mattress and the center table two overturned beer crates.

Within these walls, we made new memories and dreamt new dreams. I, for one, was going to take school seriously— okay, a little more seriously. We had four months to go to the dreaded Second MB. I borrowed Amide's notes and copied them. I scrounged around for money to replace textbooks I had never bought. And I read—not hard. I have never read hard. I read easy. I lay on my bed with the book open on my lap and, with or without Amide snoring softly on my shoulder, deciphered words like "adrenocorticotrophic hormone"—a jawbreaker that my seniors in the medical profession had wisely shortened to ACTH. I became a fake guy, a half-fledged geek. Most evenings, I remained indoors while my guys went out and came back at midnight with car park and Jowitz gist. In the mornings, I tried to make classes. Some I attended; some I missed. Thrilla, our anatomy group's cadaver, was down to only his torso and head.

The few times I went out without my guys, it was to escort Amide to the BQ she had been living in since we resumed— her parents had insisted she move out of the hostels after the attack by Mobile policemen the previous semester. I would spend an hour on her bed while she ran around the small room preparing food for me to eat. Lying there most evenings, I thought about the time I had been in a BQ alone with another girl, Tseye, and smiled to myself about missed opportunities.

I never slept in Amide's room. Her landlord was a friend of her father who took us in physiology. He took the mantle of overbearing, overprotective parent and wore it in bright, angry colors. Amide was barely allowed to entertain guests, to talk less of boys. Talk less of sleepovers.

When I did not go to Amide's place and wasn't reading, I would be in either Osaze's room in Estate or Brenda's place at Adolor junction. Brenda was my new neighbor—the former hospital was literally a stone's throw from my flat. I walked to her place in the evenings.

"But you love the girl?" Brenda asked.

"I think so—"

"You think. You think? Ha, Amide has suffered."

We were in Brenda's room. It was a converted sluice room and still showed signs of its former purpose. The deep wall-mounted ceramic bowl in which she washed plates had seen nastier things poured into it than day-old moldy food. Thankfully, at that point in time, we were unaware of this fact. I came to talk in Brenda's room about everything and nothing. My girl-bestfriend was back in my life. She was attacking my reasons for seeing Amide.

"But, Brenda, you do not understand. That girl has passed through a lot. She makes me laugh. We've never quarreled or exchanged a sharp word. It's so peaceful being with her."

"Shut up, my friend. It is so peaceful. Why will it not be peaceful when she lets you smoke? Haba, she's even a chimney herself."

"But she is a good person."

"That she is. That she is. But why don't I see that fire in your eyes when you're with her? Or when you talk about her?"

"What fire?" I knew what she was talking about, though. I knew. I had experience with fiery relationships; I had seen my parents' burn. I knew what Brenda was saying; *she* did not.

"Remember, Ewaen? Remember year one? When you used to come to my room and bore me to death about Tseye. Kai, you were a mugu then, sha. 'Tseye did this,' 'Tseye did that.' I wanted to kill you. Remember now? Did that girl kill this thing inside you?"

"What thing?"

"I don't know, my guy. But truth is, you do not love Amide. You feel guilty that she was attacked in hostel when you should have told her not to go back that night."

"That's not true—"

"But it is, Ewaen. I am not saying you should bust her o. Just be sure of your feelings."

"And what are those, do tell?"

"That you still love Tseye."

"This is why you can't find a boyfriend. All this nonsense Freud talk. I see Tseye every day in class. At first, yes, every time I saw her my heart skipped. When I saw her walking to-wards where I would soon be, I took another turn. But the last time I spoke to that girl was a year ago. I care about Amide, deeply."

"Ehn, but you don't love her."

"Gerrout!"

We both laughed. A trailer on the main expressway honked past her window. It was ten in the night and the noise outside almost drowned out our gist inside. A table lamp that stood on her reading table lit Brenda's room dimly. The read-ing table had two thick tomes on tort. One of them was open and dog-eared.

"How can you read with the noise outside?" I asked. I was leaning over and lacing up my Chelsea boots. It was time to get back. I had locked the flat, and Tambo did not have a key yet.

"It's worse in class. You know how fine girls suffer, now. The wolves no dey let us read." She shook her buttocks in front of my bowed head. I looked up from my shoes and narrowly missed her buttocks with the slap I planned to plant there.

She heard the whoosh and said, "Ha, Ewaen. You are a wicked boy."

At the gate she waited under the roof of the short walkway and watched as I maneuvered myself around their flooded front yard, up the short remnants of a fence, and tightroped the rest of the way until I hopped down on the other side of the body of water before saying, "About my lack of boyfriends, Ewaen. It will please you to know that I am presently seeing someone."

"And you wait until I have jumped your River Niger before telling," I shouted back. "Who is it this time?"

"Ha, Ewaen. This time? How many times you don know me with boys? Anyway, sha. It's Lorenchi."

"Loren . . . Brenda, you dey crase? Wait!"

She was already turning back and threw her voice at me like a ventriloquist. "Ewaen, goodnight. We'll talk tomorrow."

I stood on the spot, but my eyes followed her. It was now official. Brenda don crase. Dating a confra boy? What was wrong with her? I could already see her justifying it in our next talk with something lame like, "But he is a fine boy now." I would just break her head. That was what a boy-bestfriend was for—knocking you back in place when you fucked up.

I MET Tambo in Mesiri's room when I got back that night. Mesiri had left the reading class early and had walked with Tambo back to Osasogie. They were lying on Mesiri's bed gisting when I entered. I joined them and sat on Mesiri's reading chair.

Tambo had been stood up by a girl who left the reading class with a 419 boy. He was still fuming and ran our ears ragged with notions of what he would do when he finally had money. He would show them bitches, he said.

The 419 thing grew big that year. Suddenly, young men, recent graduates all, were awash with cash. They visited our university. They had money, and the girls rushed them, flattered by the fact that young men with money came to take them out instead of the old potbellied politicos and soldiers that used to visit. Boys were not smiling. Many a guy had lost a date because the girl in question was "sick" on the prearranged weekend. The guys unlucky enough to find out the truth in the worst possible way would see their girlfriends dancing the Macarena in a club later that night during that same "sick" weekend. We envied the 419 boys; some of us saw them as heroes and rebels. They were doing what the imprisoned MKO had taken as his pet project in the late eighties—reparations. They took the money back from the oyibos that for centuries had robbed our continent blind. And they looked good doing it too. My father would have loved them, but he was too hung up on the fact that they made easy money writing letters about lost funds, prison terms, and dead relatives.

I chilled with Mesiri and Tambo until eleven. I got sleepy and shook Tambo. We had not yet built his room, and he slept in mine or Tuoyo's.

"I dey go sleep. You dey come?"

"Yeah."

Mesiri was already asleep, so I pulled his cover cloth up to his shoulder, tucked him in, closed the anatomy textbook he had not read, and left the room, Tambo after me. Tuoyo and Wilhelm were not back yet. They would claim they were reading, but I knew they were in the hostel car park drinking and chasing girls.

I had turned off the light in my room and was listening to Nate Dogg and Warren G when Tambo asked, "When was the last time you talked with your brother? When was the last you spoke to him?"

"Yesterday. Why?"

"That your brother, him eyes no good. You know he is a fine boy. I hope he knows what he is doing."

"If you got anything to say, tell me."

He did.

"I saw Tommy talking to him. Three days ago. So if you saw him yesterday, I guess he didn't tell you. Interesting."

Osaze would have told me. Tambo was talking nonsense. Osaze would have told me. "You were obviously there. What were they talking about?"

"Ewaen. Ewaen, you know say I blend Cosa Nostra."

"Tambo."

"No worry. You guys are my friends. And besides, who doesn't know? The thing is, I have regretted it ever since. You guys—Tuoyo, Mesiri, and you—might think that we have something you don't. But I dey envy una. I look at you guys and I see freedom. No wahala. You can take a stroll anytime without wondering if one of your supposed brothers has pissed off somebody. Without looking over your shoulders, seeing in every gesture an attack, a stab waiting to happen."

"Tambo, you were telling me about Tommy and my brother."

"I'm getting there. Remember in year one when I told you guys that there was a war brewing? Between Cosa Nostra and the Black Axe?"

"Yes. You said that Black Axe would soon put the Mafia in their place. That they were upset about the new upstarts."

"Well, the wahala is getting closer. That day I arrived from town. When we resumed. You remember?"

I did.

"Did you notice Yibril?"

"Yeah. You know Wilhelm and he aren't talking. I no know say na so the guy get heart. Drinking in your joint. That's brave o, even for a Black Axe boy."

"You don't know the half of it. Frank was robbed two weeks before we resumed. He lives in Ekosodin because he has been disowned by his parents and so was here throughout the strike and closure period. He wasn't in when the thieves came. They took his clothes, his deck, his TV. They took everything. We kept it quiet because na fuck up say they rob our don. But do you know that evening when Yibril sat in Jowitz alone, he was wearing Frank's clothes."

"No."

"Yes, he was. Tommy be wan' go shoot am. Na fuck up, now."

"Hmm."

"But the main thing is that wahala is coming."

"I see where you are coming from. First, Armani harassed Frank's babe, then Yibril and his gang robbed Harry, Frank's college son. I heard they hit Lorenchi."

"Yes, they did. Then we hit Yibril. We beat him up."

"Then this is a snowball rolling down a hill. When is it going to end?"

"If TJ was still the don, the wahala would have been resolved over glasses of beer. But this Frank guy . . . he thinks he's in some gangster film. Na'im be the thing I wan' make you tell your brother—this is not time to join confra."

"Was any time ever the 'time'?"

"Ehn, I know. But not now. A war is coming soon. Somebody go soon die. Frank gave the order that Yibril should be hit again. Only God knows where this will end."

"Have you spoken to Wilhelm?"

"Wilhelm? That one has had his head in the clouds for the past two weeks. I am not even sure he still goes to Black Axe meetings. I no even sure say Black Axe know about Yibril thief-thief. Everybody frowns on stealing. My point again—if TJ had been the don, Yibril would have been serving punishment in the bush, administered by his own crew. All this tension for no dey."

"Talk to Wilhelm. I will talk to my brother."

"Yeah," he replied absentmindedly.

"And Tambo."

"Yes?"

"Thanks for the heads up."

KEN SARO WIWA was killed by the government in November. He was finally pronounced dead after five hanging attempts. The Ogoni Nine were then bathed in sulfuric acid to make identifying their remains impossible for their families. If that was not enough, the men were buried in secret, unmarked graves to prevent the site from becoming a shrine. The international community was outraged. Wilhelm's transistor carried the BBC's version of events. It was not good. Nigeria was out of the Commonwealth. Our generals and their families were handed travel bans. They could not go on their shopping trips abroad—a life-threatening inconvenience for them.

Inside the country, not a peep was heard. There were rumors that the CIA and MI6 would soon invade, but everyone knew that it was nonsense. The fount of the democratic coalition's resistance had been gunned down by armed robbers—or so the official version of events went. Nigeria was like the African countries we read about in Frederick Forsyth's novels, that we saw in films like *The Wild Geese*. We were like sheep. Bus rides into town were silent; the tuke-tukes even complied by keeping their stereos down. The junta threw everyone in jail: protest musicians, renegade politicians, and that noisy lawyer from Ikeja.

24

I LIKED the idea of staying back in school for the holidays. Our house had become an army boot camp; ever since Mom and Dad stopped quarreling, it had become increasingly difficult to get away with stuff. My parents now ganged up on their children. It was not like the old lulls between their quarrels, when we knew that a lie told to Mom in the safety of her room could be reconstructed into gospel in Dad's. They now compared notes and sat the offending child through hours of combined scolding. No. 10 Omorogbe Avenue had become a hellhole. It was so much more peaceful when Dad and Mom fought.

Mesiri blossomed into a talkative gentleman. He especially enjoyed playing psychiatrist—the subspecialty he said he was interested in was relationship counseling—and grilled me and Wilhelm so regularly about our girlfriends that we learned to play deaf. We hoped Mesiri would not change his ambition to ear, nose, and throat. Wilhelm made sure he was never alone with our blue-black-complexioned friend; it was easier to dodge private and potentially troublesome questions by pretending you could not answer because there were others around. I, on the other hand, just let him rant away. Mesiri genuinely felt he was helping and only slowed down after Wilhelm told him to get a girlfriend and stop worrying us to death with his psychobabble.

Amide spent more time in my flat but stopped spending nights because she said I did not let her get any sleep. In a strange parody of a first quarrel, I accused her of being the one who would not let me sleep and, with a huff, she left for school. It was all in good fun, and we repeated this several times over the course of the fortnight—trading accusations about love, about sex. Once, when I escorted her after laughing at the end of one such exchange, she asked, "Ewaen, we've never quarreled. Never. Don't you think that's odd? I think about it sometimes, and I wonder what our first quarrel is going to be like." Typical Amide, worrying over something as joyous as peace. Or was it a lack of passion? Did she have something to worry about?

On Christmas morning, Wilhelm and I waited for Mesiri to come back from service. While waiting, we had made a breakfast of champions: eggs and corned beef washed down with bottles of Fanta and a beer, which we shared. The three of us strolled to the phone booth run by that family that lived opposite Stores. We each placed calls home—Mesiri was upset that his would not go through—and then went to my Uncle Max's house for Christmas lunch. We repeated the same thing on New Year's Day.

The break was good for one more thing. It poured ice water on the fire that had been brewing in December. After the incident in Jowitz where Yibril had worn Frank's stolen clothes and sat down gloating opposite the Cosa Nostra boys, it became obvious to those in the know that the Mafia boys would react, violently. In early December, while on his way to night reading, the ubiquitous troublemaker was accosted by unknown assailants and stabbed in the buttocks. Wilhelm told us that they, the Black Axe, knew exactly who had ordered the hit. He let Tuoyo and me in on a secret: almost the entire exco of his confra was happy that somebody had taught the idiot a lesson. They knew he was an embarrassment to the Black Axe. Nothing was going to happen. The insiders knew this but not the rest of school.

Bikes stopped running after 9 p.m.; girls' hostel and the car park became as quiet as an anthill. The school authorities issued mimeographs warning against any breach of the peace and solemnity of the campus. The tension was there, and the fact that it was an illusion did not take away from its unpleasant infectiousness. Everyone was glad that the school emptied for the holidays. Hopefully two weeks at home would cool the fieriest of the hotheads.

BRENDA WAS one of the first students to return from the holidays. She invited me, Tuoyo, and Ejiro out for a drink two days after she returned.

I left Tuoyo and Ejiro at a restaurant on Adolor College Road that afternoon and walked the short distance on to Brenda's place to tell her that we were waiting. I met her and Lorenchi in the room. He smiled and got up from the reading chair to offer me a handshake. I had not seen him since the middle of year two—since Black Axe boys attacked him after he reported the culprits in the robbery of Harry's room. I expected scars from the assault, and I was not disappointed. He had a stained gauze bandage on his left wrist. Stained? It looked too recent for something that occurred more than a year ago.

As I smiled over his shoulder at Brenda, I asked, "Lorenchi, long time, no see. What happened to your hand?"

He turned and pointed at Brenda, saying, "Ask your friend."

Brenda was smiling. She turned back from us and gazed at the mirror. She dabbed some more makeup on and said, "Don't mind him o. He was playing hero."

"What happened?"

"You know my camping gas? My gas cylinder I keep in the corridor? It caught fire yesterday when I was preparing him food."

Lorenchi took over. "I couldn't let it explode, now." He was talking to Brenda, not me. She finished with the mirror, grabbed her handbag from the table, and hustled us out of her room. As she locked up, I could still make out the charred patch on the wall next to her door.

"Una never still tell me wetin happen o," I said.

"Lorenchi grabbed the burning cylinder with his bare hand and threw it downstairs o. I was so scared. That was when he burned his hand. Very reckless."

"It wasn't that reckless, Brenda. It wasn't the cylinder that was on fire. The hot oil in the frying pan spilled and caught fire. It was less dangerous than it seemed. Even if this wasn't so, I had to do it for my girl."

I did not say anything. I watched Brenda, jaguda girl if there ever was one, suddenly go coy. She blushed. It was not a change in color; Brenda was too dark for anything less than a purpling to be noticed. It was her stammer, her averted eyes, the way she behaved. She had actually blushed. I felt the heat rush to my face too and realized that I was happy that it was getting dark already. I was jealous. Of Brenda? I was uncomfortable. They seemed genuinely happy, and Lorenchi's closeness to my girl-bestfriend seemed to have a nice effect on him; it seemed to have smoothed out his roughness. They looked good together.

"BUT THAT guy, sha. How has he survived this long without getting seriously injured?" Ejiro sat beside Lorenchi on a cloth-upholstered couch in a restaurant. Tuoyo, Brenda, and I sat in single wrought iron chairs on the other side of the table, open bottles of beer in front of us. Alcohol has a wonderful way of shifting topics. We had in the last hour gone through two bottles each and touched on subjects as varied as music, clothes, the burgeoning pandemic in East Africa, and now we were on Yibril.

"A stab in the yansh isn't serious injury?" Lorenchi asked.

"But he still survives. People like that do not die," Tuoyo replied.

"I can't imagine what will happen should Ah-kay retaliate. This school will burn," Ejiro said. He was not worried about Lorenchi's presence. Lorenchi was cool; he was dating a member of our group. Besides, Lorenchi was a Warri boy. No confra could break that bond.

"No. I hear Yibril is in UBTH. That should keep him out of trouble for a few months," I said. I smiled at Tuoyo. He knew what I was talking about: Wilhelm's gist with us. I glanced around the table and caught Lorenchi's smiling face. In the two years I had known him, he had not lost his sense of humor. He knew that matter was done with. The Black Axe was not going to retaliate.

WE SAT there and laughed and talked late into the night. I saw Mesiri first. He stooped at the entrance to the joint, a low-slung door with a high staircase meant to clear the high water mark of Adolor junction in the rainy season. Behind him was Amide. I was not expecting her tonight. Brenda, noticeably tipsy, said, "Ha, Ewaen's girl. You've come to take our guy away?"

Amide had sat with us on a few of our sessions and knew that the thing to do was ignore Brenda. She smiled her sweetest at my friend and said, "How can you people see in this place? It's so dark and smoky. Let's sit outside. It's dry enough, and the Harmattan breeze is lovely."

The bar attendant thought we were about to leave without paying but was reassured by Lorenchi, who told her to bring our drinks outside.

I contrasted this confra boy's behavior with that of my old best friend, Wilhelm. Wilhelm could be very impatient with barmen and waitresses. I had told him once that it was shocking that somebody who was so nice in other things could be so nasty to the hired help. He had replied that they were paid to take shit from people; that his own did not smell as bad as what he knew they heard from others. I knew he was talking nonsense. It was something even his girlfriend complained about. He drew the attention of everyone in a bar when he berated a slow or incompetent waiter. And he got the best service because he was oyibo, but he was never satisfied.

"Where is Willy?" I asked Mesiri after we had spread out our chairs on the lawn outside. Amide was right. The breeze was cooler outside. The normally noisy junction was quieter at ten; the trailers passed at longer intervals, and the suya men were outside, the aroma of their ware wafting temptingly up our nostrils. Amide sat beside me and leaned over from her chair with her head on my shoulder. She lit a cigarette. While we moved our chairs outside, she told me that she had come to the house and found only Mesiri in. She had asked him where I might be. She dragged the recluse out to escort her here.

"Wilhelm came back as Amide and I were getting ready to come here," Mesiri answered my question. "He dey with Weyinmi. He said he would hook up with us."

"He should not come here with his big eyeglasses and start shouting on the waitresses o," Tuoyo said. Everyone laughed. We all knew Wilhelm.

Amide and I left the group to buy suya. My right arm was around her shoulder as she haggled with the suya man. She was so short that her head was almost beneath my chin. I bent my head and sniffed at her hair. It smelled of soap. I liked this girl; I really did. This was pleasant. It was not painful, not like with Tseye. There was nothing tugging at my chest, nothing that made me feel like I was being gutted by the devil when I did not see Amide. She exuded a confidence, and it was contagious. She was comfortable with her feelings for me. She had already said she was not sure it was love. But she was happy with whatever we called it, and so was I.

Wilhelm and Weyinmi joined us at ten thirty. Weyinmi was tall, the same height as Wilhelm. She was dark and full, and wore her hair in tresses that shook when she laughed, which was often. Weyinmi had an oblong face with slanty eyes and a small pointy nose, and she had facial marks, small scars like elevens on either cheek. Throughout the evening she kept quiet and stared at Wilhelm whenever he was talking.

"Ewaen, do you know when Tambo is planning to come back to school?" Wilhelm asked as he dipped his paws into my suya. He pretended not to know what he was doing.

I slapped his hand when he reached for seconds and said, "I saw Omogui. He said he saw Tambo in town. Maybe next week."

"Next week?" Lorenchi said quietly. "No, he is already around. He dey Ekosodin for Frank's place. I'm sure he will join you guys soon."

"That's true," Brenda said. She was suddenly animated and continued talking. "Were you guys talking about Ekosodin?"

Lorenchi cupped her face in his hands and cooed. A very nauseating spectacle.

She continued, "Darling, let's tell them about Phoebe's party now. Ewaen, make sure you come o. You too, Willy, Tuoyo, Ejiro. And Amide. You guys can't miss Harry's sister's birthday party."

She was drunk. Ejiro turned to Lorenchi and asked him, "What's she talking about?"

"Phoebe's organizing a party to celebrate her birthday and to open her new room in Ekosodin," he said.

"Ekosodin? Harry's sister moved from Osasogie to Ekoso-din? Is she mad?" I asked.

"Why?" Wilhelm asked. "What wrong with Ekosodin? No be human beings dey stay there?"

"You will defend the place, won't you?" I retorted.

"Abeg shut up, Ewaen. Lorenchi, when is the party? Or should we wake your girlfriend and ask her?" Wilhelm ribbed Lorenchi.

"You be idiot o," Lorenchi replied playfully. "In two days. On Friday, at Home Improvement Annex." He saw the clue-less looks on our faces and explained, "It's a new hostel in Ekosodin. To get there, just take a bike from the gate. It's near Green House."

"Two days," Wilhelm repeated thoughtfully. "I might be traveling o. I should be going to Abraka, but I'm not sure. If I am around, you can be sure I will make it. Shebi, you will be at the party, Ewaen?"

He was asking me? We were having our Second MB exams in two months and Willy was asking me if I could go to a party in Ekosodin of all places. I saw in his smile that he already understood that I would not go. Not Ekosodin. Not quarters. Not anywhere that was not my own place, my own house. Not even for Brenda.

AFTER HAVING a shower in the bathroom that I shared with Wilhelm, I prepared to sleep. I had the best sleeping medicine known to man: a textbook called *Last's Regional Anatomy*. It was so boring that it guaranteed sleep within three minutes of opening its pages. And we were supposed to have it crammed over the next nine weeks. Amide came into the room just as I was about to switch off the light. She had been in Mesiri's room gisting. The exasperated look on her face said it all: Me-siri had practiced his psychology on her.

"That your friend is mad o," she complained as she snuggled up to me. She wore a slip—a short satin nightie that I loved. I ran my finger along the curve of her hips. She snuggled closer, almost as if she wanted to curl herself into a ball in the curve of my tummy.

"You did not know before now?" I replied with the question. "This girl o. Shift to your side of the bed now. You want to push me off?"

"Shut up. Because I deign to bless this your yeye room with my presence."

"If I remember correctly, you said that I disturbed you from sleeping. That I—"

"Shut up and kiss me."

When we came up for air, she asked, "Are you going to Brenda's party?"

"No. The exams are too close."

"Since when did that disturb you from partying? You too lie. You're still scared about Ekosodin, aren't you? And Wilhelm is not going. What do you think he's going to do in Abraka?"

"You heard about the wahala there too," I murmured into her ear, ignoring the first half of her statement.

"My brother, Abele, is in year one there—"

"I know."

"He said it's a war between three confraternities. That it's like a world war. Everybody is fighting everybody. He is already at home. My mom has a very short fuse when it comes to school wahala."

"Because of what happened to you?"

"Because of what almost happened to me. But that's not what we are talking about; Wilhelm is going to Abraka in the middle of a confra war. What do you think he is going to do there?"

"This girl. How should I know?" I lied. "Shift for me before I fall off this bed."

She did not budge. We wrestled, and the strong girl turned me over on my back. She straddled my hips and whooped—a victory cry. We made love with the lights out and the windows open to the chilled Harmattan breeze. I did not need *Last's Anatomy* that night.

25

TWO DAYS to eternity. There is no other way, in retrospect, to describe those days in early January 1996. Amide left the next morning for her room in Doctor's Quarters after exacting a promise from me to meet her in class later in the day. Strolling back from our junction, I reveled in my joy. I could not even remember when Amide and I became an item. I remembered when we first slept together. I remembered when I first noticed her in class. But I could not place the moment in time when I knew—when I knew I would do anything for her. She was uncomfortable saying she loved me. And after Tseye, I was uncomfortable saying I loved anybody. I had heard the gist that you only fell in love once; that the lightning did not, in reality, strike twice. It was true. With Tseye, I had felt lost. I had known emptiness. But with Amide, all I felt was comfort. It felt like what Brenda and I had had in secondary school. That harmless, flirtatious warmth one shared with an attractive friend, with a girl-bestfriend. I skipped back to my flat, oblivious to the see-this-crase-man stares I got from the Okada riders and their passengers.

When I got back to the flat, Mesiri was already up and ready for school. He nodded at me as we passed each other at the door. I told him to make sure he copied notes and that I would photocopy his. I was not sure I was going to make class. In the kitchen, Weyinmi made eggs and toast. We did not have a toaster; we made the toast by coating the slices of bread with butter and holding them over an open fire.

Weyinmi handled the loss of her activist uncle well. When she first came back, it seemed as though she would never stop crying. She had an inner strength that we, Wilhelm's friends, had only guessed at. She smiled at me and asked if I wanted any breakfast.

"Of course. Have you ever heard me refuse free food?"

Wilhelm was already dressed and came into the kitchen. He had a knapsack slung over his left shoulder, ready for Abraka. He sat at the small wooden table we put in the kitchen.

I leaned on the door, waiting for my toast, and listened to Wilhelm. "I should be back in two or three days. Nothing really dey happen there o. My friends just invited me for a visit."

I wondered what lies he told his girl. But I knew that she was aware of his affiliation with one of the most violent gangs in the University of Benin. Maybe they pretended he was going for a pleasure trip; that it was not Black Axe business that called him across state lines on a useless waka.

"Weyinmi go dey here while you travel?" I asked.

"No, o. I am going to my place as soon as I am done with this cooking. You think I want to stay here with you useless boys? You guys will just turn me into a maid." She spoke with a nasal Warri accent; she confused l's, r's, and n's.

I collected my plate from her and sat next to Wilhelm at the small table. Weyinmi left the kitchen. She said she was going to get her stuff from their bedroom.

Wilhelm spoke as soon as she was out of earshot. "I like that girl o."

"I know," I said. I stabbed at the eggs on my plate, finally caught a large piece with my fork, and put it in my mouth.

Wilhelm was finishing off the last of his meal. "You are wondering what I am going to Abraka for in the middle of a confra fight?" he asked, pausing just long enough for me to raise my head from my breakfast and look at him. "Don't answer."

But he knew I would say something. I interrupted him. "Willy, when did you start carrying this confra thing on your head? You told me, in year one, that you joined only to prevent Cosa Nostra boys from victimizing you."

"Not now, Ewaen. I don't want to start that argument. I know everyone is wondering why I want to travel to Abraka now. It's our exco's decision. The don has sent us to negotiate peace. The boys over there do not trust themselves—too much bad blood. And I cannot refuse my don."

"I thought the only time you guys traveled to other schools was for hits."

"Ha, Ewaen. You still read those useless newspapers. The journalists have to sell copies. They always blow things out of proportion. There is this stupid arse called Lopez who's causing the wahala there. Na Maphite boy, but the fight has involved the Eiye and Black Axe. All because of this guy."

Why did he feel the need to make me understand? "Why you dey tell me?" I asked.

"Because—" He paused, and his color shifted, first to an angry red, and then he became pale, almost like death. "Because you are like a brother to me, Ewaen. You're the only one who doesn't judge. Tuoyo is cool too. But he is asleep now, so I can't off-load on him."

We giggled together. Tuoyo was always the last to wake up in the morning.

"I am so tired of all this wahala. Person can't read because of his 'brothers.' When we get to the head of this thing of ours, we are going to change the Neo-black Movement. Everything." He walked to the sink with the perpetually leaking faucets and dumped his plate. "Everything," he repeated.

"I know," I said. "Before that, make sure you wash your plate."

I WOKE up Tuoyo after Weyinmi had escorted Wilhelm to the bus stop. While we swept and mopped, Tambo walked in with his traveling bag. He started to say something cute but Tuoyo cut him off. "Tambo, must you fuck up? When did you enter school?"

"Are you my father? Which kind nonsense question be that?"

I said, "Tambo, quiet. Nobody wan' be your papa. The thing is that we are your friends. Your only real friends. You know how many times you've fucked up. Who always forgives you? And if you can't get it into your thick skull that the least you owe us is to be honest with us and to tell us where you are at all times, then I think that you should kuku just pack and go and stay at Frank's place."

"Ewaen, Ewaen. The speech. Don't bite your tongue o," Tambo said. His attempt at humor fell flat; no one laughed; Tuoyo and I just stared and waited for him to explain. "Look guys, sorry. But una dey always pick on me. Personally, I no feel say I dey fuck up." He paused to catch the duster that Tuoyo threw at him. He started dusting the top of the TV. His traveling bag was on the only settee in the sitting room. "But, meanwhile," he continued, "I have invitations to Phoebe's birthday party. It's in the bag. Yours," he said to me, "Tuoyo's, Mesiri's, and Wilhelm's."

Tuoyo said, "Brenda has already invited us."

Tambo seemed crestfallen. "What of Wilhelm? He still dey inside with him babe. Those two, them too like sex."

"Wilhelm don travel. He say he go spend two days."

"But the party na tomorrow night."

"That means he will miss it."

"See, you guys are the ones fucking up now o. I hustled for these invitations from Frank. And my friends can't all be there."

"Actually, Tambo," I searched for a way to let him down gently, "your friends can't be there at all. Like you said, na Frank you collect the invitations from. One, that means it's a Cosa Nostra groove. And two, it is in Ekosodin. I no fit go party for Ekosodin. Sorry."

Tambo walked to the window louvres and continued dusting them. The way he turned, tried to speak, and turned back to the window, I knew he wanted to explain that this was Harry's sister's party, not Frank's. With his back to us, Tambo said, "It's your loss, guys. The groove is going to be jumping."

I RECEIVED a scolding from Amide the next day. She was upset because I had not come to class the day before. We sat through lectures together and afterwards strolled to C6 with Fra, Oluchi, and Preppa. Preppa had heard some gist from his neighbors in town about the wahala in Abraka.

"Black Axe boys shot dead that Lopez guy yesterday evening in Abraka o," he said. Shot dead? Those were Wilhelm's people. I thought he said he was going to make peace. Fra muttered something about people getting what was coming to them, and we all agreed.

THAT EVENING, Tambo changed in my room. Mesiri, Tuoyo, and I watched as he dropped shirts, changed shoes, and harried all of us for our colognes. I had missed the moment that he and Mesiri finally settled. Tuoyo said they had started speaking as if nothing had happened.

"I hope you enjoy yourself," Mesiri said as he handed Tambo a pair of socks.

"You trust now. Have you forgotten that I'm the groove master general? I run things; things don't run me." Tambo pulled on the socks and shoes. He faced the cracked mirror I placed in front of the window and preened himself like a peacock overloaded with testosterone. "Ewaen, I fit borrow that your wristwatch?"

"Thank God none of us are following you for this groove o. How you for take dress up?" I took off the wristwatch and tossed it to him.

"What are friends for if not for these little inconveniences? And you know that it fits me more than you." He rotated the wristwatch in the light, catching a reflection that played on the walls.

After he left at 7 p.m., we chilled in my room and gisted. Wafts of dust, burning ash from the mixture of spontaneous and criminally set Harmattan fires, blew in from my open windows. I sat at my reading table and turned my swivel chair to face Mesiri and Tuoyo on the bed. Only the table lamp on my desk was on, affecting a subtle coziness that loosened tongues in the room. Tuoyo was twiddling with the dial on my radio when Mesiri spoke.

"You guys heard what happened in Abraka?"

"Yes," Tuoyo said. "I hear that it was foreign students who shot the Maphite boy at a peace meeting."

"At a peace meeting? I did not hear that part," I said.

"You guys think Wilhelm was involved?" Mesiri asked the obvious question.

I, who knew Wilhelm the longest, said, "He go dey there. I'm sure he was there."

"But wetin dey do Wilhelm?"

I explained, "Wilhelm's problem is that he never knows when to stop; he does everything until the end. You see the way he treats waiters. He claims it is because he hates oppression. When he says these things, it seems like he's joking, but he is dead serious."

"But for confra wey he no wan' join before? If not for that wahala in year one, would Willy be in Black Axe? And to travel to another school and shoot somebody? What kind of cold-blooded crowd does he move with?" Tuoyo asked the questions quickly, rhetorically; he knew the answers to each of them.

"Maybe he wasn't there when the guy was shot. Or maybe it was not his call. We can never know." Mesiri always tried to see the best side of people.

I had no such illusions. Everyone concealed a Hyde just under their Jekyll. "Maybe when he comes back you can ask him," I said.

"There is something else I want to talk to you about," Tuoyo started. "It is Brenda. I am not comfortable with her and that Lorenchi."

"I wasn't either. But you have to admit—Lorenchi's cool."

"Lorenchi is cool. Isn't Wilhelm cool? What is the news around school today? Na Lorenchi crowd I no like. See, we have survived three years in this school dodging these bastards. And now your girl is inviting people to what everyone knows is a Cosa Nostra party. Talk to her, abeg, before she enters wahala. You no know how many confra wars girls don cause for this school?"

"Guy, I know, men. What can I tell her?"

"Why are we worried about Brenda? What about the three of us, living with two confra boys?" Mesiri asked.

Good question. We chewed on that for the rest of the evening. It spoiled our night. When I finally fell asleep, I had no premonition of the number of times I would ask myself that question over the next few years.

I HAD a dream that night. I was in the bush surrounded by figures shrouded in shadow. When the hot embers around which we stood finally erupted into a bonfire, I saw their faces. They were all confra boys. TJ was there. So was Tommy, who gloated that they had finally caught me, that I must blend tonight. *Ah,* I thought, *the Cosa Nostra has kidnapped me.* But then one of the faces—was it Lorenchi's, Yibril's, or Frank's?—dissolved like a special effect from a Michael Jackson video into Wilhelm's. He walked towards me, holding a piece of firewood from the bonfire in his right hand. The end still glowed with heat, reflecting red light off his thick glasses. I stared at the reflection of the bonfire in his glasses as Wilhelm raised the stick up and brought it crashing down on my head. *Bang!* It sounded like wood on glass. Was my head broken? He did it again. *Bang!* And again.

"Ewaen. Ewaen, wake up!"

I stirred and turned towards the sound of tapping—nay, banging—on my window. "Who be that?" I asked.

"Na Wilhelm. Come and open the door."

"Willy? Do you know what time it is?" I rolled off the bed and reached for my watch. Oh, it was with Tambo. "What time is it?" I asked Wilhelm again.

"Five. Actually, ten past five. Wake up, now. Come and open the door."

"Where's your key?"

"I have it here, but you guys locked the protector from the inside."

It took me a few more moments to shake the sleep from my eyes. I walked to the sitting room door and pulled at the bars of iron. Wilhelm stood in a halo of early morning dew. His glasses were frosted, and he took them off to wipe the lenses on the tail of his shirt. He smiled and picked up his traveling bag. "Good morning," he said.

I grunted a reply even I did not hear and locked the door after him. I walked behind him down the bedroom corridor and entered my room. I slept off almost immediately.

WHO WAS that making noise again? I opened my eyes to streams of bright, healthy sunlight passing through the gaps between my curtains; I watched motes of Harmattan dust dance in the light. The voices were coming from the sitting room. I grabbed my early morning stick of cigarette from the reading table, lit up, and walked to the parlor. On the settee were Mesiri and the normally narcoleptic Tuoyo with their eyes bright, open, and gawking at Tambo. Tambo looked haggard. His blue jeans were torn and mangled. He was not wearing his shoes, and his stockings looked odd alongside each other—one of them seemed as clean as it was when he left yesterday; the other was soaked through with mud, as though he had trudged through the bush with only one shoe on.

He smelled the cigarette first before seeing me and turned from his rapt audience, saying, "Why una tell me say no cigar for this house? Ewaen, abeg, bring that smoke here."

"Why are you guys making noise? Tambo, wetin happen to you?" I asked.

Tambo took a long drag from the stick and said, "Oh boy. Wahala dey school o. Black Axe boys attacked Phoebe's party yesterday. Na bush we sleep."

I surprised myself; I took the news mildly. I left the stick with him and sat down beside my other flatmates. I whispered to Mesiri in the middle of Tambo's gist, "Where is Wilhelm?"

"He left for his girl's place at seven. Tambo just missed him."

We listened to Tambo tell us what had happened. The party had been groovy, all right. At about ten, the guests noticed some boys dressed in black scuffling with the bouncers at the gate to Phoebe's place, Home Improvement. It was a gang of Black Axe boys led by a limping Yibril. They broke into the party and started shooting up the place. They destroyed the sound system with one blast from a sawn-off shotgun and slapped around Phoebe's guests. Tambo told us that the boys forced the guests to sit on the floor. Yes, Brenda too. Then the Black Axe boys went from person to person, seizing wallets, ripping off necklaces and bracelets. Tambo apologized for my wristwatch; he said a chap who claimed to be Phoebe and Harry's cousin took it. This bastard shouted that he was going to blast Harry himself and that Harry's father was a pompous prick who disrespected other members of their extended family. Tambo said that Yibril went for Frank, pulled him up, and started threatening him with a pistol to his head. "He said he was going to blow Frank's head off." This was where, according to Tambo, Frank showed why he became the Capone of the Cosa Nostra. He wrestled the gun from Yibril and shouted for all the guests to run. During the confusion, helped in no small part by the intermittent bangs from the contested gun, most of them were able to escape, including Brenda, Phoebe, Harry, Tommy, Lorenchi, and Frank.

Tambo, as usual, told his tale animatedly. He waved his arms around, revealing scratches on his wrists that he said he got from the barbed wire fence of Home Improvement Annex.

Tuoyo spoke first. "But this doesn't make any sense. Wilhelm told us that the Black Axe weren't going to retaliate for Yibril."

"That's well and good. But I saw the boys myself. They were Black Axe men," Tambo said.

"What about Brenda?" I asked.

"We were in that bush till six this morning. Frank felt it was wise to wait because Ekosodin is Black Axe territory. I escorted Brenda home this morning. She is shaken but otherwise, nothing do am. She's okay."

"Thank God."

"But that's more than I can say for any Black Axe boy we catch today," Tambo said.

"Why? What's supposed to happen?" Mesiri asked.

"Frank stepped down last week. The new don of the Cosa Nostra is Tommy. He issued orders to all Mafia boys yesterday; he said that since the Cosa Nostra could not feel safe in Eko-sodin, then any Black Axe boy found in Osasogie today would have himself to blame."

"That's what he said?" I asked.

"That's what he said."

This was not good. What kind of wahala was this? Two of my flatmates were officially at war. And this was the worst thing that could have happened; the new don of the Cosa Nostra was Tommy?

Tambo was still talking. "That's why I came here. I'm going to town. I am not going to be around for this wahala. I will not be expelled when the shit hits the fan. Abeg, make I leave message for Wilhelm. I was surprised to find out that he was back from Abraka. I thought you guys said he would be away for two days. It's bad that I did not meet him." He was talking too fast. He almost hiccupped and stopped. Then more slowly, he said, "Tell him when he comes that he shouldn't sleep here tonight. It won't be safe."

THE GIST was all over school. I looked out for Wilhelm all day, but he did not come to classes. What did I really expect? We never went to school. I hoped Tuoyo was having more luck. He had said he would go to Weyinmi's place and warn Wilhelm about the trouble.

In class, Amide was bothered. She said I was distracted. She asked if anything was wrong. Nothing, I replied. But I felt a premonition. Something bad was going to happen. I stayed in school until afternoon physiology practicals. I stopped at Es-tate to see my brother at around three that afternoon. We went to Jowitz for lunch. The Cosa Nostra stronghold was strangely quiet, if not empty. Boys stood, draped in long overcoats, at corners in the Stores compound. I saw Tommy, but, unusually, he did not approach to harass me over blending. He frowned at my brother and me and walked past us. Osaze and I rushed through our lunch and left. I told him what was happening, and he told me to be careful and that nothing would happen. I hung out with him and Edosa until six that evening. I told them about year one, about the party in quarters, about the hole in the fence that led into Ekosodin, about TJ, Tommy, and Frank. I told him about our old oyibo friend from Warri—Wilhelm.

I got to our flat at six thirty and was surprised to see Wilhelm indoors with Weyinmi. I greeted him with what I was sure was a shocked look on my face. He smiled as if there was nothing hanging over his head and continued with his business. He said he wanted to repair the torch in his room and that the batteries were always going out. I left him and went to Tuoyo's room.

"You didn't tell Wilhelm about what Tambo said?" I asked.

"I did o. Hours ago. I went to Weyinmi's place and told him. He said he had already heard and that it was a rogue faction under Yibril that organized the hit. He said that peace moves were already being made."

"But he is not sleeping here tonight," I said, hoping.

"No. I'm even surprised he is still here. But you know Wilhelm. He go soon comot. No worry. Where you dey go?"

"I dey go talk to am."

"Guy, cool down. See your face. If you go now, both of you will just end up having a shouting match. Willy knows what he's doing. He will soon leave."

I exhaled loudly. Emptying my thoughts to my younger brother and cousin had made me angry with Wilhelm. Angry and irritated. Why was he always so cavalier about things? Fuck him. "I'm going to my room," I said. "I have exams in a month. I dey go read."

"I fit come play radio for your room. No worry, I go use the earphones."

I tried to read, but I could not put the dance of letters in front of my eyes into words that made sense. I picked at the hem of my white inner shirt, played with the loosening strands of yarn, and chewed on them. I looked at the LED clock on my radio from time to time. Every thirty minutes or so, Tuoyo put down the earphones and walked out of the room. Each time he came back he had something to say, which in other circumstances might have been funny.

7:30 p.m. "He says he will soon leave. That he wants to finish with the torch. And he say make I ask you wetin make you dey frown."

8:15 p.m. "He says I should let him bathe first. That he will leave immediately after that."

8:45 p.m. "Ewaen, I don tire for this boy. Now, he says his girlfriend wants to have a bath too. That after that, they will leave for her place."

We heard them at nine on the dot. Weyinmi's screech. Mesiri's shout, "They are beating him o! Ewaen! Tuoyo! They are attacking Wilhelm o!"

26

FRAGMENTED IMAGES flash in my head as I remember what happened next: Tuoyo and I racing out of my room; the *thud-thud* of Weyinmi's footsteps as she ran past us, wet and naked, her towel abandoned at the bathroom door; Mesiri, frantic and shaking, meeting us halfway in the corridor; and the bad fluorescent light in the sitting room casting our shadows as flickering, changing ghouls on the tiled floor around us.

"What happened?" someone asked. Tuoyo, I think. Or maybe me. The three of us crouched in a huddle in the middle of the corridor. We heard nothing but the sounds of our own heavy breathing, the sobs coming from Wilhelm's room where Weyinmi had run into, and the rumbling of the compressors from the air conditioners of the University Palace Hotel.

"I heard them," Mesiri said. "They are still outside."

We were directly beneath the naked bulb in the corridor. The lights were on everywhere in the flat. Anyone outside could see us.

"Turn off the lights," Tuoyo whispered. "Turn off the lights, Mesiri. Ewaen, you lock the kitchen door. I'm going to peep through Mesiri's window in front."

I ran to the kitchen, switched off the fluorescent, and slammed the iron protectors shut. The shadows in the house changed positions rapidly as my friends flicked off the light switches and finally merged into one body of darkness when the last bulb died. The house was in total darkness. Still I heard nothing.

Wilhelm. Willy.

What did Mesiri shout when I was in my room? They are killing him? They are beating him? Trouble! We were in big trouble. I felt my way back to the corridor. There were now four of us in the dark and narrow place. Weyinmi, I could see in gray of the dim light of the UPH's streetlights, wore one of Wilhelm's shirts. She was trembling.

I asked her, "Weyinmi, what happened? Where's Wilhelm?"

"He went outside to meet them," she whispered between choked-back sobs. "I was having my bath when I saw these men . . . through the window, I saw their shadows. I thought they were armed robbers—armed robbers like in Lagos when they killed my uncle. I was naked, so I ran to Wilhelm. He said he knew them and that I was being silly. He went out to meet them. I wanted to call you, but I was naked. He said I was being silly."

Just then, we heard the scream—one voice, a dark gurgling scream that screeched on and on until it lost steam and became a moan—and then ungodly sounds like the onomatopoeias of newsstand comic books. I was so afraid. Though deep down I knew what was happening, I still asked myself, *Were we being robbed?* I had always been afraid that our bungalow was too isolated, too far away from other populations of students. What were we going to do? Who was going to hear us cry for help? Who was going to answer?

"I didn't see anything from Mesiri's window. Weyinmi, you said Wilhelm went outside with them. Which side of the house did they go to?"

Weyinmi mumbled something. I did not hear. Tuoyo shook her. She shrank deeper into the part of the wall where she now crouched, hugging herself. She looked like a baby. Mesiri told him to stop.

"Na Mafia boys. I heard them talking with Wilhelm outside my window. Then I heard the sounds of fighting and Wilhelm screaming," Mesiri whispered.

Tuoyo grunted. He crouched on all fours and crept towards the kitchen. Was he mad? What was he going to do? Beside me, I heard Mesiri muttering. "They came to hit him. They have come to wound Wilhelm, Ewaen. We don die. School will expel all of us."

So it had come at last. I went numb, shockingly calm. I told this fool, Wilhelm, to leave the house. I told him. I followed Tuoyo to the kitchen, but I did not creep. I walked upright. My eyes hurt when he turned on the fluorescent light. Through the protectors, I saw Wilhelm running towards our back door. There was no one after him, but he hobbled; I knew he was hurt.

"Ewaen, open the door, quick," Tuoyo shouted beside me.

I heard him. I slid the bars back and pulled the door open. In the corner of my eye, I could see Mesiri and Weyinmi at the door to the kitchen. Wilhelm was almost at the back door. He wore a plaid shirt, a lumberjack that was open at the front, its collar askew and stained with mud. I saw something. It looked odd sticking out of his back like that. He collapsed into my arms. He was wet; the sticky wetness made him slip from my arms onto the kitchen floor tiles.

There was a handprint of blood on my white shirt. I stared at it as I was pulled down to my knees by the rush of bodies, Tuoyo, Mesiri, and Weyinmi, who hurried to pull Wilhelm into the kitchen. I saw the black leather-clad handle of the knife sticking out of Wilhelm's back, his shirt ripped around the hilt of the blade. Wilhelm, doubled over in pain and on his knees, screamed, "Ee dey pain o! Ee dey pain!" We let him down gently on his side. It was a Hausa dagger.

"Ha!" Mesiri shouted.

I screamed silently. What to do?

Tuoyo and Weyinmi seemed to be waiting; they held their hands hovering above our friend, afraid to touch him. Wilhelm was on his side shouting in pain. It was not like the movies where stab victims went down quietly. My friend was shouting. He was begging us to stop the pain, the hurt. What did doctors do? I did not know. I was in pre-clinicals; I was completely ignorant.

Tuoyo made a decision. "Let's remove the dagger so we can lay him on his back."

I said nothing. Mesiri said nothing. We lifted up Wilhelm's torso and watched as Tuoyo pulled on the handle of the dagger. It took so long. The dagger was so long. When it clanged to the floor beside us, we heard Wilhelm give a sputtering, wet cough. He seemed relieved; he became quiet, his glasses were misted with the damp from his tears. Through the tears, I saw his eyes open, moving from me to Mesiri to Tuoyo and resting on Weyinmi.

After laying Wilhelm on his back, I shouted to Weyinmi, "Get help! Run outside and get help." Wilhelm's grip on my hand was still strong. *He should be okay*, I thought.

I looked up and saw Weyinmi, watching and frozen, still standing above us. She was silhouetted against the fluorescent tube, her shadow fuzzy on Wilhelm's supine and writhing body.

I shouted again, "Weyinmi, go! Fucking move!"

Her glazed eyes came to life and she moved. She ran out the back door, screaming for help.

She was not the only one paralyzed with fear. Mesiri, since seeing Tuoyo pull the dagger out, had turned into a blithering idiot. He leaned against the ceramic tiles of the kitchen wall, alternately shouting and mumbling about how Wilhelm was dead, about how we should have left the dagger in place, and about our imminent expulsions from school.

I was bent over Wilhelm, giving him the kiss of life, when I heard the first of four police officers at the kitchen door. They were from the detail that kept guard at the University Palace Hotel, our next-door neighbor. One of them, a sergeant, had Weyinmi's hand in his. He spoke to the three of us, "Is he alive?"

Tuoyo said, "Yes!" He looked at me after he said that. Wilhelm had gone strangely quiet soon after Weyinmi ran out. But he was still breathing, wasn't he? Yes, he was. He was . . .

The policeman barked out orders to the other three. He told them to stop any car on the road and that the Good Samaritan would carry us to the UBTH.

IN THE car, a blue station wagon Peugeot 504, I held Wilhelm upright in my arms. I was leaning against the door; his legs were on Tuoyo's and Mesiri's, the other occupants of the back seat. Weyinmi sat in front between a policeman and the driver—a complaining, tall, dark chap. She glanced back at the sound of a clap; I had slapped Wilhelm twice because he was sleeping.

"Wake up! Wake up!" I said. "Wake up," I whispered.

We got to the teaching hospital within minutes and were waved in by the security men at the gate. They pointed out the emergency room to us. Mesiri was praying. Tuoyo stared straight ahead, quiet. My shirt was soaked through. The front of my trousers was wet, and my boxers were wet and sticky. I bent my head backwards through the wound-down side window and pulled in a long, deep breath. I could not think. I could not think.

When the station wagon screeched into the elevated drive-through in the emergency department, everyone jumped out except me. My friends shouted, "Help us! Help us o!"

Tuoyo ran to my side of the car to help me open the door so I could climb out and help put Wilhelm down. A nurse shouted, "No! Leave him there! Let the doctor come and see."

"But he is a medical student," Tuoyo shouted. "He is a medical student. Make the doctor hurry, please."

A man in glasses and a white long-sleeved coat walked up to the open door of the car. He was not in a hurry. He stood at the door opposite me. Wilhelm's unfolded feet almost touched his shins. He asked the others what had happened as he pulled on rubber gloves. Then he leaned into the car. He avoided my eyes and put a stethoscope to Wilhelm's chest. I waited and watched his face. There was nothing there, just a deep concentration and aloofness. He pulled out a small pen. No, it was a torch. He shined the light in Wilhelm's face, one side then the other, rolling Wilhelm's head on my bloodstained chest. The doctor shook his head and finally looked at me. I stared back quietly. I knew what he had just told me with his eyes. I heard him telling my friends and the policeman, "There is nothing we can do. He is dead."

I knew. I had known for about ten minutes. I had known before Weyinmi came back with the policemen. Mesiri screamed and started crying. Tuoyo stood to one side. Weyinmi walked to him and collapsed in his arms. I had my dead friend on my chest in the car. They had forgotten about me. I felt so confused. The annoyance that I had felt earlier in the evening when I saw Wilhelm back in the house instantly turned into soul-sinking guilt. I questioned everything we had done over the past two days. Nobody I knew had been through what I was suffering. My only points of reference felt hopelessly inadequate. What would an action hero do? What would my heroes, the fighters and gunslingers of video game *lore* do?

"NO O." The nurse was shaking her head at the policeman. "You can't put it here. We do not take BIDs."

"What is a BID?" Tuoyo asked. He had finally come to my side of the car and was helping me out.

"Brought in dead. We do not accept corpses from outside into the hospital mortuary. You will have to go elsewhere."

"He is a medical student. There must be something you can do. Help us, please?" I was in front of the nurse now, beside the policeman, who said nothing more to try and convince the woman. "But there is a policeman here. He can sign whatever paper you want signed."

"Sorry, I can't help you. The problem is from the police. Tomorrow they will turn and arrest someone here for treating armed robbers."

"Ma, he is not an armed robber. He is a medical student. Armed robbers attacked him in our house. Please help us."

She looked at me. It was comforting to see someone working at a hospital who still had some humanity. Her face was kind, and her eyes had this shine as though they were filled with incipient tears. She paused and reached for my face with a small gauze square. It smelled of methylated spirit, and it felt cold when it touched my face, chilly. She wiped at a spot and said, "You should get cleaned up, my young man. Look, I cannot do anything. Tell the policeman to take you to Central Hospital. Take him there. They will accept your friend."

It was the first time since the doctor saw us that she referred to Wilhelm as a person.

COLD REALIZATION slowly descended on us. Our flat had been attacked in what was clearly a cult-related assault, and somebody had died. How would the school authorities hear the news? What would our parents say if we were expelled? The owner of the station wagon had been persuaded by the policeman to take the corpse to the police station at the old Housing Authority Estate opposite the university. Curiously, we were not under arrest. All the policeman said he needed was one of us to follow him and give a statement so they could use their police van to take this "victim of armed banditry" to a proper morgue. The police still thought it was a robbery

attack. Tuoyo decided that Weyinmi and Mesiri would go with
them. He pulled Mesiri and me aside and explained what he
had in mind.

"There is this guy, a friend from Warri, Nesta."

"I know him. He went to FGC," I said. "He was me and
Wilhelm's senior."

"Yes. And he is the sergeant major of the Youth Defence
Cadets. They get direct line to the dean of student affairs. He
go fit help us. So, Mesiri, follow them go the police station.
Take care of Weyinmi. No worry. Everything go dey okay."

Mesiri sobbed, "I hear."

We had to bring Wilhelm out of the back seat and put him
in the back of the station wagon; the owner of the car did not
want a dead body leaking blood and God knows what else on
his upholstery. I was dead inside and noticed that Mesiri had
stopped crying. The policeman stood aside as the three of us
carried our friend. Wilhelm was heavier than when we had
pulled him into the car at the house; there is nothing as still
or as heavy as death. He smelled of piss and blood. It was not
like the antiseptic smell of the anatomy class. I thought about
Wilhelm's mother, who did not want her son to develop rashes
from sleeping in hostel in year one.

There was so much to do, so much to worry about. It felt as
though I were on a swing being pushed by a schoolyard bully.
I went higher and higher; I got dizzier and dizzier. When the
driver tried to shut the hatchback of his car, it bounced back
after a sickening crack. Wilhelm's arm had slipped out of the
position we had placed it in. The policeman cursed and folded
our dead friend's arms himself.

I WALKED behind Tuoyo along the corridors. We were taking
a shortcut through the teaching hospital. Tuoyo was strong. He
seemed to have concluded that the best thing to do was make

E G H O S A   I M A S U E N

sure that none of us, innocent as we were, followed Wilhelm
out of school. I hugged myself, self-conscious of the ogling
from everyone we passed; I made quite a spectacle. I had on
my inner white T-shirt, light blue jeans, and one slipper, a gray
flip-flop that was on my left foot when I first heard the screams.
The front of my body was a mess of red that looked black in the
aseptic fluorescent lights of the hospital's open-air corridors.

"Tuoyo, what will Black Axe boys do when they find out
that Willy is dead?"

"They know that we are not confra boys."

"You think the gist is already spreading?"

"Ewaen, I don't know. Maybe it is, maybe it isn't. When we
get to hostel, we will find out."

"You sure about Nesta? I mean, can he help us?" I met the
gateman's stare. He said sorry to me as he pulled the cord on
the iron bar. Tuoyo and I ducked under it and continued walking. We were on the other side of the UBTH, on the road that
connected Pharmacy to Osasogie.

"There are three things we should be worried about, Ewaen.
One: the school and the police might feel that we were somehow involved and conclude that we are cult boys and expel or
arrest us. Two: the Black Axe boys might think we betrayed
Wilhelm—"

"But they know we are not confra boys. Omogui is a member. When last you hear from am? I sure say he go dey hostel
car park."

"Yes, but you never see these people when they don smoke
weed. Do you think it was normal people that killed Wilhelm?"

"No," I said. "God! We really dey big shit o!"

"And three: the Cosa Nostra boys who Tambo warned us
about may feel we saw them. At least they know that Weyinmi
saw them. Look at all of it; we will go to hostel. We will see
Nesta in the car park. That's our best hope. Na our only hope."

252

"I know."

We walked out through the Pharmacy gate and elicited the now-familiar word from its gateman: sorry. He wished my injured relative the best. The University of Benin Teaching Hospital was sited along an expressway. Anyone seen bloodied was immediately assumed to be a victim of a road traffic accident.

I walked past a group of my classmates taking a break from reading in the Pharmacy lecture hall. They stared. Then I saw Preppa. He ran towards me, asking what happened. Tuoyo and I told him. I told him to go to Amide's BQ for me and to make sure she heard it first from him that I was okay. I had forgotten my brother. I had been with Osaze earlier this evening. What was wrong with my head? I was a Bini boy, a son of the soil. I had family in this town.

Preppa was about to leave when I told him, "Abeg, you go see Amide later. First, go to Estate. See my brother. Tell him what happened. Tell him to go to town and inform my uncle that we might be arrested tomorrow."

When he asked where we were going, he understood that seeing Nesta was a good idea. I also told him to tell his Black Axe neighbors in town—any of them not yet expelled from school—that we were Ju-men.

We spent the next hour looking for Nesta. We saw him in Dreams. He was having a beer with some friends. A hush fell over the drinking joint and spread palpably through the entire hostel area as I walked into the light. Tuoyo told me to stay in a dark corner and went to where Nesta was sitting. Nesta cried when Tuoyo told him what happened to Wilhelm. They were bunkmates from FGC Warri. He lamented Wilhelm's stubbornness. He said he knew what to do. We followed him in his car.

With each retelling of our story, Tuoyo and I slowly reached a consensus on what we would tell the authorities.

Without speaking about it, we knew that Mesiri would be saying the same thing right now at the police station. Some people had come to our flat. People whom Wilhelm knew because he opened the door and went out to meet them. Then they stabbed him to death. No, we did not see anything. No, we did not know if Wilhelm was in a cult. No, we were not in any cults. We repeated this tale to the dean of student affairs, a small dark man I knew only from his picture in the twice-monthly school gazette.

At the school gate, where we were advised to go and make the official report, I sat on a bench under the streetlight and tried to ignore stares from passing car drivers. I saw a few faces I knew. One of them, a party animal who lived in Benin, mouthed the question at me, "What happened?" I waved him on when I saw that he was going to park. There was nothing to tell. Some years later, I would run in to this same fellow. He would tell me that at the time he thought that I was a thief who had been caught and beaten by a mob enforcing jungle justice. But by then he would already know what really happened. The security men told us that we were free to go at around twelve that night. Nesta drove us to Estate. Tuoyo and I had decided to sleep in Osaze's room.

Estate was asleep when he dropped us off. Osaze answered when I rapped on his window. He came around and let us in.

"I just came from Uncle Max's house."

"You spoke to him?" I asked.

"Yes, I did. He almost crase. He was so worried. He asked who the guy was. He wanted to know how you came to live with this kind of guy."

"What did you tell him?"

"I told him that it seemed as though the guy was a secret cult member. The operative word being 'secret'—that you could not know if he was in any confra. He said he would make some calls. He wanted me to spend the night, but I said I had to go back to see what had happened to you. He talk say he go drive come school tomorrow morning."

"What of Edosa?"

"Uncle Max did not let him come back with me."

I stood in the middle of Osaze's bedroom. I did not want to stain anything with my bloody clothes. Tuoyo had already flopped down on the bed. He lay on his back with his eyes wide open, and he was quiet. Osaze walked towards me and helped me out of my shirt.

"Ewaen, pull this off. I will put water on the fire so you can bathe."

"What are you going to do with the clothes?" Tuoyo asked.

"I'm going to burn them."

I AM *working a busy evening shift at the hospital. It's an hour to the time I get off. A patient is rushed in with a blue station wagon. Two young men and a policeman jump out of the car. I raise my head from the patient I am suturing, a thickset guy with tough skin who was slashed with a broken bottle. I continue trying to puncture his torn skin with therapeutic stab wounds, joking that since he had juju against metal, what would it have cost him to extend the supernatural insurance to cover broken glass? Then he would not be here.*

A nurse calls my name. Emergency! Get someone else, I say. Doesn't she see me working? She shouts back that I am the first on call. That she thinks the chap is dead and that it is a stabbing. I walk to the car. On the driver's side of the back door, a pair of feet sticks out. One of the toes on the right one is rubbed raw, peeling and oozing yellowish-brown fluid. I stand for a moment, listening to the others as they tell me what happened.

What?

They pulled the dagger out?

I lean into the car. I notice a pair of hands wrapped around the victim's chest. I see a head, but I do not look at either the face of the victim or his friend's. It is something I have learned the hard way. Until you are sure you can save them, do not get attached. I listen to the chest.

Nothing. I pull out my pen torch and check for reflexes in his pupils, both of them.

Nothing.

I look at the face of the friend holding the victim's head up. I look into his eyes to tell him silently that his friend is dead. I look into the face behind the victim, and I see my face. Me!

And then the victim shakes his head, spraying blood on both my faces. Wilhelm is fair, fair with light-brown eyes and light shaggy hair. Where are his glasses? Wilhelm says to me as I hold him up from behind, "Thanks, Ewaen. But I think you should shift o. Your belt buckle is shooking me in the back." He straightens himself up, turns back to me with the stethoscope, and says, "And you, Dr. Ewaen. Thank you o. I thought I was going to die. I thought because I shot that Maphite idiot, Lopez, in the mouth that I was going to die." He laughs, "Nemesis is a bitch, eh."

Suddenly, Wilhelm is in front of both of me. He is wrapped in bandages. He tells both of me that there was nothing wrong with helping Tuoyo pull out the dagger from his back and that, as I can see, he is not dead. He turns his back so I can see the wounds on his back. He is silhouetted in bright light; his skin seems translucent. I can see the light through him. He looks like a painted window. The light gets brighter as Osaze pulls the curtains open.

"Ewaen, it's morning o! Wake up!"

Then I wake up.

27

DREAMS. I hate them. I have heard people say they give a glimpse into the future, or at least they tell you what you want to see in the future. I guess the latter is true. As I roused, staring bemused at Osaze for longer than normal, I expected Wilhelm to jump in with a joke or two about girls and sex. Then I shook the last vestiges of sleep off my eyes and remembered everything. The nightmare, the limp body I helped fold into the boot of that station wagon, and the sound of Weyinmi sobbing.

"Guy, how far now?"

I rolled my head over to the right and looked at Tuoyo. He sat by Osaze's reading table, already dressed. The light reflected off him in a haze, making him seem as though he were lit from within, like Wilhelm had been in my dream. The light was shining on me too; I should have felt warm, but instead I shivered and was about to pull the blanket over my head when Osaze said, "Ewaen, get up. No let the air conditioner deceive you. We have let you sleep long enough already. Get up."

"Where to?"

Tuoyo spoke, "We are going to the flat. We have to make sure Weyinmi and Mesiri are okay."

We had to do that. Osaze lent me a shirt and a pair of jeans. On our way out, he told us how he learned about what happened yesterday. I had assumed Preppa told him, but I was wrong.

"I ran into Harry last night. He said he had been at a party at Brenda's."

"I thought the party was at Phoebe's in Ekosodin."

"No, Tuoyo. They held a repeat party at Adolor. They used them Brenda's lobby. He said he left the party early, around 10 p.m., because he did not like the crowd there. That was when he told me about what happened the night before. But come, Ewaen. Na true say dey shoot Big Boy's radio?"

"Na true."

Osaze paused for a moment, shook his head and continued, "Anyway, Harry said that as he was walking down FGGC Road he noticed the crowd gathered around your front gate. When he heard what had happened, he was sure that the guy-men who killed Wilhelm left the party at Brenda's and strolled down the same path he had taken. When I met him, he was packing up to go to Port Harcourt. He told me about Wilhelm. That's when I decided that going to see Uncle Max would be a good idea."

"Wait," Tuoyo said, "they threw the party again? After what happened at Ekosodin? Did Harry tell you if he saw Tambo there? Wait, don't answer. You wouldn't know. And Harry said he was leaving for Port Harcourt last night?"

"Yes o. We even climbed on a tuke-tuke together. He gisted me about Frank's party and that Yibril guy. Harry feels that Black Axe will connect the dots to him. He said he was leaving the school for good and that his father did not send him to university to die."

"He should speak to our dad," I said.

"I am sure Uncle Max is telling Daddy now. Maybe they will be in town today."

"No worry, Osaze. Wherever we go, I will leave a message for you at the hotel next door. Ask the hotel's gateman."

"Who will tell Wilhelm's people?" Osaze asked.

"I do not know," I said. "Osaze, I do not know."

WHEN WE got to the flat, the police were already there. Two officers sat in the parlor. Mesiri told me they had conducted a search of the property for any confraternity memorabilia. They found none. The police officers told us to get ready, that we were not under arrest but would have to follow them to the Force Headquarters. Force Headquarters?

"What were we going to do in Force Headquarters?" I asked them.

The first one, a light-skinned mustachioed sergeant who said he was the investigating police officer, the IPO, told us that this was not a simple break-in. This was murder. No, our local police station could not handle this. It was a case for the Criminal Investigation Department.

KA-POW!

There is no other way to describe the sound of an AK-47 going off in an enclosed place.

"Ehen!" the policeman interviewing us shouted. "You get am, Abdul."

The man who had just fired the shot grinned at us and continued shouting at the chap he had just scared, literally, shitless. He and another policeman, uniformed in white T-shirts and monogrammed Kevlar vests, picked up the man they were escorting through the courtyard.

"Who was that?" Tuoyo asked.

"Oh, that guy? Did you see how he looked?"

We did. The prisoner had been brought in about an hour after we started giving and writing down our supervised statements. We were kept in a room on the right in the square courtyard of the investigative department of the police headquarters. I had been the first to be questioned and had taken the pen from the policeman who was interviewing me; he had trouble understanding how fast I was speaking. I found out I had more trouble writing because I was shaking so badly. It had been Mesiri's turn when we heard the van pull into the middle of the yard and offload its passengers, the two policemen and a disheveled, bleached-to-Caucasian young man who had shackles around his feet. One of our interviewers had nudged the other, and they had smiled. The AK-47 had been fired when the prisoner would not move fast enough.

"Can't you see how artificially fair he looks? He is a wanted criminal, an armed robber. He has been holed up in a flat in Sakponba trying to change his appearance. My colleagues got a tip-off this morning and now they have arrested the bastard." He shook his head and continued, "Just imagine if they had reached there a day or two late. He would have vanished."

Now he was dead, I thought. My mind traveled to Thrilla, my anatomy class cadaver. Maybe he was an armed robber caught like this after a tip-off to the police. I watched the prisoner shuffle away faster. He had a map-shaped stain on his pants that the smell traveling across the yard proved to be excrement. He had shit himself. I did not blame him. I had almost done the same when the gun went off. By the van's tires was a crescent-shaped crater where the bullet had lodged itself.

I remembered what I had written down. It was identical to what Mesiri was saying now. It was identical to what Tuoyo and I agreed we would say. We were cutting our connections to Wilhelm fast. There was no time now to grieve. I leaned on the bench under the squeaking ceiling fan and glanced sideways at Weyinmi and Tuoyo. They were both calm. I did not try to think about what was going through their minds; mine was in overdrive. Osaze had said that Uncle Max was going to be at Osasogie to check on me. Well, the flat was locked. I hoped he would check on Osaze and that both of them would drive down to the police station.

The reassurances of the IPO had helped little in clearing up my anxiety. He had told us that he was sorry about what happened to us. He did not seem to think that we were in any way involved. This was good, I know. But from what little experience I had—I remembered the Nigerian axiom when dealing with the Nigerian Police Force was NPF: No Permanent Friend—I suspected that Sergeant Patrick's sympathies could turn into persecutory glee should we give him any need to suspect us. I had seen the way he whooped when the other policeman fired his gun at the bleached armed robber. I wanted Uncle Max to be here. I wanted anyone who knew anyone to be here so the NPF men would know that we had people and so they would not turn us into other Thrillas for future anatomy students to dissect.

WHEN WE got to the police station earlier that morning, we had first walked to Central Hospital along Sapele Road. We were going to the morgue to identify Wilhelm. We walked in a silent single file: Sergeant Patrick in front and Tuoyo, Mesiri, and I following him close behind. We had told Weyinmi to wait at the hospital gate. We had insisted even after the sergeant said all of us would have to identify the body. We followed the policeman across asbestos-roofed corridors and across denuded lawns to the backend of the hospital, where the mortuary stood alone like a hut in a too-empty hamlet. It was Saturday, which was not a clinic day, so the hospital was quiet. We met the attendant, shirtless and scrawny, smoking a menthol cigarette at the door. He had a tortoise-shaped head, bald, and possessed the look you'd expect to see in Igor, assistant to many a mad scientist from Frankenstein to Dr. Jekyll. I half expected him to be hunchbacked, and when he stood,

I was surprised to find him surprisingly tall and straight. He crushed the cigarette butt with the heel of his thin slippers and spoke with the policeman. Yes, the body was here. They had been waiting for his relatives to come so they could start embalming. No, of course they hadn't started embalming; they knew it was a police case, a murder.

Mesiri leaned towards me and said that they must have changed shifts because this wasn't the attendant who had been here when they dropped off Wilhelm's body the night before.

"Okay, boys," Sergeant Patrick said. "Follow me."

As we entered the morgue, I understood why the attendant burned the aromatic incense of menthol cigarettes: the place smelled horrid, to the degree that it blurred the boundaries between smell and taste—that smell of corrupt meat, of the abattoir late in the evening, long hours after the meat has been butchered. It did not smell of formalin, of the anaesthetized and sterile anatomy lab. We passed a thin corridor made thinner by the corpses that lined its right side. Nothing is as still as death.

The attendant, walking in front, turned back slightly and without stopping said, "No space for those ones; their relatives never come negotiate for drawer space."

What did he mean by drawer space? I did not ask aloud, thankful that we had made the right decision to insist that Weyinmi remain at the hospital gate. I glanced back at Tuoyo. He was stoic, his face expressionless until he attempted a smile of reassurance at me, behind which I saw the minutest hint of pain and discomfort. We had all lost a friend. I did not worry about Mesiri; he was a medical student, and he had seen corpses before, up close, even if those had flesh stained green and gray by formalin and arrested decay. He had been here yesterday.

Wilhelm lay on a steel stretcher on the floor in the middle of a dimly lit room that had walls lined with what looked like the overlarge drawers of a huge filing cabinet. Some were half pulled open; I saw the ends of legs with paper tags tied to the big toe of each right foot. Wilhelm's arms were still flexed at the elbow in the position that the officer from last night had placed them when the hatchback of the station wagon had cracked against my friend's hand. My oyibo friend's straight hair was matted with blood, bunched into a single thick plait on the right side of his face.

Sergeant Patrick spoke. "You," he pointed at me. "Is this Wilhelm?"

I nodded. Sergeant Patrick looked at Tuoyo, then Mesiri, with the same question in his eyes. I followed his gaze and saw my friends nod; yes, the corpse was Wilhelm, had been Wilhelm.

"Okay," Sergeant Patrick said. "Two of you . . . yes, you two." He pointed at Tuoyo and me. "You said he was stabbed in the back. Turn him over and show me."

I noticed Tuoyo hesitate. I looked at Mesiri. Mesiri came forward, in front of Tuoyo, and both of us approached Wilhelm's body. We knelt on our dead friend's left side and tried to turn him over. I almost recoiled at the coldness of his skin. I expected this, had been trained to expect this, but this was my friend. He was cold and hard, the muscles rigid in rigor mortis, his glasses were gone, and I saw the face I only noticed early in the morning—eyes squinting in a smile that said, *There is no worry in the world.* I remembered my dream from last night; I remembered seeing Wilhelm swathed in bandages, telling me that it had been a close-run thing. I looked at the dead body of my friend; his eyes were closed, taped shut with paper masking tape. I grunted as a sign to Mesiri that we should get this over with. We had turned him over. The skin on his back was black where the blood had settled. A silly intrusion in my mind told me Willy would have laughed at the joke; he was half-white, half-black, properly half-caste. Out of a gash between his shoulder blades, blood and water leaked out in a slow trickle. There was no scabbing, no failed blood clot. It was like a tear in cloth. A stitch in time saves nine, *a stitch in time saves nine;* for some insane reason, that thought, that oddly apt parable, repeated itself on and on in my mind.

MY HEART had been beating loudly and quickly ever since we left the morgue for the police station. It went up a notch when the IPO interviewed Weyinmi. When he heard that her uncle was the dead pro-democracy activist and that she had been in the house when he died, he did not show any sympathy. He just stared back at Weyinmi's sad eyes and told her that she must be cursed to lose two loved ones in six weeks. Weyinmi's questioning had taken the longest. They asked about other lovers she might have had. They asked her very odd questions. It seemed that her relationship to the slain democracy activist was making the policemen smell blood.

WE FINISHED with our statements and were told to go. We would have to report at the headquarters every morning until the case was cleared—except Weyinmi. She was placed under arrest for conspiracy to commit murder. We shouted for the first time that morning, all of us. What was happening? Why her?

The IPO said, "Well, we think she had a clandestine lover in the state university at Ekpoma. She admitted that much to us."

When? How?

He continued, "So we feel that her and her lover ordered assassins to kill your friend, Wilhelm, out of jealousy. You should be happy. The killers will soon be found."

I felt so bad. Should we tell them all we knew about Wilhelm and the Black Axe and the Cosa Nostra? Would this make any difference, apart from making us seem more like confra boys and thus suspects? Tuoyo stepped forward and hugged Weyinmi. She told him not to worry and that her family would take care of everything. She made us promise to call a number in Lagos. The IPO promised that she would be treated well. We stayed until they put her in a cell. We emptied our pockets for the Presido's fee that they said she would have to pay in there to avoid being beaten up.

AT ONE of the ramshackle restaurants by the gatehouse to the police headquarters, we sat and shared cigarettes. Even Mesiri, whom I had never seen cop a drag, lit up. We stayed there, thinking aloud about what we were going to do. It was a Saturday morning. What would we have been doing now if none of this had happened?

Mesiri said, "Tambo would have heard by now."

I nodded and agreed, "Yeah. He has heard. He don run to Port Harcourt with Harry."

"Harry run to Port Harcourt? Why?"

Tuoyo and I told him about Harry's sister's party in Ekosodin, about everything we thought we knew.

We spent the next few minutes arguing about the merits and demerits of our statements to the police, especially now that Weyinmi had been arrested. We all agreed that it was for the best. That the police were looking for bribes from a rich family by keeping Weyinmi in detention on useless speculation. They had to produce a suspect for their ogas, but Weyinmi's people would take care of her. Every one of us ignored the question of who would tell Wilhelm's family. I knew I would have to make the call, but I hoped that Wilhelm's many cousins in school would have already heard and that Willy's mother had heard too.

The IPO smoked. He walked outside the station, crossed the road, and joined us under the shade of the tree where the mama-put served food. Tuoyo offered to pay for his cigarettes.

This seemed to warm his heart towards us, and he asked, "Which of you is Chief Omorogbe's nephew?"

Dumbstruck, I put up my hand.

"You're lucky. Your father's brother called my boss, the deputy commissioner of police: anti-crime. That's why we were so light on you boys. But apart from that, I have seen that you are good boys."

"Then why did you arrest our friend?"

"The girl? Hey, that was orders from above. Everyone knows your flatmate was a member of a secret cult."

"Oga, you're making our point for us. Why did your people arrest her? Is it because of her family? Do you guys think you can milk some dough from them?" I was shocked at the boldness in Mesiri's questions. Were we not planning to leave this place free?

The IPO laughed. "This is why I know you are not bad boys. You are such Johnny-just-comes. It is not for the family's money that your friend is being detained. Her identity has reached the ears of some very big people. You have to be very careful in that university of yours. You must know that some of the people you think are fellow students are actually state security personnel. The order for Weyinmi's arrest came from the SSS office in our compound. They want to use her to frustrate her family. They regard all of them as enemies of the republic."

There was nothing to say to that. We sat in silence and finished our cigarettes. The IPO was a good man. He told us that nothing would happen to Weyinmi; that we should keep on with our daily visits to the station until the whole thing blew over. "Don't worry, in a day or two, they will tire of this case and free your friend."

WEYINMI SPENT two weeks in detention. It took a full-page advertorial by her family in the papers before she was freed. Throughout that time, a lot more happened in Uniben.

Wilhelm's father came to the flat the Sunday after his son's death. Willy's mother did not come, could not, he said. He asked for the place where his son had fallen. We showed him the stain on the floor of the corridor; we traced the trail of dark stains from the kitchen wall, along the kitchen floor, to the corridor. We told him about the ride to the hospital; we told him about Central Hospital and the police station. He said nothing. He just sat in the parlor across from us with his son's luggage, a brown traveling bag, two shoe cases at his feet, and shook his head from time to time. Wilhelm's father said nothing. He shook our hands, asked me how my mother and father were doing, and he left.

On the Monday after Wilhelm's death, two Black Axe boys walked into the law faculty and shot Lorenchi. The shooters were chased down by a riot of students and were almost lynched. University security rescued them, and they were taken to the male cell beside Weyinmi's, where the cell occupants, hardened armed robbers, beat them up some more. Lorenchi died in Brenda's arms. She was broken. She left for home. I did not get to see her until weeks later. She left the University of Benin and was enrolled into a school in the UK by the end of that semester.

Tambo snuck into the flat one night and packed his things. I thought he had already traveled to Port Harcourt with Harry. He told me he was moving into a place in town until the wahala blew over. He had to. He was a marked man. Even his boys in the Cosa Nostra had abandoned him. Tommy, the new don, told him to his face that since he lived with Black Axe boys and Ju-men, he was not a bona fide wise guy. Omogui, our friend from year one, warned Tambo that almost all Black Axe men felt he was the one who fingered Wilhelm.

Omogui also told us about Yibril. The thief, the cause of all this, had traveled out of Benin the morning after Wilhelm died. Nothing was going to happen to him. Nothing ever happened to the bad people. It was a myth, our training. All we learned as children growing up were lies. Nemesis, she was too slow. She was a crippled, ineffective, bitter old bitch.

Amide was the best thing that ever happened to me. I heard that she fought a girl in our class who said that I was a confra boy who deserved to be locked up. She moved into my flat and even helped us wash off the bloodstains from the wall in the kitchen where Wilhelm had slumped and died. She held me to sleep when I finally broke down. I cried a week after Wilhelm had died. The monotony of taking a bus to town every morning, sitting outside Weyinmi's cell, talking with her, and waiting for the police to say we were free to go finally got to me. It allowed the grief and the tears to wash out the dirt and grit of pain that had held me.

My parents came to Benin two days after Wilhelm's death. My father had finally had enough—although I found out later that Uncle Max had so insulted him that he was forced to reach this decision. I was going to leave the University of Benin. He made the calls. Osaze and I would not finish the year here—we would resume school in the UK in September; Eniye would join us later. Meanwhile, Mesiri and I kept on reading. The Second MB exams would begin in a month. I was surprised that the school was not closed. Two students had died, but around the campus, unless you were directly involved, it was as though nothing had happened.

And the Africa Cup of Nations was held in South Africa that January. Nigeria did not go; our great general said he had been insulted by Nelson Mandela and withdrew the Super Eagles from the football tournament.

I WAS in my room with Amide that afternoon, bent over my books, when Weyinmi came home. I heard Tuoyo shout her name, and we rushed out of my room to meet her. None of us expected her. We had been to the station the day before and had felt nothing out of the ordinary. Our visits were no longer necessary, we had been told by the IPO the previous week, but we still went. So how had she come out?

Weyinmi had lost weight. She wore the same pair of jeans from two weeks ago. We gathered around her in the parlor: old friends, new friends, brothers, girlfriends, Tuoyo, Mesiri, Amide, and me. I sensed the presence of everyone who wasn't there. I looked above Weyinmi's face as she spoke, and I saw Omogui, Oliver Tambo, Kayode, Harry, and Brenda. We listened as Weyinmi told us how she was called into an air-conditioned office to see the state's SSS director. He had harangued her about her family—how people who felt they were untouchable, who felt they were know-knows, always fell. She said she had stared at him and listened without saying a word. When she saw the spittle flying from his mouth dry up, when she saw him lick his lips, she knew she was free. He told her she was free to go.

"Just like that?" Amide asked.

"Just like that," Weyinmi replied.